About The Poet,
The Professor, and The Redneck

Reading The Poet, the Professor, and the Redneck *is like*
looking deep into the lives of my fellow bikers. The characteristics
of fellowship, loyalty, compassion, willingness to help,
and to be heroes without a second thought.

—Len Lambert
Nonprofit Finance Professional, Genius with Numbers,
Long-Distance Biker

Acclaim For *Freedom's Rush I* and *II*

A completely charming and delightful ride-along
with an amazing story-teller. —(L. J. K.)

This will really move you. Great insights. Great stories.
Kinn's ability to put [Freedom] into words is astounding. —(A. C.)

Loved this book and Kinn's writing. [It's] a motorcycle version of
Bill Bryson's "A Walk in the Woods." —(A. H.)

Felt like I was right there on each trip. —(S. H.)

Just think a mixture of Garrison Keillor, All Creatures Great and
Small and Harleys. Good hearted, never demeaning and
always entertaining. Very worth while. —(T. P.)

Brilliantly written, nothing like the feeling of the wind in your face
and the road below your feet. —(C. R.)

He's the real thing. He's one of the few authors that really captures and communicates the experience. —(C. M.)

Foster Kinn reads like an old friend. —(D. R.)

Great book!! Fantastic stories! —(M. K.)

Kinn's writing skills make me want to throw a leg over my Harley and ride along. —(W. T.)

I recommend this book to anyone seeking the meaning of life. Insightful and thought provoking, often funny and always entertaining. —(K. H.)

Kinn is a first-rate storyteller who will keep you turning pages. —(R. J. K.)

I love how Kinn can create a story that makes you feel like you're on the same adventure. —(C. S.)

I love this book!!!! —(A. A.)

Having read several books in this genre, this one is far and away one of the best. The writing is excellent. —(P. D. P.)

As a rider of over 40 years who traveled cross country many times, it reminded me of those days. —(G. H.)

Wow, [Kinn] is an awesome read! —(M. C.)

[Kinn] is a must read for anyone whose soul yearns for freedom. —(J. G.)

Great book. Great writing. This is the kind of stuff I love. Down home, folksy humor, heartfelt, perfect. —(A. C.)

His made me feel I was right there with him all along the way. I think this will be what finally pushes me over the edge to get that motorcycle I've always wanted. —(S. M.)

Very powerful. —(J. S.)

Great Read! Great Writer! Great stories! —(M. M.)

I found this a thoughtful, gentle book. [By] the conclusion I personally felt the author had answered the question—why we ride. —(F. S.)

So well written you can feel the travel experience of bad weather, good people, great scenery. Loved it . —(R. F.)

If you have a passion, if you love to travel, or if you just like a good book, this is it!! —(G. H.)

Be careful, because if any book will make you want to hit the open road and explore America (or anyplace else) by motorcycle this book will do it! —(R. W.)

This is about the pure joy of riding, warts and all. Everything that can and does happen to us is masterfully covered. —(C. R.)

This might be the best current book on what it feels like to ride a motorcycle solo for medium to extended time periods. —(K. C.)

I'm left feeling like I've just eaten a very satisfying meal— just perfect when I finish. —(L. F.)

This book captures 100% of the reality of long distance lone riding and it does so with reflective humor and a keen eye for the sparkles and contrasts that are out there. —(H. S.)

The only thing I can say is this is a must read for anyone whose soul yearns for freedom. —(J. G.)

THE POET,
THE PROFESSOR,
AND THE REDNECK

How Men Die, How They Live

for my superb friend ALEX

FOSTER KINN

JCB 2021

BANYAN TREE PRESS

Published 2020 by Banyan Tree Press, an imprint of Hugo House Publishers, Ltd.

ISBN: 978-1-948261-28-9

Library of Congress Control Number: 2019916931

Cover Design and Interior Layout: Ronda Taylor, heartworkcreative.com

Cover Photos: Melissa Manning (Back of the Poet)
                 Dwight Mikkelsen (Road in Montana)

Interior Photo: Dwight Mikkelsen

Editorial Supervision: Patricia Ross

Editing: Diane Austin

Proofreading and Editing: Rose Albano

www.BanyanTreePress.com
BANYAN · TREE · PRESS

PROLOGUE

The Road.

The Road is a lonely, dangerous, and uncompromising place.

Too, it is comforting. Gratifying. A place where dreams come true.

It's that place where you meet all that exist, all who live.

It is malice and love, death and life,

Right there,

Rushing beneath your boots.

PART I

ONE

· · ·

H E WAS AN OUTSIDER CHASING THE UNKNOWN.
A blend of sounds surrounded him, muffled and directionless. Fans blowing in air conditioning ducts. People talking. A shriek and a laugh. Traffic lumbering by underneath.

When he exited the enclosed walkway, he heard a sound more immediate. Crisp and urgent, like a suppressed squeal, its location unclear. He turned toward the stairwell that led down to the third floor where his Road Glide was parked.

He heard the sound again. It came from somewhere in front of him. He stood motionless, the helmet in his right hand gently swinging. He heard it a third time then walked to the outside of the stairwell along a smudge-covered wall.

The shirtless man was large and muscled and wore a dark blue bandanna. He stared intently at the young woman who was on her knees. She shook her head left and right as he tried to force his erection into her mouth. On her right side was another man who had the look of a cartoon character with a triangular face and a wide and disfigured mouth. Short and lean. White t-shirt. He was videotaping and giggling.

The Outsider silently ran toward them, and that's when he saw the third man, who was kneeling behind the woman with a twisted wad of her hair in his left hand. The gun in his right hand was pressed against the bottom of her skull.

Still running, the Outsider thought, I can handle the first two but by the time I get to the third one, the surprise will be over. And he's the one with the gun. I'm fucked. He kept running. None of the other four noticed him. Three strides away, he screamed a high berserker wail.

1

The shirtless man turned in terror as the Outsider bull-rushed him. They careened toward the low cement wall at the side of the parking structure and the shirtless man landed on his back on the top edge of it. His body wracked with spasms.

The Outsider turned toward the second man who waved his arms in front of him like he was fending off a swarm of wasps, the video camera still in his right hand. The Outsider threw his right arm back and set his helmet in a large forward arc. It hit the left side of the second man's head knocking his eye down to his cheek. He crumpled to the cement. Parts of his brain pulsed where his eye had been.

The Outsider ran toward the third man, the man with the gun, who was backing up on his feet, butt and hands. When his elbow hit the wall behind him the gun accidentally fired. The bullet sliced the Outsider's left cheek and whipped his head to the left causing a sharp pain at the top of his neck. He stopped for a few moments then haltingly turned his head forward and again ran.

The third man shot wildly and rapidly. The Outsider counted: two-three-four, the bullets ricocheting off the cement ceiling and the few cars behind him. Five-six. He was one stride away when the seventh bullet went into his left shoulder and lodged against the skin on his back. The blow pushed him backward to the ground. It felt as if his shoulder had become riveted to the cement.

He went over the situation. Even if it's just an eight-round clip, I'll be dead within a minute. Unless the gun jams, but that would be luck, good luck, and today is not a day for good luck. My only chance is if the woman has a gun of her own, uses it and is a better shot than the man coming toward me. In his peripheral vision, he could see her shaking violently, clutching her large purse to her naked chest. She has to have a gun.

Blood pumped out of his cheek and down his neck where it merged with the blood that came out of the hole in his shoulder in intermittent bursts. The two streams flowed down his armpit forming a warm puddle under his shoulder blade.

The third man was standing above him, the pistol barrel pointed between his eyes. The Outsider looked past the barrel and into the man's face. Eyes crazed, sweat dripping from his nose. He was screaming. "Gonna fuck you up! Gonna fuck you up, asshole! Those're my fucking brothers asshole, gonna fuck you up!" The Outsider closed his eyes and thought, good Lord,

2

the man's entire education has come from watching bad cop movies. I'm about to be killed by an idiot.

For a few moments, the Outsider looked again at the young woman. She frantically rifled through her purse. *Good, she does have a gun. But she's shaking. She needs time. Settle down, find the gun, shoot it. She just needs a little time.*

He looked back at the third man, his fuck-you-up mantra a whisper now. *He's afraid, but that twitching finger could end my life at any moment.* He closed his eyes—*she just needs some time* – then opened them. He lifted up his right arm and in a friendly voice said, "Okay. All right. Just give me a few minutes. My shoulder is terribly uncomfortable."

The Outsider's calm demeanor froze the third man and halted his fuck-you-up mantra, but his body soon went into a rapid tremor. Bloodlust flooded into his eyes. His trigger finger convulsed as if it had a life of its own. *Any moment now.*

The Outsider saw me as I walked to the woman and placed my left hand on her left shoulder. My old brown leather vest and my long and straight silver hair. His eyes were filled with sweat and I appeared translucent, like a reflection on glass. He thought he was hallucinating. The woman stopped shaking.

The shot was different from the others. Higher and more piercing. The bullet glanced off the back of the man with the gun, twisting him and he fell face-up. He screamed maniacally, like a wounded wolverine backed into a corner. "Gonna fuck you up, gonna fuck you up!"

The Outsider let out a guttural bellow as he raised himself up, the pain from his shoulder tearing through him like a blast furnace. His helmet landed like a wrecking ball on the third man's face. Then again and a third time. Silence.

The Outsider fell back and winced when his shoulder hit the pavement. The gun tumbled out of the third man's hand with a light double click on the pavement. The young woman quietly sobbed.

TWO

•••

THERE WAS NOTHING REMARKABLE ABOUT THE ACCIDENT. A COUPLE riding two-up on a big motorcycle were on their way to meet some friends in Branson, Missouri when a slow-moving blue Chevy Cruze broadsided them. There was little blood. Some in their cars slowly passed, some parked and looked, others came out of diners.

Some minutes before, Billy Balcomb was sitting in a diner next to a window enjoying a plate of bacon and a lemonade when a young duck jetted out the window of an old red pickup looking for its owner, its path ragged and unpredictable. Traffic stopped and a cacophony of honking horns commenced. Billy ran outside and he and several others ran in oblique circles like drunken merrymakers, bumping into each other, trying to catch the quacking runaway.

I thought about helping them but catching ducks is something I know nothing of. Besides, the sight was rather funny.

Finally, a tall and slender old man wearing a beat up John Deere baseball cap exited a hardware store and knelt in the street. The duck waddled to him and jumped into his arms.

Breathing heavily with his hands on his knees, Billy looked at the man, his eyebrows scrunched. "Yer holding it like yer in love."

"She's my baby."

"She's yer baby?"

"Yeah. We got a bond."

Billy straightened up then wiped off the sweat from his forehead with the front of his t-shirt. "Well okay. What's her name?"

"Nine."

"Nine what?"

"Ducks don't have last names."

And that's when they heard the accident.

Billy ran to the woman. Her leathers were covered with bling and her hair was mostly gray but she had the kind of pretty face that hadn't grown old for twenty years. She was lying on her back crying, "Oh-oh-oh" over and over. He said, "Name's Billy. Ya got anything broken? Anything causing a sharp pain?"

She stopped crying and looked at him. "I, I don't know. I don't think so. Is John okay?"

"Don't know yet. Let's move yer legs and arms a little. See if yer okay first." Billy helped her move them and she began to relax. "Comfortable as you can get?" She nodded. "What's yer name?"

"Annie."

Billy looked her over one more time. "Well okay, Annie. It don't seem like nothing's broken. Y'all just stay right here. Leave yer helmet on. Just be as comfortable as you can be. I'll go check on John."

John was lying amid a ragged gathering of onlookers, most of them taking videos with their cameras. Billy pushed through them and knelt beside him. He was breathing deeply and rapidly and a blotch of blood was growing on his left leg. He looked at Billy. "Where's my Annie? Is she okay?"

"She's lying right over there. Scraped up a little but don't think anything's broken. Unlike you. Yer left thigh bone's poking out of yer pants."

The man raised his head and looked. "Oh god." He quickly took three deep breaths. "Are you sure Annie's okay?"

"As sure as I can be. Are ya as comfortable as you can be? Anything else causing discomfort?"

"My left shoulder. It's like it's turned the wrong way."

Billy looked at it. "It does seem a little not right. Probably dislocated. I can punch it in if ya want."

"Yeah yeah, okay. Do it. It's happened before. Gotta get it before the swelling."

Billy felt around the shoulder and without a warning, jammed it back into place. John winced for several moments then slowly relaxed. "Thanks."

"Sure thing. Ambulance'll be here in a minute or two. Just relax as best ya can. Want some water?"

"I'm okay. Are you sure Annie's okay?"

"Gonna go check on her right now."

Two

Five prolonged minutes passed before the police arrived. The EMTs arrived just afterward but by then Annie was jaundiced. Her injuries were internal. And serious. As they lifted her into the ambulance, she died of heart failure.

A cleanup crew arrived and a half hour later, all evidence of the accident was gone except for a few puddles of water.

Billy rode east. Less than an hour later he walked into another diner and spent a long time drinking a cup of coffee. He paid, left, then stood next to his motorcycle, his eyes and doleful thoughts wandering. He took a deep breath. The afternoon was getting on and the hot air sat above the town like a wet tarp so he got a room.

Once in it, he sat on the bed and pulled out his keychain on which were two, narrow three-inch steel vials. He held them in his hand and felt their coolness and their weight. He closed his eyes and rubbed the shallow grooved surfaces with his thumb. He wept.

Ten minutes.

THREE

...

THE NEXT MORNING, BILLY POINTED HIS ROAD KING BACK WEST AND spent the next day riding throughout the relief-filled Ozarks. The round and verdant mountains were as sentinels as he pushed it hard on the weaving roads, scraping pegs and drifting around sand- and pebble-covered curves. Crows would caw and race alongside before arcing away, horses would snort and nod in approval, burrowing animals would crouch and watch as he passed.

The few cars required scant attention and they soon became nonexistent, and as the miles disappeared under his boots, his mind became more and more untethered. Vital and electric. Eventually, the road behind him was forgotten, lost to the wind; the road in front a desire, a promise, a destiny, and he came to own the earth.

He had at last emerged from his sorrow-filled memories, the gray of his past, and into the bright sun of living. The air was a warm comfort, the few clouds were like beacons of liberty, and the sound of his engine a siren of joy.

He rode faster then faster again until the road and the wind's white noise became all there was. Every sinew, muscle and bone was alive with ecstasy, every movement unbridled, every thought like lightning. He was invincible.

And he rode faster and faster still so that at last he looked through the eyes of angels and his mind was cleansed of all earthly effects and he reached that higher realm of light in which all things are holy and pure.

...

FOUR

...

THE OUTSIDER WAS GOING IN AND OUT OF CONSCIOUSNESS. IMAGES OF blood and brain flashed left and right. The immediacy of bullets. The thin clanging of shells dropping on cement echoing louder and louder. A terrified young woman. A man with long silver hair. The gray and red and white of cracked skulls. An eye dangling in space.

He heard running footsteps. The first to arrive was an old biker and his lady. The biker gasped, "What the..." His lady kept saying "Oh no, oh no, oh no." After them came a security guard who was yelling into a small, black plastic box attached to his left collar. "Ambulance, fourth floor! Blood everywhere! Ambulance! Ambulance!"

The police and EMTs arrived within minutes. Then more police and another ambulance. The young woman explained everything to the police and the news quickly spread into the ever-gathering crowd. More police arrived then a local TV news crew.

A young paramedic taped gauzes on the Outsider's shoulder and cheek. The press of onlookers stifled the air and the heat in his body rose like water coming to boil. The biker, his lady and the young woman stood close by. He gave the biker his helmet, told him the license plate number and said, "Third floor, black Road Glide, keys in my left front pocket." The biker retrieved the keys and said, "We'll take care of it, son, don't you worry." His lady said, "We'll take care of you, too, when you get out of the hospital."

The Outsider, being the least injured, was the last taken to Sentara Norfolk Hospital in Richmond, Virginia. As the paramedics lifted him into the ambulance, the young woman looked into his eyes and clutched his right hand so hard it hurt. Tears flowed down her cheeks. She said nothing but didn't need to.

The Outsider lay on a low hospital bed in the emergency room. His heart rate slowly returned to normal. The cut on his cheek had been glued shut and there was gauze taped over it. He was miserable but mostly uncomfortable and it was worse than the pain, which had become more of a constant pressure.

A doctor and a nurse were tending to the three men he had bludgeoned, the other doctor and two nurses ministering to seven other patients in various stages of agony.

He glanced at the nameplate of a short, rotund nurse as she walked by. "Excuse me, Kendra. Would you please tell one of the doctors that there's no need for an operating room, that it would be best and quickest to simply put some numbing concoction on my shoulder, slice a small cut, pull out the bullet, then staple me back up?"

The nurse, wearied with bloodstained arms and smock, looked at him a few seconds. "You sound like a college professor." He smiled.

Some minutes later, a slender, middle-aged doctor came over and together with the nurse lifted him to a sitting position. He winced when the doctor felt the bullet under his skin. The doctor continued to look and feel. "You want me to numb the area, cut and remove the bullet, and staple you up?"

"That's the plan."

The doctor looked over the emergency room. Understaffed. He was tired. Too tired. Ten hours and counting. He took a deep breath as he turned his attention back to the Outsider. "How's your liver?"

"Fine."

"Meds?"

"No."

"Allergic reactions?"

"No."

He took another deep breath and one more look around. "Kendra, you know what I need. You do the stapling, okay?"

Kendra returned with some Lidocaine, a stapler and an array of scalpels, while the doctor talked to another patient. She helped the Outsider onto a high steel table. He asked her, "So what's the damage report on those guys?"

Kendra looked at the three men then back at him. "I don't suppose you're part of the family?" He smiled. She leaned over and in a conspiratorial voice said, "One of 'em's top two vertebrae are smashed to bits. Still convulsing when he got here. Bit his tongue off, crushed his teeth and fractured his own jaw. Probably won't live long enough to be introduced to a wheelchair. One of the others lost an eye and a good part of his brain. Doubt he'll make it."

She gazed at the third man who was lying motionless under a gray, bloodstained sheet, the IV drip-drip-dripping. She took a deep breath. "Last one's in a coma. Had his face fixed into his skull. Brain damage. Don't know how much. Even if they live, none of 'em'll ever be right. Far as I'm concerned, they got what was coming to 'em." She placed a hand on his good shoulder. "Ya did good, college boy."

The doctor came back and had him lay on his right side. The Lidocaine did its magic and he could feel only a momentary sting from the cut, and there was a quick suction sound as the doctor removed the slug. Kendra stapled three times and it hurt more than the cutting.

"Only three?"

"I'll put more in ya if ya want."

He smiled. "Three's good."

"Don't wanna fix ya up too good 'cause then you'd never see the scar. Ya do know the ladies like a man with a few good looking scars, doncha darling? They probably don't teach ya that in college. Anyways, don't worry, I did ya up right." Kendra helped him back to the hospital bed and covered him with a sheet and a blanket.

Damn, he thought, all I set out to do was ride a motorcycle for the rest of my life and in only nine months this happens. He remembered a saying Maarku, a martial arts instructor and the father of a high school buddy often said: Bones heal, muscles mend, skin grows back; fight the good fight and it's worth it. He laughed under his breath. If I'd trained with him more, I'd be riding my bike this afternoon instead of stuck to a hospital bed. Kendra brought him a second pillow and he plunged into a dark sleep.

Soon, the man who had been videotaping the attempted rape regained consciousness for twenty minutes then died. No one heard his pleas for forgiveness. The following morning, the man who had lost his top two vertebrae died after two hours of painful convulsions.

FIVE

...

T HE NEXT DAY, BILLY RODE NORTH INTO AN AREA STREWN WITH HILL-ocks covered with thick grass and cattle grazing and trees of medium height and wooden houses and fences. Scattered across the sky were white clouds intertwined with gray and dark gray, and every now and again a drizzle would cool his face.

A few hours later, he passed by an elementary school in Rogersville. Through the thick maple and walnut trees, he caught glimpses of a baseball field where a number of kids were playing, and he could see some adults, too.

A half mile later, he stopped at a stop sign, put his bike in neutral and sat and reminisced about the years he played little league and American Legion baseball. All the other games, too. The smell of the grass, the hot air, the excited shrieks, the smell of his sweat-stained leather glove, the slight pressure of his baseball cap, the sound of his rubber cleats when he walked on cement. If I had to choose only one thing America would be remembered for, he thought, I'd choose baseball.

He paid no attention to me as I turned in front of him and rode by the school.

He turned around, went back to the school, walked over to the field and halfway up a wooden bleacher that was scattered with flakey strips of old white paint hanging precariously, but you knew they'd never fall down until you passed the back of a finger over them and hear the faint snaps.

He sat and watched. He guessed the kids' ages to be between nine and eleven and they were having fun, which was good, but it seemed that only half of them knew anything about throwing, catching and hitting.

The more he watched the kids' lack of skills the more dismayed he became. Five minutes later he was downright indignant. Baseball is sacred, he thought. Baseball is America. How can American kids be so clueless about the fundamentals of the game?

Furthermore, no one was organizing the practice. Where's their coach? Why isn't he teaching them anything? I need to have a talk with him. He looked and looked but didn't see anyone coaching. A few of the parents, who were all mothers, were trying to instruct but they were as clueless as the kids. Billy couldn't take it any more and walked down to the field.

The closest mom was wearing a maroon shirt on the front of which was written Mom's Marauders. "How ya doing, name's Billy."

"Hi, I'm Daisy."

"Wanted to ask ya, which of you is the coach?"

"Oh, none of us are. We're just the moms."

"So he's not here today. Or she?"

Daisy swatted away a fly. "No. He had heart bypass surgery a little bit ago and won't be back until after our second game. His name's Mick and he's a sweet old codger and he played in something called the minor leagues for a few years, I forget where or what their name was, so he knows a lot and we were really looking forward to him being our coach. But then he had that surgery so we're doing our best to teach the kids ourselves but, as you can tell, we have no idea what we're doing. Do you know anything about baseball?"

"Played a little, know a little."

"Oh that's wonderful! Could you help us out?"

"Well, I don't want to push myself onto nobody."

Daisy swatted at the fly again. "Oh, you wouldn't be doing that. It'd just be for two weeks, just until Mick gets back. You'd be doing a really good thing. All our kids are from single mom families and they're all good kids and they're dying to learn and they'll work their little hearts out."

Billy closed his eyes. He was eager to keep riding, but when he thought of kids needing help with America's pastime, kids who needed a coach and really wanted to learn how to play, he couldn't turn his back on them. "Well, tell ya what. Lemme see what I can do for the next hour or so and then we'll talk about it some more."

He gathered the kids around and introduced himself and, as Daisy had said, they were good kids and attentively listened. The first thing he told them was to not close their eyes when a ball was coming at them, whether it was a ground ball, a fly ball or a pitch. "Ya gotta look the ball into yer

16

glove or onto yer bat and ya can't look at it if yer eyes're closed. It's kinda like yer guiding it yerself, sorta like the way ya make one of them remote controlled cars do what ya want it to."

One of the kids asked, "What happens if the ball hits you in the arm or something? Or the eye?"

Billy looked at him. "It'll hurt."

Another kid asked, "What if it hurts a lot?"

"Then it'll hurt a lot."

Still another asked, "What if it breaks a bone or something?"

"Then ya got a broken bone or something. But ya see, the body does this thing when it gets hurt real bad. What it does is it sorta shuts down the pain thing so what ya mostly feel is the pressure from the swelling. The best thing to do when ya get hit is to just look at where ya got hit. Look at that spot and say to yerself, 'I got hit right there, well whaddya know.' Do that and you'll feel as little pain as possible, maybe even none."

He paired them up and had the first kid of each pair roll the ball into the second kid's glove, then the second kid would roll it back. He had them do this back-and-forth until they all did it with their eyes open. Next, he had them bounce the ball, then had them throw the ball underhanded, then overhand, and finally increased the distance until every kid was throwing and catching the ball from thirty feet away.

He explained the fundamentals of base running then showed them the proper way to hold a bat and how to swing, and kept telling them over and over to never take their eyes off the ball. They all got the hang of it quickly and they would hit and laugh and hit again.

Except for Norma. Norma could throw and catch well but could not get the concept of hitting a ball no matter what Billy said or showed her. Every time she would tightly close her eyes and the more Billy told her to keep them open, the harder she'd close them. It got to the point where Billy thought she was going to give herself a headache or, worse, squeeze her eyeballs out of their sockets.

Norma's actual swing was remarkable because it was about as wrong as wrong can get. She'd lift the bat as high as she could and would then come down like she was splitting wood with an axe.

After the practice was over, the mood was upbeat and all the kids thanked Billy and called him Coach. The mothers thanked him profusely, too, and he agreed to hang on for two weeks.

Billy worked the kids hard every day for the rest of the week and each of them improved in every aspect of the game. Except for Norma and her hitting. No matter what Billy tried, he could not get her to stop pounding home plate with her bat. However, she had a fine throwing arm so he made her the starting pitcher.

That Saturday they played their first game and largely due to making fewer errors, Mom's Marauders won with a score of 24-9. The handshake line showed true sportsmanship and Billy got a tear in his eye while watching it.

SIX

•••

I T WAS LATE AFTERNOON WHEN CAL AND DENISE, THE BIKER AND HIS lady who were the first ones on the scene in the parking garage, drove the Outsider back to their home from his last interview with the detectives. The last of the would-be rapists, the one who no longer had a face, had had a severe brain hemorrhage and died the night before so there were "loose ends to tidy up" and forms to fill out and sign and more questions and good wishes and hands to shake.

So. It was done. The blood and the healing, the killing and the talking of it. The compression of rooms and the press of questions.

Cal and Denise had taken good care of his motorcycle and good care of him, too, just as they'd promised. He'd stayed with them six more days than he'd needed to, but Denise was a damn good cook and as Cal had said many times: A man could live and live well on nothing but her biscuits and gravy.

As the Outsider looked out the window and watched the wooded neighborhoods pass, he reflected on his current life. He knew he couldn't truthfully claim to be a denizen of the road – that would take a full cycle of seasons, he felt – so he still needed to ride, to go, to turn and stop and go again whenever or wherever, to drink, to eat, to sleep alone and with women, to fight if he had to, but mostly to ride and see mountains and rivers and trees of hickory, oak and pine. Now, nine and a half months after he'd left his other life behind, the reality of being a true inhabitant of the road still awaited him.

Dinner that night was the only subdued one they had had. He couldn't stay forever, they all knew that, but the saying of goodbye to friends is always a melancholy affair. He would leave in the morning but promised to visit every now and again, and he would. Good people.

He went to bed early and, as was his habit, woke up at 3 a.m., that quiet and uncertain time when the night begins to die. He walked out the back door and up a small hill. The sky was moonless, the silhouetted trees like a charcoal drawing on gray construction paper, the constant and quiet sounds of night muffled by the warm air.

On the left side of Orion's Belt, Alnitak shone through the eons just to the right of an upward flowing hickory branch, and he decided to stay there until it passed behind the branch then appeared on the other side. It was only when he marked time like this that he felt attuned to the earth and her inhabitants. To life.

There was a vast peace around him as he contemplated what he'd done two weeks prior. The violence and the killings didn't bother him. The nagging thought he had was just that, that he wasn't in the least troubled by them. He kept expecting nightmares or a wash of guilt or sleepless nights, but they never came. He wondered why.

On the third afternoon following the incident, a gaggle of photographers, videographers and reporters crammed into his bedroom at Cal and Denise's to record the mayor giving him a key to the city of Richmond.

Nine days after that, the FBI arrested thirty-four people involved in an international rape and child trafficking ring due in part to the data found on the computers of the three would-be rapists. The Outsider was certainly pleased with the news, but like the killings, it didn't connect with him on an emotional level, either.

Jam Smith, the young woman's father, had visited him. He assured Jam that the rape had never occurred and noticed a relief in his eyes. Jam was a large man with bulbous jowls and long, bushy sideburns, who wore his protruding belly like a royal sultan. He said, "Found the gun in the rubble of a house in Kuwait when I was scouting for the army back in the 90s. Twenty-five caliber snub-nose, pearl handle. Gave it to her for her protection."

"I'm glad you did."

Jam looked around the room and stroked his chin. "Except I'm worried, man. It's not registered and I might have to give up all my other guns."

"I wouldn't worry. No one remotely connected with politics, common-sense or justice will charge you with anything. All you have to do is get in touch with the woman detective on the case, forgot her name, and she'll get it back to you."

"But it's evidence, she can't do that."

Six

"Two of those guys are gone and the third one is on his way. There won't be a trial. Besides, things go missing in evidence lockers all the time." The Outsider looked into the eyes of the big man like he was an old friend. "That little girl of yours, Jam, grew up to be one hell of a woman. She saved my life."

Alnitak disappeared behind the hickory branch and his thoughts again turned to the fact of his not being affected in the least by the killings. He felt the presence of the Dark Companion, the thing or non-thing that claimed his life during his violent acts and that kept him from feeling any emotions about them. From all he'd learned in his forty-two years, the things people do should affect them, especially killing other people, justifiably or not. Why am I different?

Originally, he had thought the Dark Companion was a lacking in his soul, an absence of what should be. Some years later, he viewed it as a thing that actively caused that absence, a constant presence that haunted and pursued him. But once he abandoned his old life for a life on the road, he began to see it as the other way around, that it was now something he pursued.

Alnitak's glow appeared to the left of the hickory branch that posed in dark silhouette. He contemplated the possibility that mankind's basic problem was that we move in spurts, sometimes slowly, whereas the universe moves always, and that, perhaps, this component of life was irrevocable because were it not to exist, mankind would be like the non-living things that crowd the universe: the rocks and sounds and waters and distant suns that light our nights. Perhaps this was what it meant to be divine. Or dead. Perhaps this is what happened when the Dark Companion claimed him.

So far, the times the Dark Companion had replaced his life had been temporary but that didn't exclude the possibility that it would become permanent, something that terrified him. Whatever it was or wasn't, the possibility of an existence without emotion was real to him. What would it be like, living without introspection, without guilt or shame, without pride or sense of accomplishment? Living without knowledge of living?

Alnitak was fully clear of the hickory branch but for an inexplicable reason, as the lonely hoot of an owl filtered through the scattered sound of crickets, his attention went to the northwest and he stared in that direction for several minutes before going back to bed.

21

SEVEN

...

THE OUTSIDER RODE PAST HARD-PACKED HILLS COVERED WITH TREES and grasses and small animals that watched warily with black eyes, and birds who flew in short arcs and chittered in halting phrases.

The cars faded behind him and the ever-present middle line gave way to the will of the curving road, which was his will. The engine rumble snaked up his body like a beast that feasted on marrow, the gas tank warmed his legs like a siren begging for pleasure, the asphalt flowed under his boots and reached up to him, wanting him to meld with their hard death; the wind howled like an ancient crier reading a register of those who had gone and those who would soon be gone, and the clouds looked down like feeble gods assembled for the viewing of him alone.

He stopped for gas but did not get off his bike, and he rode away without returning the looks of those left behind. He kept riding until he again needed gas. When the tank was full, he crossed the street to a diner whose name he did not notice, sat in a booth next to the door and a front window and watched his bike while he ate, looking as a man intent on conquest. Or a man waiting to be possessed.

He made his way to the Blue Ridge Parkway and into the Smoky Mountains. His senses flowed through the thick vegetation and swirled with the rising smoke to the layered and darkening mountain ridges that cut askew into the sky. The road beckoned a wildness from him like a sorceress leading to extravagant rooms filled with strange creatures and exotic pleasures that disallowed all familiarity.

The shadows lengthened and they were like newly grown hands of the Dark Companion that grasped at his boots and jeans and vest and hair, and he rode through them and over them, and still they grew and grasped until the shadows consumed the sun as a substitute for his soul.

EIGHT

...

AFTER TAKING SUNDAY OFF, BILLY WORKED THE KIDS HARD THROUGH-
out the following week and their improvement was remarkable, though
he worried a little about Norma, who was hard on herself because of her utter
lack of being able to handle a bat. But most of the time, the fact that she was
the starting pitcher, and a damn good one, overshadowed her frustration.

The second game was against what everyone said was the best team
in the league, Dad's Destroyers and, similar to Mom's Marauders, all the
parents were single dads. Billy admired their skill but was off-put with their
unfriendly attitude, especially that of the other coach. When Billy went to
introduce himself, the man just stared and wouldn't shake hands. Billy said,
"Well all right, there ya go."

Billy and Mom's Marauders soon found out how good Dad's Destroyers
were. Through the first three innings, they had yet to get a hit and were
trailing 6-0. The opposing pitcher was the coach's son and his fastball was
faster than any of them had ever faced and his curveball curved more than
any of them thought possible. He looked too old to be in the league, so did
most of the team, but Billy decided to let it pass.

The one thing that really riled Billy was when the opposing players
snickered at Norma when she was at bat. He got really heated when the
other coach mocked her swing, which made his players laugh out loud.

At the end of the third inning, Billy had noticed that the other pitcher
seldom threw a curve ball for a strike. He noticed two other things as well:
He threw his fastball with the exact same rhythm every time and was tipping
his pitches. When he stood in the middle of the pitching rubber, it was a
fastball; when he stood on the third base side, it was a curveball.

Billy first showed his players how to time the fastballs. "Wind-up, 1-2-
pitch." He also showed them how the pitcher was tipping his pitches and told

them to never swing at a curve. The kids began to silently count in rhythm with the pitcher, stopped swinging at curves, and at the end of the fourth inning the score was 8-3, and at the end of the fifth inning it was 9-6, thanks to Norma catching a line drive hit right back at her with the bases loaded.

The score was 11-10 at the end of the sixth and in the top of the seventh inning, Dad's Destroyers went ahead 13-10.

In the bottom of the seventh, the last half-inning, Mom's Marauders quickly scored twice then got two strikeouts. After a single and an error, Georgie was the tying run on second and Mario was the winning run on first.

It was Norma's turn to bat. She was standing in the on-deck circle staring at the ground on the verge of crying because she so much wanted to help her team but knew she had no chance to do anything but strike out. She also knew that Billy really had no choice but to replace her with a pinch hitter. He walked over.

"Norma."

"Yessir."

"I wanna win this game bad, real bad. You do, too, right?"

"Yessir."

"So I'm gonna tell ya something."

"Okay."

Billy got down on one knee and looked directly into her eyes. "I believe in you. I believe yer gonna walk up to home plate and get yer first hit of the season."

"You do?"

"I do."

"You think I can get a hit?"

"I do. I know you will. I believe in you, Norma, I really do. Now get yer butt up there and show me I'm right."

"Yessir!"

Billy looked at the other coach and read his lips when he said, "Now that was just stupid," and he knew he was right.

The dust in the air made the sky a pale blue and the sun out of focus. The grass was dry and threw off heat like a cotton quilt. A dust devil in left field spun around a crushed paper cup. Billy looked at the people in the stands. Most wore sunglasses, some wore hats, others wore both. A few fanned themselves with magazines and now and again all of them would swat away flies and gnats.

The younger kids who had been playing pretend baseball games behind the grandstands were now watching in silence. The kids who had been warming up in the next field were now leaning against the low fence along the right side of the field, their arms hanging down on the inside of it. Norma's mother was praying with her hands over her mouth and her eyes closed.

With the weight of the world on her shoulders, Norma was visibly shaking. Billy thought about the impossible position he had put her in. In two games she had had fifteen at-bats and had struck out every time. And now she was up there by herself feeling like the loneliest person in the world, knowing that it wouldn't be long before the other team would be laughing at her. Only by some miracle would she get a hit and when she didn't, she would cry and blame herself for letting everyone down and losing the game.

On the other hand, for the rest of her life she would remember that her coach had believed in her, that her teammates had rooted for her, that her mother had prayed for her, and that, most importantly, she hadn't backed down.

No one moved or spoke. Above the centerfield fence, a small bird chirped once like it was lost. The first pitch hit the dirt in front of home plate. Norma closed her eyes and swung her vertical swing well after the ball hit the catcher's mitt. The umpire had no choice but to call it a strike. The second pitch came straight down the middle but Norma was crying and shaking so badly she couldn't move.

Billy called to her. She looked back at him, her every muscle taut, tears on her cheeks. Billy took off his sunglasses and looked directly at her for several seconds then smiled. Her shoulders and face relaxed, her arms, too. She wiped away the tears. Billy smiled and nodded slightly. Norma took a deep breath and stepped back into the batter's box.

The next pitch was also right down the middle, straight and hard. Norma squeezed her eyes shut and swung down like Paul Bunyan splitting a giant oak. The ball went straight up and hung in the air, spinning so hard it looked like a UFO getting ready to zoom off. It landed inches in front of home plate, shot to the backstop and caromed toward the first base dugout. Norma stood with her mouth open in shock. Billy exploded out of the dugout, "RUN! RUN! RUN!"

The catcher chased after the ball while Georgie rounded third like a hurricane wind. Norma, still holding the bat with both hands, scampered to first and stayed there, wondering what had happened. The catcher threw the ball to the pitcher but Georgie slid in under the tag. The game was tied.

Mario was now the winning run on third. He was the smallest kid on the team and had only moderate speed, but he had an instinctive knack for the game. Freddie, one of the two best hitters, was up next. Billy walked over to him. "Freddie, I need you to give up one for the team."

"What do you mean?"

"I want ya to do something ya wouldn't normally do."

"Okay. What?"

Billy got onto one knee so their eyes were level. "On the first pitch, whether it's a strike or not, I want to ya swing as hard as ya can and miss."

"Miss?"

"Yeah, miss. And swing so hard that the bat goes flying outta yer hands toward the third baseman."

"Let go of the bat?"

"Yeah, but don't make it obvious. Make that bat fly outta yer hands like a rocket right at the third baseman, okay?"

"Okay."

Billy gently put his hands on Freddie's shoulders. "And then walk on over to it real slow and pick it up and walk back with yer head hanging down like yer really mad at yerself, like yer ready to explode. People might be laughing at ya but don't pay 'em no mind 'cause we got a plan here. Okay?"

"Yessir."

Billy put his hands on his own knees but kept Freddie focused. "Now on the next pitch that's a strike, gotta wait for a strike, I want ya to bunt half way down the third base line. Can ya do that?"

"Yessir, I can."

"Just half way. A nice soft bunt that just dies in the grass."

"Yessir."

"Good. Do that and we win."

"Yessir!"

Billy went back to the dugout, took off his sunglasses and looked toward third base. When the third baseman looked away to his left, Billy winked at Mario to let him know something unexpected was about to happen.

Freddie missed the first pitch by a foot and the bat went flying at the third baseman, who barely got out of the way. The other team and some of the fans were laughing, including the other coach.

Mario retrieved the bat and handed it to Freddie, who was walking the way Billy had asked him to. The third baseman backed up several feet and Billy again winked at Mario.

The next pitch was to the inside corner of the plate and Freddie laid down a bunt along the third baseline. The pitcher, the third baseman and the catcher stood frozen and stared as it died on the grass. Mario crossed home plate without a problem. Mom's Marauders won, 14-13.

NINE

• • •

THE OTHER COACH WAS FURIOUS, KICKING GLOVES AND BATS IN THE dugout, screaming profanities. When he refused to let his team join in the handshake line, telling them they weren't even good enough to congratulate someone else, Billy looked at him and thought, you and me, bud, we just might be having us a talk.

As everyone was getting ready to head over to Daisy's house for the victory barbecue, Billy saw the other coach leaning against his Jeep, arms on either side of his son's head. He loudly berated him and slapped him over and over. Billy walked over. "Ya better stop that."

"Who the fuck are you?"

"The guy telling ya to stop that."

The other coach looked Billy down and up. "You're just a fucking hillbilly. Go back to your stinking shack and fuck your cousins and your dogs."

"Now that there is a real clever insult. Think of it yerself or did ya read it on one of them interweb things?"

"Fuck you."

"Nah, ain't gonna happen."

The man stood up and faced Billy. "You'd better watch it, asshole. I have a fourth degree black belt in Tae Kwon Do."

"A fourth degree black belt in Tae Kwon Do. Now don't that sound real pretty."

The man stood ready, veins pulsing in his arms and neck, sweat glistening on his forehead. "I'm telling you, you'd better leave."

"Not till I'm done saying what I gotta say. If I see ya hit a kid just one more time, especially if it's yer kid, I'll take ya down so fucking hard you won't wanna come back up."

"Fuck you. I can do anything I want to my kid."

31

"No, I don't believe so."

The man stared at Billy several seconds then whacked his son's face with the back of his hand. The kid fell down on one knee, crying, with a bloody nose.

Billy exploded forward, kneed the other coach in the stomach then delivered a downward right to the top of the man's left eye. He fell back onto the dirt. Billy put his boot on his neck. "Now I'm going easy on ya because yer a stupid fuck, but I promise ya this: If I ever see ya or even hear about ya hitting a kid, any kid, just one more time, trust me, you ain't never getting back up. Do we have an understanding?" The man nodded slightly.

A woman came over to the boy and helped him up. "I'm his mom, I'll take him home with me."

"Sounds like a good idea." He looked at the boy, "Don't worry, kid, you'll be all right." The boy nodded and brushed away a tear. Billy bent down and looked at him kindly. "A coupla other things, son. Ya got a lot of potential but yer fastball's too easy to time and ya gotta learn to throw a curve for strikes. And ya gotta stop tipping yer pitches."

TEN

...

THE OUTSIDER STOPPED FOR THE NIGHT AT A ROADSIDE MOTEL IN Swannanoa. The woman at the check-in desk was around fifty years old, tall, smelled of lavender, and dressed like a hippie from the '70s. Feather earrings, silver and turquoise bracelets, Native American and butterfly tattoos, a shirt with fringes. A child of Mother Earth. At one time she had had a taut and full figure but now much of it was sagging and soft. There was a sensuousness about her, however, so he let her carry on the preponderance of a long conversation.

After unloading he went back to the office. "I'm going out for dinner. May I bring back something for you?"

"Oh, that's okay. I only eat organic."

The Outsider nodded. "I'll bring you a piece of pie."

An hour and a half later he placed two Styrofoam containers on the desk and told her, "One's lemon meringue, the other's cherry. You don't get to know which is which, but you do get to choose." She chose the lemon meringue but when she curled her nose after the first bite, he gave her the cherry pie and took the lemon meringue.

He let her talk more but didn't listen much to what she said, only nodded or shook his head or lightly laughed at what seemed like the right places to do those things. When her shift was over, they went for a walk in the sparse woods behind the motel.

Later, they were in his room. Before going to sleep, she reached over and turned on the radio. He asked her why. "I like it. It gives me better dreams."

The following morning, the Outsider rode back west, then continued south and west on the Blue Ridge Parkway. He got a room at the Cherokee

Casino, went for a walk along Soco Creek, gambled a little, drank a lot and slept alone. The following day he reversed his route and headed back to Swannanoa.

He imagined a story he would tell, if he ever got around to writing a book. It would be years ago in some bar in New Mexico where an old timer told him: Every road is two roads. Ride one way on it and it's good; ride the other way and it's as different as a different road. If I ever do write that book, he thought, I'll need to come up with a good name for that old-timer. Zachary or Elijah, something biblical.

Again he spent the night with Mother Earth Child. When he came in after his 3 a.m. ramble, he heard the last line of the chorus of an old song, something about pie and levees and whiskey and rye and the day the singer will die.

ELEVEN

...

BILLY RODE TO DAISY'S FOR THE VICTORY CELEBRATION. SHE HAD JUST started up the barbecue when the President and Vice President of Rogersville Little League showed up. The conversation was civil but the demands firm: Billy was to never coach in their league again nor attend any Rogersville Little League games for a year.

He told them he understood and that if he were in their position, he would do the same. "I know I used untoward language within the hearing of children and that should not be tolerated."

The President was a tall and handsome woman in her thirties. Black and tightly-coiffed hair, hazel eyes, scarlet lipstick. She wore a dark blue business suit, a pearl necklace and burgundy Cole Haan loafers. "Well, there was more than that."

"You mean when I busted that piece of vermin filth in the gut and face and threatened him with future violence if he ever hit a kid again?"

"Yes! Violence can never be tolerated."

"You seem like a nice lady and I respect the fact that ya do the work ya do for Rogersville Little League, but I'm afraid I disagree on that point."

She crossed her arms. "But violence never solves anything, Mr. Balcomb."

"Sure does. It stopped that piece of slime from hitting his kid again and it gave his ex-wife good reason to sue fer full custody."

"Well, yes, but violence is just, well..."

"Sometimes necessary."

She stomped her foot. "That's not what I was going to say."

"But it is the truth."

The President, flummoxed, stared at Billy with her mouth open. Billy said, "Tell ya what, why don't ya both hang out for a while, eat some of them burgers, have a few beers and we'll do that agree to disagree thing."

"I don't think it's right to drink alcohol in front of children."

"Why not?"

An exasperated curl of hair fell onto her forehead. "It's a bad influence, they might get the idea it's okay to drink."

"Well, if yer an adult it is okay to drink."

"But they'll get the idea it's okay for them to drink."

Billy looked at her, at the kids, then back at her. "They ain't that stupid. First off, they've already been told that kids ain't allowed to drink alcohol. That communication thing works, doncha know. Second, they can see the difference between a kid and an adult. Third, it gives 'em something to look forward to when they grow up."

The President didn't know what else to say and with a look of disdain, she and the Vice President turned to go. Before they left, the Vice President whispered into Billy's ear. "Off the record, I'm glad you did what you did."

TWELVE

· · ·

THE FOLLOWING MORNING, THE OUTSIDER HEADED WEST WITH THE adrenaline rush of a ride with no destination. He turned south onto a narrow state route through the Nantahala National Forest where the oaks, hemlocks and poplars followed him along a road scattered with hairpins.

He stopped just after Chimneytop Gap in South Carolina for a smoke and to watch three deer foraging, who looked at him with only mild interest. Not long afterward, he made his way to a side road, walked down to Reedy Cove Creek Lake, took off his boots and socks, rolled up his jeans and cooled off his feet in the waters, letting the mud squish between his toes.

He continued south on a two-lane highway enjoying the easy curves. The steaming humidity was like a thick soup and covered him with a fine mist of sweat. Nevertheless, the passing air settled him into a comfortable temperature. The trees were southern-lush and there were a few maples with crimson tufts still clinging to them. Once, he rolled through a patch of maple seeds and they billowed up and out behind him, then helicoptered their way back down.

When he stopped, he would mostly just stand and look, often toward the north. Something's there, he thought, but whatever it is, is a destination and I'm not interested in any destinations right now.

Once, he wondered if his decision to never take any photos was a wise one. True, it would be fun to someday sit in an easy chair and look at them and relive all the places he had visited, but he honestly and firmly didn't plan on doing anything but living on the road for the rest of his life. Besides, he loved the freedom of not being connected to any one place or person and photos were a substitute for that, for being connected, and they are a constant enticement to go back, and going back was contrary to going forward, which is what he wanted to do.

While he was stopped at a light in Pickens, I passed in front of him. There was no way for him to follow me but he did give me a quizzical look.

He ended his day at a motel at the southern end of Pickens. For dinner, he walked to a pizza joint a few blocks away where a little league team was celebrating a victory. One of the kids had hit a home run. "I knew it was gone as soon as I hit it."

"Sure went a long ways."

"Soon as I heard the crack of the bat, I knew it was a goner."

"Me, too."

"Clean over the fence."

"Ain't never seen a ball hit like that."

"Easiest swing I ever did."

He smiled and relived his first over-the-fence swing and how it was just like the kid described: an easy swing. Easy and sure and straight-through. It was then that he realized the blessing that baseball had been in his life. The sweat, the teamwork, the camaraderie, the hours with his dad. All of it.

His thoughts turned into a satisfying reminiscing. I loved playing third base, the hot corner, and hitting, though I never quite liked the sound of an aluminum bat. Wood is the best, like the way Frank Thomas made it sound like compressed thunder. Will there ever be a better nickname than the Big Hurt?

Dad used to talk about Mantle and Mays and I wish I could have heard them, too. He talked about Musial, how he said that whenever he was in a slump, he'd just try and hit it straight up the middle, surgical, like a great fly fisherman's cast, and the crack of his bat was a quick snap, clean and precise.

Damn, I love baseball. Every weekend dad and I would go to the school-yard, he'd measure off sixty feet six inches then throw me curve balls. He'd been a top pitching prospect in college and I wonder if he'd have made it to the majors if he hadn't broken his right elbow and knee in that car accident. Like to think so. But he could still throw a damn fine curve.

Eventually, I learned to hit them and ended up with a .441 batting average my first year in college and there was no one to thank for it but my dad. Wonder if I could have played third base in the majors. Like to think that would have happened, too, but then so does every guy in the country. But then, there aren't many who can hit a curveball.

He went to bed early and alone, and after reading a good chunk of Faulkner's Light in August, realized that Mississippi was the one state that fetched his imagination more than any other. There's something mysterious there, he thought, something out of reach and out of sight, impenetrable and forever moving. A pilgrimage in constant twilight.

Early the following morning, he continued south. Soon, he stopped next to a small abandoned shack then walked along a narrow and muddy creek. There was nothing there that fit any common concept of beauty, but for some reason, he continued walking. When the heat rising from the weed-covered soil stifled his thoughts and the small black flies ramped up their flesh-nibbling ways, he went back to his bike and continued south.

He stopped in Liberty for coffee and a stale blueberry muffin, then rode back roads and farm roads for the next few hours, some of them only dirt, and the local citizens would look up and wonder if he was someone they knew. Some would wave and they all watched him until he passed out of sight.

He made his way on roads he didn't notice the names of and eventually found himself north of Anderson where he observed students from the local university. It was easy, too easy, to see them as those who were condemned to a slow and numbing death, their souls disemboweled by a gradual lack of meaningful thought, much like what had happened to him.

He was disconnected. From the students, from the buildings, from the gaiety and the seriousness, from everything around him. It was a familiar feeling but was now more pronounced than ever before. He wondered if the cause was the Dark Companion. He didn't know, but because he had no other answers, he assumed it was.

He walked to his bike but before mounting, took one more look at the students and silently wished for them lives worth living.

When he got to Sadler's Creek State Park, he sat on a bench next to a wide section of the Savannah River, the bitter smell of the mud bank filling his nose. A few boats were lazing about, as were the flying insects. He ate a bag of trail mix, drank a bottle of water and smoked several cigarettes while reading more of Faulkner's keen observations of life in Mississippi. It was then, inexplicably, that his attention, instead of going west to Mississippi, again went north. Again, he wondered why.

He left an hour later, made his way across a river into Georgia and at Royston began zigzagging westward through the daytime shadows, the needled trees, and the steel lattices of a bridge that reminded him of barred windows.

When he got onto Interstate 75 North at Resaca, he rolled on the throttle until he was cruising at over a hundred, the wind and the pressure of it taking him forward and away from all he had known.

THIRTEEN

•••

WHEN BILLY WALKED BACK TO THE VICTORY PARTY HE SAW FIVE OLDER boys huddled together, one of them being Lance, Daisy's older son. Evidently, Lance had fallen in love and was the object of some good-natured razzing. Billy listened. When the subject changed to the boys giving Lance useless teenaged advice about girls, he decided to intervene.

He called Lance and told him to sit across from him at a wooden table. "How old are you, Lance?"

"Turned eighteen last month."

"Okay, yer old enough to talk to so lookie here, I'm gonna tell you how to ... " He glanced at the mothers standing around the table, one of whom was Daisy, and decided to sanitize what he was going to say. "I'm gonna tell you the proper way to get a woman to go out on a date."

"Okay."

The mothers relaxed and the boys leaned in. Even the buzzing insects slowed their frantic ways as if they, too, began to take heed. "Now, lemme ask you something first, Lance. This lady yer interested in, what color are her eyes?"

"Uh, brown. Or light brown, I think. Or green. I don't know."

"Okay, that's bad, real bad. Next time you see her, get to know that color real good. Just flat out memorize her eyes."

"Okay."

Everyone's eyes darted to each other wondering if this was the real deal or not. "So what's this girl's name?"

"Bev."

"Everybody call her Bev?"

"Yeah."

"Okay. One important thing is to say her name often and when ya do, say her full name. Everybody else says Bev, you say Beverly. Never call her Bev, always say Beverly. If she asks ya why, just say Beverly is a prettier name and fits her better than Bev. Got it?"

"Yeah."

Lance's friends leaned in closer, the mothers sat down. "Next thing is ya gotta listen to her. And I don't mean just sit there not saying nothing. Ya gotta really listen, keep track of everything she says and it don't matter what she's talking about, it's important. Concentrate."

"Okay."

"All right. Now you gotta be sincere. All the time. Women know when yer not sincere and there ain't no way for a man to fake it. You can fake it with guys but not with women. So be sincere.

"Say she wants to play her favorite song and it's New Age music. Listen to it all the way through, absolutely, but when it's over, thank her (that's just good manners) then just say yer not a fan of New Age music. Don't be mean or derogatory, just say yer not a fan."

"What if I like New Age music?"

"Don't even think of going there, Lance. New Age music is okay fer a woman but fer a man, it leads to only one of two things: mass murder or slow suicide. Got it?"

"Yes."

The mothers smiled wryly. "Okay. Now, you got to learn the art of paying a compliment. Ya gotta be natural about it. Ya don't have to be smooth, just natural. Real natural. And the timing has to be right. The way ya do that is to wait for a silence of at least three seconds. That's important. Without those three seconds, yer compliment will never get there."

"Okay."

The attention on Billy was now complete. No one else spoke or moved. "Okay, now here's a good compliment technique: Interject the compliment in a non-sequitur way. Know what non-sequitur means?"

"No."

"It means 'does not follow.'"

"Okay."

"Now, say she's talking about her job and her stupid boss and her back-stabbing co-workers. Let her finish, wait three seconds, gotta get those three seconds, then say something like, 'Y'know, every time I look at you,

Beverly, yer eyes sparkle with the sweetest color. Just takes me away.' Do that, and you'll take the breath right out of her."

"Okay."

The mothers looked at each other then at Billy like he was some sort of romance god. He went on. "Now here's the big secret about compliments that every woman knows but only a few men do. Ready?"

"Yeah."

"The best compliment you can give a woman is on her shoes."

Lance scrunched his nose in doubt. "Her shoes?"

"That's right. Compliment a woman's shoes and yer more than halfway there. But ya gotta do it real natural. Don't say, 'Hey, nice shoes, Bev.' That's better than nothing but pretty lame.

"Say yer walking along together and ya get them three seconds of silence. Stop walking then she'll stop and look back at ya like she's saying 'What's up?' Ya got her full attention now, see? Look off to the left, not the right 'cause looking to the right means yer lying or insincere. Look off to the left then look right into her eyes, real kind like, like they're the softest and sweetest sight there is, and say something like, 'Y'know, Beverly, every time I see ya, yer wearing a perfect pair of shoes. Like them there are as cute as a kitten in clover. I do not know how ya do it.' Ya do that, pull it off real natural and sincere-like and she's yers."

"Okay."

At this, Lance's friends' mouths slowly dropped open as if discovering an ancient wisdom. "But ya still gotta close the deal and here's how ya do that. Don't ever ask for a date. Never, never, never ask. Never. Asking a woman out on a date shows her yer weak and unsure of yerself." The mothers now looked a bit skeptical. "What ya do instead is state your desire. State, don't ask. State, don't ask. Make a mantra out of it if ya have to. Know what a mantra is?"

"No."

"A mantra is a sacred phrase or sound ya say over and over till it becomes part of you."

"Okay."

"So the mantra is 'State, don't ask. State, don't ask.' Lemme hear ya say it."

"State, don't ask. State, don't ask."

The mothers raised their eyebrows. "Good. Now it works like this. Let's say ya wanna take her out fer dinner. If ya say something like, 'Hey Bev, wanna go to dinner?' well, that's just stupid. Now, if she's a good woman she'll forgive ya fer it and may even agree to go, but ya might as well hang a sign from yer ears that says Yokel. Know what a yokel is?"

"No."

"A yokel is an unsophisticated and uneducated person."

"Okay."

"What ya do instead is state yer desire. First get yer three seconds then say something like, 'Y'know, Beverly, it would be a perfect evening fer me if I could treat ya to a nice dinner.'"

"Okay."

"Got it real good?"

"Yeah!"

"Good, 'cause I tell ya what, Lance, you do all that, know the color of her eyes, say her full name, be sincere and natural, wait fer those three seconds, compliment her shoes, state yer desire, and ya got yourself a date. Guaranteed."

"Okay. Thanks!"

The mothers looked at each other, smiling again, wide-eyed with wonder. Lance's friends began whispering among themselves. Billy raised his hand and everyone stopped. "Now hold on there. There's one more thing."

"What?"

"The first kiss."

"Oh."

"Yeah, the first kiss. The first kiss is important, real important."

"Okay."

Again, Billy was met with laser-like attention. "Now, the first kiss has to be a proper kiss and a proper kiss is in five stages: surprise, pause, deep, look, soft. Say 'em after me. Surprise, pause, deep, look, soft."

"Surprise, pause, deep, look, soft."

"Good. Now ya still gotta get yer three seconds. That's not one of the five stages but ya gotta get those three seconds."

"Okay."

"Now, the surprise part is to start when she's not expecting it. It's like that non-sequitur thing we talked about before. Remember what non-sequitur means?"

"Yeah, it doesn't follow."

"That's right, that's good. The surprise is when yer just walking or just standing around, three seconds have gone by and, bang, ya wrap yer arm around her waist, just one arm, and bring her in real close so yer lips are almost touching. It's important to hold her firm but not tight. Ya don't wanna be forceful, just firm. Okay?"

"Okay."

"Good." Lance's friends' eyes glazed over with imagination. Billy continued. "And then the pause. Yer lips are real close but ya pause before the kiss. Look directly into her eyes fer at least three seconds. Yer there with one arm around her waist, firm-like, and yer real still and not breathing and ya look real kindly into those eyes ya already got memorized. Okay?"

"Okay."

"Good. Now for the deep part." Billy leaned toward Lance and lowered his voice. Everyone else leaned in closer as well. "Put yer other arm around her waist and kiss her long and deep. Passionate-like, with yer eyes closed. Don't squeeze her, just keep yer hold nice and firm, and it's important to make it last. Ya make it last by slowly moving one of yer hands with the fingers stretched out right on up her spine and when it gets to between her shoulders, slightly increase your firm hold and it'll be like she folds herself into ya and ya'll feel one of the most thrilling feelings a man can feel. Okay?"

"Okay."

Everyone was barely breathing. Even the flying insects had settled down and stopped moving. "Now the fourth step: the look. When the kiss is over, don't release yer firm hold, just keep her lips real close and look into her eyes like before. Just hold her with yer fingers stretched out and look into her eyes real kind-like. Okay?"

"Okay."

"Last is the soft kiss. Now this kiss is a short one so don't linger with it. What ya do is keep yer hands and fingers where they are and keep yer eyes open and kiss her so soft ya can barely feel it. Ya don't even pucker, ya just lightly touch yer lips to hers and keep yer eyes open looking into hers and hold it there fer no more than three seconds. And while you're doing it, breathe in her breath, real light like. Got it?"

"Yeah."

The mothers all silently sighed with wishful reverie; Lance's friends each entered his own world of future romances. "So there ya go, Lance: surprise, pause, deep, look, soft. Do those five steps real good and you'll be a legend she'll never forget. She can go off and marry somebody else and have seventeen children and seventy-four grandchildren and three hundred great grandchildren and she'll never forget that kiss."

"Okay."

"Got all of it?"

"Yeah."

"Real good?"

"Yeah!"

"All right. Now I gotta grab me a bacon burger and a beer."

FOURTEEN

•••

WITH THE OUTSIDER'S FRAME OF MIND AS IT WAS—NO SCHEDULE, NO *destination—it was an easy task to guide him to a specific place, which happened to be a modest roadside motel outside of Dalton, Georgia. After he unloaded, I lured him about a mile north to Sadie's Tavern. He sat at a small, round table while I sat out of sight at the end of the bar.*

It took a while for Sammie, a tall and sultry waitress, to come over but the way her ample and well-proportioned curves were scantily covered made it worth the wait. "What'll I get ya Biker Man?"

"Have Beefeater gin?"

"Got every kind of gin there is."

The Outsider smiled appreciatively. "Excellent. I'll have a Beefeater and tonic and a PBR in a bottle, please."

Sammie smiled then walked away and he couldn't help but admire her seductive gait. When she brought back his drinks, she leaned over farther than she needed to and stayed like that longer than she needed to. He took the opportunity to admire the deep cleavage between what looked like two harvest moons covered with cream and specks of vanilla. His gaze followed her lavish figure as she walked back to the bar where she turned around and smiled.

He finished the gin and tonic then went to the restroom. When he stepped out, he was looking at the back end of a hefty man leaning over a pool table lining up a shot. He stood still and quiet. The man missed the corner pocket by a foot then turned to him and yelled, "Fuck you, motherfucker!"

The man swung his pool cue, missing his head as much as he had missed his shot. The Outsider hadn't even ducked, but when the man lunged at his face with a glass he'd just grabbed, he slipped to the right, stopped him with a left to the solar plexus, winced a moment at the pain that shot through his left shoulder, then delivered a right cross to the man's face.

On the way down, the man fell into two of his buddies, broke one of their pool cues and the leg off of a stool, and ended up rolling around on the floor gasping for air and clutching his nose.

The Outsider walked to the bar and asked Sammie if he could talk with the owner. When the owner came over, he held out five twenty-dollar bills and said, "Enough to cover the stool and the pool cue?"

"Ain't necessary. That stool was a rickety accident waiting to happen and all them pool cues is as crooked as a timber rattler. Besides, the guy had it coming."

The Outsider nodded as if to say "all right" then put two twenties on the bar and asked Sammie, "Think you could take him another glass of what he's been drinking?"

"Doncha think he's had enough?"

He looked at the man, who was still on the floor but sitting up. One of his friends had just taken the car keys out of his pocket. "Yeah, but his friends will take care of him. Take him the drink and he'll think about it in the morning." He half-smiled and looked into her eyes. "The rest is a tip

for a fine lady."

When the Outsider got back to his table, he thought of the first time he had gotten violent. It was a Friday afternoon, just after my fourth grade class had spent an hour painting with watercolors. The teacher was outside comforting a girl who was crying and eventually walked her to the principal's office, leaving the rest of us unattended. We all lined up to wash our hands.

Rob, a kid I never liked, pushed his way to the front of the line with two thugs in tow. A chorus of protests arose. Rob told everyone to either "shut up or do something about it." A girl, Deanna, told him it wasn't fair and he should stop being a bully. Rob pushed her and she fell against the counter, scraping her elbow on the way down.

Deanna was a small girl, frail, and it was a known fact that she fainted at the sight of blood and that's what happened then. Everyone was shocked into silence except Rob who lightly kicked her ribs then bent down and yelled in her ear, "Wake up, stupid!" His two minions laughed.

Something snapped inside of me and I pushed Rob down then punched him in the stomach. He did his best to not cry. The other two did nothing.

After school, Rob and his two minions were waiting next to the bike rack. Rob challenged me to a fight. I ignored him and tried to ride away but he blocked my path. All the other kids gathered around. The fight, like most fights, lasted no more than a minute and neither of us ever really landed a punch. I felt restricted by my thick coat and walked over to my bike to take it off. Instead, I inexplicably got on it and rode home.

Normally, I would spend all weekend playing baseball and hunting with my bow and arrows, but that weekend I stayed in my room, embarrassed, trying to find a justification for riding away, for being a coward. When Monday morning rolled around I'd somehow managed to forget the whole thing. Until I got to school.

Rob and the other two were unmerciful with their insults and would never let an opportunity pass. Every recess, every lunch, before school and after. Their taunting continued unabated throughout the week and even some of the other kids joined in, calling me a sissy and a coward.

After school on Friday, when the taunting started up again, I had had enough. I threw down my books and ran after Rob, who was on his bicycle. Across the football field, through the opening in the chain link fence then on top of the bank of a small ditch. Rob was having a tough time with the mud and the uneven surface. A block later, he dropped his bicycle and ran into an alfalfa field. When I caught up with him, the pounding began.

Everything I was, every thought I had had, every civility I had been taught was supplanted by an unthinking, bloodthirsty darkness. Rob was on his back, crying and pleading, vainly trying to stop the blows, but I kept delivering. When my arms got tired, I went to kicking; when my legs got tired I went back to my fists. My body heaved wildly with every breath, the skin on my knuckles ripped off and Rob's face was splattered with blood, saliva and mucous.

Most of the dozen or so kids who watched were frozen with horror but a few ran back to the school and told the seventh grade teacher, Mr. Reese, what was going on. By the time he got there, Rob was almost buried, covered in a thick, reddish mud. Mr. Reese lifted me away but I twisted out of his grasp and gave Rob one last kick across his face. Mr. Reese tackled me and that was the end of it.

The next afternoon, my father and Rob's father met with the school principal, who had already talked with all the other fourth graders. The three agreed that I had gone too far although Rob, who had been bullying the other kids for months, had instigated the whole thing. Rob was in the hospital for six weeks and didn't return to school until the following year.

My father was a quiet man, tall with hard built shoulders and arms. After the meeting with the principal and Rob's father, he walked into my bedroom and sat on a chair opposite me. For several minutes, we sat without saying a word, my father scanning the books on the shelves and the baseball posters on the walls.

Finally, he said, "Let me see your hands." My knuckles were covered with newly formed scabs, each of them framed with a thin, scraggly circle of blood. "Try not to bend them too much. It'll keep breaking the scabs and take longer to heal. Besides, you might get a scar or two."

My dad then took a deep breath. "Two things. One, you did right by defending yourself and Deanna and I'm proud of you for that. Two, you went too far. You hurt him bad, son, real bad. He'll be in the hospital a long time and may never be right, body-wise or head-wise. Remember that. Remember what one man can do to another."

Afterward, I would occasionally remember how it felt when my soul had been displaced with an automaton of brute force and it terrified me. But the thing that always stayed with me, the thing that shaped my early life as much as any other was that even though I was only nine years old, my dad had referred to me as a man. From that day, I always tried to be the master of my own life and answer up to my own failings and was proud of doing so.

Until I abandoned baseball and got caught up in the Ivy League life and hid behind my degrees, the "respect" of a professorship and the fallacious importances of upper education. The intellectual bigotry of it all is embarrassing.

Sammie brought him a fresh PBR. "That was really something. Don't believe I ever saw anybody take somebody down like that." He half smiled and nodded. She went on. "You ain't from around here, are ya? Wait, lemme guess." She looked at him closely as if to divine the one minuscule attribute that would reveal his origin. "Connecticut. That's my guess."

He tipped the beer bottle toward her and said, "How did you know? How did you do that?" And therein began the protocols, the unstated negotiations, of setting up a future rendezvous. He enjoyed the game and, when he succeeded, the prize at the end.

When Sammie was serving other customers, he went back to reminiscing. I did change my life after beating Rob, but it was a gradual change. I still played basketball, football and my favorite, baseball, and I loved those hours of my dad throwing me curves. Beautiful. But as the weeks and months passed, the time I spent practicing and playing became less and less.

I remember the summer after my first year of college when I went to a Denny's with my mom and dad. Rob and his parents walked in and Rob still looked broken, loose-fitting, like a retired rodeo cowboy. They didn't see us and though I was afraid to look at him, I did. The sight of him should have torn me up, but even back then, it didn't hit me on an emotional level. But it did terrify me that part of what I was, was capable of damaging another person like that without remorse.

And what did I do the next semester? Hit the books instead of curve balls. My conversion from athlete to literature geek was complete. The thing is, I loved those books, got so totally immersed in prose that I didn't even realize what I'd done, that I'd taken a divergent path. God, how I fucked myself.

FIFTEEN

•••

THE OUTSIDER'S REVERIE WAS BROKEN WHEN AN OPEN BOTTLE OF BEER was slammed on his table. He looked up and saw a wide-shouldered man wearing a worn black leather jacket and an old t-shirt on the front of which was written, "Live Free, Die Free." He wasn't tall or bodybuilder strong but more like lifting-one-hundred-pound-cement-blocks-all-day-long type of strong.

With a big smile he said, "I like a man who takes care of business, straight up with no boasting. At first, when I seen you sitting here with yer back to yer personal punching bag and his buddies, I thought you was either stupid or had no sense of personal safety. But then I saw that mirror back of the bar giving ya a clear view. I like a man who's smart, too. Name's Billy." He reached across the table with a thick hand. The Outsider took it and had trouble matching the grip. Billy sat down.

With friendly eyes, the Outsider said, "Name's Wyatt," He waited for the inevitable "Like Wyatt Earp?"

"Wyatt, huh? Hmph. Never met a Wyatt before. Good name, I like it."

The man with the broken nose was being helped out by his friends, one of whom looking as if he was going to bash the back of Wyatt's head, but a stern look from Billy disabused him of the idea. Billy watched them struggle out the front door. "Now that there's something I never understood."

"What's that?"

"Ya busted his nose and there he is limping like a newborn colt with one leg missing."

"Maybe he hurt his leg on the way down."

Billy shook his head. "Nah, he fell on his shoulder. Besides, I seen it before. A man gets his nose broke and starts limping. Ain't no sense to it."

Wyatt turned to look at the man. "It is curious, isn't it? Never noticed that before."

Billy took a long drink of his beer. "Y'know, Wyatt, I don't mean to pry but I'm wondering, what's your last name?"

"Youngblood."

"Middle?"

"Hazel."

Billy scrunched his eyebrows. "Hazel?"

"Mother's maiden name."

"Makes sense. So your initials are WHY."

Wyatt smiled. "Yes."

"That's pretty funny."

Wyatt finished his beer. "What's your last name?"

"Balcomb."

"So you're William Balcomb."

Billy got a proud look, like he was introducing his first-born son. "Actually, the first name's Baxter."

Wyatt raised his eyebrows. "Baxter?"

"Yep, Baxter Balcomb."

"Middle?"

"Got two, Oliver and Oscar."

Wyatt thought for a few moments. "So your initials spell BOOB and you think mine are funny?"

"Yours are funny, mine're fucked up."

Sammie brought both men another beer and they each nodded a thank you. As she left, she gave Wyatt a seductive smile on the sly. Billy took a long drink then said, "Y'know, from the way you talk, I'd take you for some kinda teacher."

Wyatt sighed regretfully. "Used to be but I quit."

"What'd ya teach?"

"Literature."

"Where?"

"Yale."

Billy slammed his hands on the table looking as if he just reeled in a sixty-pound catfish. "Sheeit, that's all right."

"Not really. It sucked the life out of me."

Billy dipped his head. "Now that is regrettable. I only finished seventh grade myself and barely managed that, but I read a lot."

"What kind of stuff?"

"Novels mostly. Some history. Not big on science fiction. Read a lot of the classics."

Wyatt threw back his head, eyes wide open. "Now that's all right. What are your favorites?"

Billy squinted his eyes and openly assessed Wyatt's character. "Well, usually I make something up that's, you know, acceptable to the person I'm talking to, but since you've read more than me and seem like a man I can trust, I'll tell ya the truth. Promise not to make fun?"

Wyatt grinned. "No."

Billy sighed. "Well all right. I love that chick Jane Austen, wish I'd met her. Edith Wharton and George Eliot, too. Read Silas Marner four times. Now that there was a good man. That wedding makes me cry every time and always will. Crime and Punishment twisted me inside out. Anna Karenina ripped my heart out. Madame Bovary, too, like at the end when Charles says to the guy who was the first one to fuck his wife, 'I wish I were you.' Killed me."

Billy continued, his excitement growing. "But my all time favorite is Les Miserables. The shit that Valjean went through, damn!, but he always made sure Cosette was taken care of and he never lost his dignity, even though those fucking assholes Thénardier and Javert kept fucking with him. Cried every time I read that book, too, especially at the end when Valjean forgives his new son-in-law, forget his name, and tells Cosette about her mother and then dies. A finer man never existed in my opinion."

Normally, this kind of emotional outburst would come from someone in a drunken stupor, but Billy was looking straight at Wyatt, fully sober, his eyes unwavering. Wyatt thought, Christ, I'm in a biker bar and run into a man who didn't even go to high school and in two minutes he declares more passion for literature than I saw in seventeen years at Yale.

And what about you, Mr. Ivy League College Professor with tenure? Where's your passion? Buried without protest in academia, that's where. God, I'm pathetic.

Wyatt looked around at the people drinking together and those sitting alone. The undulating drone of talking and laughter, an occasional shout. The signs with witty sayings: Beware of Pickpockets and Loose Women; It

Takes More Love to Share a Saddle Than to Share a Bed; When Freedoms Live, We Ride; When We Ride, Freedoms Live.

Then he saw me, sitting at the end of the bar, my long silver hair flowing down the back of my brown leather vest.

Something clicked inside of him and suddenly the drone of voices became a clear counterpoint, his vision focused on near and far alike, and in the random positions of the patrons he could see complex patterns like three-dimensional fractals. Heat rose from within him, like pungent wisps of smoke from an old pile of painter's rags in the corner of a studio on a steaming August afternoon. He thought, here I am in a bar, talking with a man who barely made it through grammar school, setting up a rendez-vous with a voluptuous woman and I am set alight. And it all began with breaking a man's nose.

Wyatt looked back at Billy and quoted Victor Hugo's own description of his masterpiece. "A progress from evil to good, from injustice to justice, from falsehood to truth, from night to day, from appetite to conscience, from corruption to life; from bestiality to duty, from hell to heaven, from nothingness to God."

Billy finished the quote. "The Hydra at the beginning, the Angel at the end."

SIXTEEN

· · ·

SAMMIE BROUGHT TWO MORE BEERS. SHE STOOD LEANING OVER WITH her right hip angled out, her ample bosom pulsing with the pull of gravity. Without hiding the fact, Wyatt looked appreciatively at her breasts and noticed she had removed her bra. He raised his eyebrows and gave her a friendly smile. She opened her eyes fully and cocked her head. "Getcha a little something else, Hun?"

The way she dragged out "Hun" sent a warmth through his loins. "Oh don't worry darling, you may just find out everything I want." She half closed her eyes, breathed slowly and deeply, her breasts reaching for Wyatt. She winked and walked away.

Billy said, "Dang! That woman wants you! The way she said 'Hun' and leaning over and showing off those big tits like that. Damn!"

"Yeah, I'll be getting lucky tonight. What about you? No woman on your arm and here you are wasting your time talking to me."

Billy again smiled that big smile of his. "Oh I'm all set. Nina, the kitten-cute waitress with a tight ass at the no-we-don't-serve-no-liquor-here cafe down the street. Had me a fine roast beef dinner with mashed potatoes and gravy and a side of bacon, graciously served by Nina herself. I just came over here for a beer. She gets off at ten."

Wyatt extended his hand. "I'll cover your tab, Billy, it's already twenty after."

"Shit." Billy shook his hand, "See ya 'round, my friend," and rushed out the door.

Wyatt walked up to Sammie to pay his and Billy's tabs. She pulled out a dozen or so receipts from her pocket and as she fumbled through them, he appreciatively looked her down and up. "Know what I'd really like?"

"What's that, Hun?"

"This is my first time in Georgia and I would so enjoy a ride with someone who knows their way around, someone who can take me to a place where I could get a good look at the night sky."

She looked up and smiled. "Shit, I could do that."

"Working late?"

"It's Wednesday. I get off at midnight, takes me twenty minutes to cash out."

"Meet you out front at 12:20. You sure?"

"Yeah. But, you ain't gonna hurt me are ya?" She did look a little worried.

"I won't hurt you, Sammie."

She relaxed and assumed a coy look. "'Cept for the good kind of hurt?"

By chance, Wyatt and Billy met at a coffee shop the following morning. They had each decided to stay another night. (Billy summed up their reasoning: When it's good, it's just goo-ood.) After a bit, they decided to ride together for the rest of the morning and into the afternoon. Billy paid for the coffees and when he came out, Wyatt was standing next to his bike looking at the gas station on the other side of the street.

Billy asked, "What're you staring at?"

"That guy across the street. The one with the long silver hair. His back is to us."

"Oh yeah. He was in the bar last night."

"Yes, he was."

The traffic light turned green and a number of cars and a few delivery trucks passed in front of them. When the traffic cleared, Billy asked, "Know who he is?"

Wyatt flared his nostrils at the faint smell of diesel fumes. "No. But I've seen him before."

"Now that ya mention it, I have too. When I was turning left into my motel yesterday, he passed me on the right. Funny thing: I was planning on ordering a pizza, but right then decided to go out for a meal and a beer. Where'd you see him at?"

"Up in Richmond a month or so ago. I'll tell you about it sometime." He scanned the tops of the trees across the street then closed his eyes and slowly opened them. "The thing that's interesting is that he's come all this way and doesn't have any saddlebags. Hell, he doesn't even have a fork bag or a blanket roll."

They watched as he screwed on his gas cap. Billy said, "There used to be top and bottom rockers on his vest. A middle patch, too. Can you make out what it was?"

"No, it's too faded to tell. Whatever it was, it was taken off a long time ago. What kind of bike is it?"

"Oh hell, it's just a rat bike. So many different parts that there ain't no make or model fer it. It's a kickstart."

I'm always a little nervous when bikers watch me start my bike. Sometimes that kickstarter just doesn't want to take hold, know what I mean? But this time, thank goodness, everything went perfectly and the two men watched me until I disappeared around a corner.

SEVENTEEN

...

W YATT AND BILLY HEADED EAST ON A DIVIDED ROAD THAT WAS
slightly curved here and there. It was fairly well trafficked but mostly
by working men and women so it was relatively sane. Crossing two bridges,
they caught only glimpses of the Coahulla Creek and the Conasauga River,
their muddy green waters blending with the thick overgrowth, the under-
growth filling the air with their half-rotted reek.

The white and gray clouds traveled perpendicular to their route but the
cool winds that moved them did not reach down to the road. They angled
southeast and rode past typically lush and well-maintained Georgia lawns.
Road workers paused in their duties to admire the loud motorcycles, which
once muted the sound of a jackhammer. Some would wave or nod. The two
men topped off their tanks in Chatsworth then continued east.

The road became windy a few miles after they entered the Cohutta
Wilderness and about a half-mile later, they pulled over and removed their
helmets. It was then that the two men entered a world of their own devising
where danger and speed and time become afterthoughts.

They slammed past angled banks of tawny-colored dirt spotted with
sage-colored grasses and brushed against supple tree branches, and their
perceptions spread out like wings on enormous, prehistoric flying beasts,
and birds of all available species and colors and songs would fly away in
short, upward arcs, suspend for a few seconds as the bikers passed underneath, then land from where they had taken off.

In the periphery they would admire the occasional tulip tree in full bloom
of pink or yellow, the plane-like green of small meadows, the forever parallel
power lines above and the asymmetrical weeds to the left and right. And
they smelled the fecund earth with its heady mixture of lilac and gardenia
and the cinnamon scent of rhododendron.

In their sinews they would feel every bump and nick in the pavement, the pockmarked patterns in the double yellow line, and the patches of dirt and sand that made their tires momentarily slip left or right. And they came to realize the ultimate thrill of settling into that precarious balance between centrifugal force and the pull of gravity.

They turned left onto a small road then right onto a smaller road. They passed a square, wooden gazebo covered with a red roof and fronted by a small pond and a small meadow, all surrounded by a roughly hewn three-rail fence.

Soon, they pulled to the side and cut their engines. Without saying a word, Billy got out his royal blue Colt Python and Wyatt his Ruger. They each loaded up and walked along a small stream. A couple of minutes later, Billy spotted an old target nailed to a tree forty yards away. He squatted on the wet dirt and fired all rounds, three hitting the bulls-eye, the other three within a foot of it. Wyatt nodded with approval.

Wyatt stood slightly angled so his left shoulder was a little closer to the concentric circles and put six of his ten rounds in the center circle. Billy said, "Damn."

They got back on their bikes, helmet-clad, and made their way back to the highway. They soon passed a station wagon parked on their left. Inside were two children, outside a mother and two other children were sitting on the grass facing away from the road. The two bikers passed them then U-turned back. The kids were quiet and still, the mother looked up. Billy said, "Y'all need some help?"

"Nah, we's okay," said the mother. "Pulled the kids outta school so's they could run around and get away from them damn computer pad things. Margie's forgetful and her gas gauge don't work so we run out. She's walking back to Ellijay with the gas can."

Billy nodded. "All right, we'll be back," A mile and a half later they pulled over in front of Margie, who was walking with an old red and rusted gas can in one hand and a small blue purse in the other. She had a look on her face as if she had been expecting them. Wyatt said he'd get the gas so Margie handed him the can. Billy told her to get on the back of his bike and he took her back to her kids.

When they arrived at the car, the four kids and the mother were still sitting in sullen silence. Billy, forever annoyed with idleness, said, "Hey, you kids, follow me." He led them to a graveled area, pointed to a hemlock tree thirty yards away and said, "Let's see which one of you can hit that tree."

The first rocks were thrown half-heartedly and fell far short. Billy made them each throw another then others. The mothers joined in and soon everyone was giggling and laughing and the rocks were thrown with enthusiasm, some of them even hitting the mark.

Wyatt returned with the gas then poured it into the gas tank. Both women offered to pay him but he refused. Billy got into the car, pumped the gas pedal a few times and the engine fired up on the first turn of the key.

Wyatt and Billy followed them back to Ellijay and when Margie turned into a gas station, all six of them waved and smiled.

EIGHTEEN

• • •

THE TWO MEN MET THAT NIGHT FOR DINNER AT THE NO-WE-DON'T-serve-no-liquor-here cafe where Wyatt got a good look at Nina. Height and girth considered, she was on the small side and tightly packed with penetrating blue eyes that would send any man into a heterosexual flush. She was friendly, efficient and attentive, mostly to Billy, but Wyatt also noticed a bit of an insistent push from her. After dinner, Wyatt passed on dessert and told Billy he'd meet him at Sadie's.

There were no hostilities at Sadie's that night and, instead, the atmosphere was a little celebratory. The owner nodded and smiled at Wyatt. Sammie, whose dress was fully buttoned up to her neck and extended below her knees, smiled and winked and pointed to a table in her section.

Wyatt looked for me but I remained hidden.

Sammie came over with a Beefeater and tonic and a PBR "Worked it to get off early tonight so's we can spend a few more hours together."

"Now you are some kind of sweet lady."

"I'll be home by nine-thirty but if you can wait till ten, I got a surprise for ya."

A surprise usually meant some sort of sexy lingerie or a dress with easy access, which Wyatt never found particularly inspiring – he preferred pure nakedness – but he knew that for whatever reason some women believed that dressing in such ways made them more desirable, which made them more aroused, which made them more willing, so he always went along with the game. He smiled and said, "I cannot wait."

When Billy arrived, he also looked for me.

The two men sat mostly in silence paying only casual attention to the goings-on around them, each contemplating, as they each had many times before, the fact that a night in a tavern is never as satisfying as a day on the road.

They again met late the following morning at the same coffee shop, sat outside, and drank their coffees in philosophical silence. For a minute, Wyatt's attention was again pulled north. He then noticed that Billy's Road King was loaded up and strapped down. "I see you're getting ready to take off."

"Yeah."

"Problems with Nina?"

Billy took on a vexed look. "Yeah. She started hinting at marriage."

"Marriage?"

"Yeah. Said she needed a new dining room set and showed me her baby pictures."

"Fuck."

Billy gravely looked at Wyatt. "Then the kiss of death."

Wyatt looked back at him like he was waiting for the test results from a full body MRI.

Billy, fully serious, said, "She baked cookies."

"Shit."

"Couldn't get outta there fast enough."

Wyatt leaned in. "What kind?"

"Chewy oatmeal."

"Raisins?"

"Yep."

Wyatt fell against the back of his chair. "Damn. I love chewy oatmeal with raisins."

"Me too. They're my favorite and that's what scared the bejesus right outta me."

"Take them with you?"

"Hell yeah! Want some?"

"Absolutely."

Billy retrieved two large plastic food bags and gave one to Wyatt. They ate in silence as if contemplating an existential essay by Kierkegaard. When the cookies were half gone, Billy said, "You the marrying type?"

"No."

"Me neither. The only time I think of marriage is when I see a woman with scars and tattoos."

"But Nina does have another quality."

Billy adjusted his body looking philosophical. "Good point. Lemme amend my statement. The only marrying kind of woman has scars, tattoos and a tight ass and Nina's got only one outta three."

"I'll agree about the tight ass."

"And a damn fine tight one it is. But no scars or tattoos."

Wyatt slowly shook his head. "That is a shame."

"It is that." Billy washed down the last of a cookie with his coffee. "What about you? Staying or leaving?"

Wyatt sighed. "Oh, I'm taking off."

"Was Sammie talking marriage, too?"

"No. Well, in a roundabout way, I guess. Turns out her husband is coming back from a business trip this afternoon."

"Husband! Shit, I don't mess with married women."

Wyatt looked at his coffee, the way it slowly swirled, ribbons of cream snaking through the dark liquid. "My own policy is to stay away from them."

"Well don't feel bad. Once they start jiggling those tits in front of yer face like she did, it's easy to forget to ask about their marital status."

"That is true." Wyatt looked at Billy and admired the man. "Where're you off to?"

"Wanting to head up to Maine. Probably take my time in Vermont and New Hampshire. Maine is beautiful and friendly. Lotta lakes, only two interstates and that Acadia Park will make ya gawp-jawed. Did you know that Maine has more coastline miles than California?"

Wyatt wondered how anyone would even know that. "Something I did not know."

"Yeah, they got all them fjords or whatever the American word for it is. Where you headed?"

"Something beckons somewhere north of here, maybe in Michigan, but I don't know what. Maybe I'll check it out. But then I'm thinking of riding around the Ozarks a while, take in the local culture."

Billy smiled with reminiscence. "There's some good music happening there."

"That's what I heard."

"Good food, too. And you can get a plate of bacon any time, day or night."

"Something else I didn't know."

For some minutes, the two men sat in silence watching the small town goings-on. A father and his four-year-old daughter walking hand in hand, she holding a large, green and purple stuffed toy dragon; a small dog weaving through pedestrians; an elderly couple arm in arm, leaning into one another and a lifetime of memories.

For a few moments Wyatt's attention was again pulled to the north. Finally, he took a deep breath, finished his coffee, and stood up. "Well, good man, thank you for the cookies and if we ever meet again, it'll be a fine day."

"That it will, my friend." Billy stood up and they shook hands. "Keep the shiny and the rubber where they belong."

NINETEEN

...

I *BRIEFLY CONSIDERED GETTING* W*YATT* *TO FOLLOW THE DRAW TO THE* *north but to be honest, he wasn't yet ready. Instead, I watched him con-* *tinue west.*

He scooted west into Mississippi and spent the night in Tupelo. The next day, he meandered on any road with no more than two lanes, sometimes riding on dirt paths. The people there noticed him but none acted surprised.

The tree-covered roads held more shadows than sunlight and the shadows held the mysteries he somehow knew he would find but never find out about. All along were deserted homes and trailers, weed-wealthy creeks and smaller paths leading to darkness.

Sometime in the afternoon, he happened upon a flat and open area. Up ahead on his right was an old country church and he slowed down as he approached it. The building was wood paneled, painted white decades ago, and a brown cross hung above the two front doors, the left of which was open. Toward the back were two extensions that stuck out left and right so if someone looked down from above, the whole church looked like a cross. He silently praised the design.

About ninety people were exiting. The men and boys wore suits, the women and girls wore dresses. The preacher, an old thin man with short gray hair, wore an old black suit, a white shirt and a red bow tie, and walked with a spry but broken gait.

The men and the older boys were setting up tables and chairs outside the church on the left side of the dirt parking lot while the older girls covered them with cloths of different designs, and on them they laid tubs of silverware, piles of plates and red plastic cups. Younger children ran among them, laughing and shrieking.

Wyatt stopped while women crossed the road to their cars then crossed back carrying big pots and large plates filled with food. They smiled and waved and said, "God bless." Wyatt smiled and rode on.

Several miles down the road, just before a sharp left turn, he saw in his rear view mirrors a new blue Chevy pickup quickly coming up behind him so he pulled to the right side of the lane. When the pickup passed, it missed his left handlebar by inches then swerved in front of him forcing him to the dirt shoulder amid a cloud of dust. He heard laughter. Someone threw something out the passenger side window. The driver honked and the tires squealed as he sped around the corner.

At the same time, Wyatt caught a glimpse of me as I turned the corner going the other way. I have to say I was feeling good and looking fine that day, my hair waving behind me like an elongated flag of silver. Wyatt found a solid piece of ground for the kickstand, dismounted and looked back but by then I had all but disappeared into the distance.

Wyatt stood for a while to catch his composure. He looked around and saw that what had been thrown out of the window was a purse, its contents scattered about in the weeds. He gathered them, blowing the dust off of each one. Old tins of makeup, a small and worn booklet of bible verses, an old book of phone numbers, two translucent amber bottles of prescription pills, some receipts and a wallet.

Inside the wallet was a Medicare card, a picture ID, and discount cards for a local market and drug store. Wyatt unsnapped the left pouch and found some coins but didn't count them. The right pouch was unsnapped and empty.

He put everything into the purse, got out two bungee straps, strapped it to the luggage rack, rode back to the church and pulled into the parking lot opposite the tables. Three women walked up to him and bid him good afternoon.

He replied in kind, got off his bike and pointed to the purse. "I found this purse in the weeds down the road a bit."

"By the grace of God," said the first woman. The three looked up at him with wide-eyed wonder.

"It belongs to a Mildred Sadler. Would you happen to know who she is?"

"By the grace of God," said the first woman again.

The second woman said, "And you've come to return it. Aren't you a miracle."

Wyatt smiled. "Well, I don't know that I'm a miracle, I'm just trying to return a purse to its owner. Is she around?"

The three women leaned toward him with their hands clasped, as if they beheld a heavenly wonder. The first woman said, "She's inside praying to the Lord and the Lord has answered."

The third woman said, "She's old and rickety and can't stay in the sun too long."

Wyatt unstrapped the purse and put away the bungee cords. "There's a photo ID of her inside the wallet so I can just find her myself and not bother anyone."

Just then, the preacher walked over and extended a hand. "Preacher Jack, pleased to meet you."

"Name's Wyatt, pleasure's mine."

"What a blessed name," said the first woman. The other two women nodded in agreement.

The preacher said, "I see you found Millie's purse."

"I guess. Got run off the road and someone had thrown it into the weeds in front of me. Thought she might want it back." The three women continued to stare.

"What a fine thing to do!" Preacher Jack said. "You are indeed blessed and we are blessed to have you here."

"Well, thank you, I do appreciate that."

Preacher Jack hesitated a few moments. "May I ask a question of you, sir?"

"Yes."

"Inside the wallet, was there any money? Thirty-three dollars to be exact. The reason I ask is that Millie has been saving a dollar a week so as to buy a weekly planner for her great-great grandnephew who's about to start his studies at the local junior college. He's to be the first one in her family to go to college."

"That's a fine idea for a gift but I'm afraid there was no money except for some coins." Wyatt got out the wallet and showed them. "Thirty-three dollars you said?" Wyatt reached into his left front pocket and pulled out his money clip. He put his right arm through the purse handles, flipped through the bills pulling out a twenty, a ten and three ones. The women looked at him as if he were a vision.

The first woman said, "Millie had all ones."

"Now don't you go bothering him with that," said the second woman.

71

Wyatt replaced the bills with a ten, two fives and thirteen ones. "That's the closest I can get." He folded the bills in half.

The first woman said, "Millie folded her money in threes."

"Now you just hush," said the third woman.

Wyatt folded the bills in thirds, put them in the wallet's pouch, snapped it shut, then put the wallet back into the purse. "That's the best I can do."

"You are a blessed man," said the first woman. The others nodded.

Wyatt and Preacher Jack walked to the church. Inside, the only light was the sunlight coming through the door and through narrow rectangular windows tucked under the ceiling so that it was almost completely dark at the floor and as his line of sight went up, it got lighter and lighter until the light at the ceiling was almost blinding. Wyatt admired the architectural metaphor for earth and heaven.

Mildred Sadler sat in the front pew, bent over with eyes closed, her lips moving in sync with her silent prayer. She was five feet tall, weighed maybe seventy-five pounds, wore a pillbox hat and worn black leather shoes tied tightly. Below her knees, the lace end of a white slip showed just past the hem of her dark blue and flowered dress. Wyatt and Preacher Jack waited.

When she opened her eyes, Preacher Jack said, "Millie, this gentleman has brought you something." Mildred slowly turned her head, peered through large glasses with thick lenses and gasped when she saw Wyatt with his long hair and full beard. It was as if she beheld Jesus himself. Wyatt waited some seconds then said, "I found your purse."

She sat for a full minute without moving, a tear slowly coursing down her cheek. "Oh Lord, oh Lord, oh Lord!" She struggled to get up so Wyatt instinctively stepped forward to help but was held back by Preacher Jack. He whispered, "She insists on doing everything herself. She'll hit you if you try to help and it hurts."

Mildred haltingly walked over to Wyatt and gave him a hug, her face resting on his chest. "Thank you, dear boy, thank you. The Lord has blessed me and you are his blessing. Our God is a loving God."

TWENTY

•••

B ILLY RODE NORTH OUT OF DALTON. HE WAS EAGER TO GET UP TO MAINE but often pulled over to take photos. He stopped for the night at the Cherokee Casino and except for dinner, stayed in his room and slept several hours. As he lay between the cool sheets, he thought about how he had come to this place and how being an itinerant biker had never been in his plans.

Like his father, grandfather, and great grandfather, he had joined the Army on his eighteenth birthday, then for the following six months, knew nothing but the bliss of commitment, sacrifice, and duty.

His only disappointment happened when he was ordered into the Commanding Officer's office, where the CO and two other officers waited for him. The CO asked Billy what he intended for his military career. Billy answered with a controlled shout. "Sir, to kill the enemy, sir."

The CO barely held back a laugh and under his breath said, "Whatever." The disdain on the other two officers' faces was clear.

Billy was fuming when he brought up the meeting with his drill sergeant, a hard-cut man with laser-like gray eyes. He told Billy, "He's a pile o' hog shit if you ask me. But his daddy's a bigwig state senator and had his son join the army so's it'd look good on his resume when he goes on to become a bigwig senator himself. Just another thing to put up with in the army, son."

Three weeks later, Billy bought his first high-end camera. As he walked back to his barracks, he became engrossed in all it could do and as it hung from his neck, he fiddled with all of its different functions, paying little attention to where he was going. He walked into an unmarked building intending to use the bathroom.

He had unknowingly set the camera to take multiple shots, and just as he opened the door, his hand glanced the shutter button and ten flashes went off, one right after the other. Instead of sinks and toilet stalls he found himself standing in the doorway of a vacant office. There was nothing in it except for a large metal desk against the middle of the back wall and a swivel chair against the right wall. The CO was sitting in the chair, his pants at his ankles, getting a blowjob from a naked, five-year-old Puerto Rican boy.

Billy ran across the room and busted the CO in the nose, sending him to the floor. He took off his camera then beat the CO to a bloody unconsciousness. He told the boy to get dressed then took him off the base to a Lutheran church two blocks away. He explained to the minister what had happened and the minister agreed to watch after the boy and Billy's camera.

Billy went to his barracks and sat on his bunk. When it gets to a court martial, he thought, it'll be the word of a redneck at the end of basic training against that of a respected commanding officer who is the son of a wealthy Louisiana state senator who will hire the best lawyer available. Even if the boy testifies, his testimony will be twisted and made irrelevant. Eventually it would be made to look like I had set up the whole thing and it was the CO who had been molested.

It didn't take long for Billy to be arrested, but the military police, barely hiding their smiles, were mild in their handling of him. The truth of the matter was that most everyone on the base was happy about the thrashing the CO had gotten.

Three days later, Billy was taken out of his cell to a holding area where his hands were cuffed to two upside down steel U-bolts protruding out of a metal desk.

After a few minutes, the CO's senator-father and his lawyer sat across from him. With a grave voice, the lawyer said, "Hand over all the photos and the charges will go away. Never say anything about the incident and you'll get promoted up the ranks quickly." He glanced at the senator. "And we'll sweeten the pot with fifty thousand dollars."

Billy remained silent, thinking about the hackneyed cliché. "Gimme a day to think about it."

The next day, the senator and the lawyer were waiting for Billy and watched solemnly as he was handcuffed to the U-bolts. Just after the policeman left and before either of them could speak, Billy looked at the lawyer and said, "Four things. The boy'll be adopted somewheres where a Louisiana state senator cain't never find him. I'll set that up myself." He looked at the senator like he was a reprimanded dog. "Yer son is no longer in the army."

He looked back at the lawyer. "I get an honorable discharge and I'll need a million fer my troubles. Do all that and you'll get the photos."

Billy easily adapted to incarcerated life, mainly because he had access to thousands of books and the guards made sure he ate the best food available, which included a plate of bacon every day. Even the wife of one of the guards sent him chewy oatmeal with raisins cookies.

One day he was asked if he'd like spiritual counseling. He said, "Sounds like a right fine idea. If ya could get the minister from that Lutheran church a coupla blocks away, I'd appreciate it."

The next day, the minister told him, "He's a sweet kid. Laughs a lot. Wants to learn everything there is."

Billy asked about the possibility of the boy being adopted with no trace of his origins. The minister didn't think it would be a problem and said he would get right on it. A few months later, he informed Billy that the boy had been adopted by a Lutheran family who lived on a farm in Wisconsin and that the paperwork was "lost."

It took several more months for the senator to follow through with the honorable discharge and the million dollars. The first thing Billy did after he was released was to see the Lutheran minister, thank him, and retrieve his camera.

Billy finally got his first look at the photos. He chuckled then laughed out loud, even got up and started dancing. He messengered a flash drive with all ten photos on it to the senator. The senator immediately called Billy.

"What the fuck is this?"

"Them's the photos I promised to deliver."

The senator breathed deliberately. "There's nothing on them."

"Well, there's a door and a floor and an empty desk, and the back end of a coupla feet."

"God damn it, where are the rest?"

"The rest of the feet? There's just them two."

The senator exhaled a cold wrath. "The rest of the photos, Billy. Where are they?"

"That's all there is."

"So I paid a million dollars for nothing."

"No. You paid a million dollars to rid the Army of yer perverted son and to set that kid up to have a decent life. And who knows, maybe when he's all growed up he'll tell the world what a fucked up son you raised."

Billy felt the senator's foul smile. "You're not getting away with this."

"I ain't getting away with nothing. You did what you promised to do, I did what I promised to do. We're all square."

The phone went dead.

Billy half smiled as he lay on the bed, the muffled sounds of the casino stealing through the walls. He was unable to fully recover the elation he had felt then, the passage of time diluting colors, softening edges, and melding details into vagueness, like cream diffusing throughout a cup of coffee.

He pulled the two steel vials out of his pocket and squeezed them in his fist. He opened his hand, looked at them, then caressed them like they were a puppy, soft and fragile. The smile had left his face, replaced by a longing, an aching that could not be soothed, a sadness that could not be assuaged, and for some time, he was in the inescapable shadow of a sorrow.

Ten minutes.

TWENTY-ONE

...

PREACHER JACK INSISTED WYATT EAT WITH THEM SO THE TWO WALKED outside and joined the line of parishioners eager for a Sunday afternoon feast. The first two tables were jammed with ham and bean stew, beans and cornbread, beans and greens, thin slabs of fatback, pork sausage, fried chicken, rice, and gravy. The third table was full of desserts. Sweet potato, pecan, peach and lemon meringue pies, and coconut, chocolate and hummingbird cakes.

The children gathered around Wyatt asking all sorts of questions about his motorcycle and because he was a patient man, he answered all of them. When he finished eating, they followed him to the bike. "First," he said, "Those two long, chrome things on either side are called pipes. They get sizzling hot so don't touch them."

"Hot enough to fry an egg on?" asked one of the kids.

He smiled. "Yes." Then he showed them all the main parts of a motorcycle and explained the function of each.

An eleven year-old boy asked, "Can I go for a ride?"

"As long as you have permission." The boy looked at his dad and the dad nodded. Wyatt handed him his helmet and the boy said, "I don't need no helmet."

"My bike, my rules. You wear a helmet." All the parents were relieved and nodded agreement.

For the next two hours, Wyatt gave rides to all the kids, the mothers safety-pinning the girls' dresses between their legs so that they looked like fancy pantaloons. After their rides, the girls' smiles could not be bigger, and the boys each walked an inch taller.

As the sunlight waned, Wyatt helped with the cleanup then went to the kitchen where Preacher Jack was washing dishes. "I believe it's time I headed on. Wanted to say thank you for your hospitality."

"It's been an honor, son. Where are you staying?"

"Don't know. I'll find a place somewhere."

Preacher Jack scraped the suds off his arms and leaned against the tub, his hands on either side of it. "Well, if you're not finicky about your accommodations, there's a spare room just off the altar."

"Thank you, Preacher Jack, but your generosity has been more than I deserve."

Preacher Jack slowly stood up straight and faced Wyatt. "Not to Millie. She and the others are claiming you a miracle."

"Hers is a sweet soul, but really, I'm just an itinerant biker."

"That may be, but my offer stands. Be proud to have you lodging for a night."

Wyatt accepted the offer. He unloaded his things into the small room, lay down on the thin-mattressed bed and read sixty pages of Larry Brown's Faye, his descriptions of Mississippi life like the slow and inexorable rhythms of the great river that dominated everything around it.

At 3 a.m., instead of going for a walk, he sat where Mildred had, and looked at the altar. Above it was Jesus nailed to the cross. The bloodied hands and feet. The emaciated body. The anguished look.

He heard the door to his left open. The screws holding the top door hinge were loose so Preacher Jack had to pull up the doorknob then push the door against the jamb.

Preacher Jack carefully closed the door then sat at the opposite end of the pew from Wyatt. He bowed his head and prayed, then leaned against the side of the pew and stretched out his legs on the pew itself. "Wyatt, would you object to a personal observation from an old preacher?"

"Not at all."

"All right." He swallowed a breath like great grandfather just before crawling out of bed. "Now, I do not say this with malice, but I do not take you for a believer."

"I would say that's an accurate assessment."

"What in your life turned you away from the Lord?"

Wyatt raised an eyebrow. "A more pertinent question would be if there was anything that had ever turn me toward the Lord."

"I see." Preacher Jack nodded knowingly. "Is it that you see mostly evil in the world?"

Wyatt looked at Preacher Jack, his eyes gentle. "Not at all. In fact, I see much the opposite. You often hear about evil but only because it's the anomaly, the uncommon. The usual, the normal, the garden variety, the every-day are not newsworthy. If you hear about something, it's almost always not that which is common.

"It's not just the news, either. It's people, too. People will talk about a fight in a bar. Why? Because if you consider the millions, hundred of millions, of people who go to bars every day, bar fights are actually a rare occurrence. Same could be said for armed robbery, extortion, rape and murder. In the main, Preacher Jack, people are good."

Preacher Jack pressed his lips together in thought. "You're an intelligent man, Wyatt, educated, too, and you speak well. Are you a teacher?"

Wyatt looked at the altar again. "I was. I quit."

"Why?"

"I had become something I was ashamed of."

"What was that?"

Wyatt, fatigued by the inability to escape his past, closed his eyes and sighed. "I was a professor of American Literature and had lost my passion for it, but at the same time I was held in esteem for being a champion of it, an icon of artistic integrity. It was a sham and I was a charlatan."

"Who or what made you see that?"

"An accumulation of things, of events, some small, some large. I came to realize that there is a limit to the number of deceptions a man can hold and when he reaches that limit, he is faced with two options. He can fool himself into thinking his deceptions were necessary thereby justifying them at which time he becomes an illusion, a nothing, a deception of deceptions, a reflection of a shadow, and can no longer truly enjoy the adulation he receives."

Wyatt slumped into a resigned attitude. "The other option is to face up to his deceptions, see them for what they are, see himself for what he is. And what he will see, and what I saw, has very little worth, if any. Only then, however, can he begin to build another life."

With a measure of compassion in his voice, Preacher Jack said, "And you started your life anew."

"I did, though I can't say I've built much."

"Have you considered that it was the Lord who made you see this?"

Wyatt looked at Preacher Jack, his kind demeanor and comfortable presence. "I like you, Preacher Jack. You're a good man. I'm not going to argue your beliefs, but I will say that I did consider that, but it was a conclusion I didn't countenance."

Preacher Jack nodded, gazed at Jesus on the cross, then reached into the inside pocket of his coat. "I do believe the Lord is understanding enough to countenance someone smoking in his church now and then." He pulled out a pack of cigarettes, a small aluminum ashtray and a box of matches. "Care to join me?"

"Sounds good." Wyatt crossed his legs, lit a cigarette and cuffed his left pant leg for an ashtray.

They had been smoking for a while when Preacher Jack broke the silence. "You see, many look for a sign or a proof or a certainty before they will believe, when it's really the other way around. Certainty grows from belief.

"A young man believes that someday he'll be a doctor or a young girl believes that someday she'll be a ballerina. They work at it and work at it and one day, they are a doctor and a ballerina and those are facts of which they are certain."

The curling smoke from their two cigarettes made Preacher Jack appear translucent, like an ascended prophet. He continued. "Many things went into that, of course. Reading, learning, practicing and so on, but the constancy throughout it all was belief. It's similar to the way that belief will lead to certainty of God's existence and his mercy and forgiveness."

Wyatt pondered Preacher Jack's words, the wisdom of them. "That's an excellent analogy and it does make sense, Preacher Jack, it does. But the certainty they each have is a personal one; one that, through belief, they each created. But wouldn't God, by definition, or at least the way I understand the definition, be a certainty that exists independent of man, prior to and beyond man? And if a man were to realize that certainty, how would he distinguish it from a personal one?"

"Are you expecting me to say 'through belief' thereby creating a circular logic?"

Wyatt laughed. "Oh, you're too smart for that, my friend."

Preacher Jack smiled, took a long puff and again looked at Jesus. "I am certain of God, Wyatt, of his existence. But I can't convince you or anyone else of it and I don't try. All I try to do is get others to look, to just look, and hope that they, too, will someday be certain. Sometimes, true, it comes as a revelation like when Paul was on the road to Damascus or when Martin Luther made his pilgrimage to the Vatican. With nearly everyone else, however, it's a path, a journey, individually taken and oftentimes long."

"A journey taken with the constancy of belief."

"Yes, with the constancy of belief."

Wyatt tapped a long ash into his cuff. "But 'belief' is intransitive. Doesn't the belief required to reach that certainty actually have to a be a belief in something?"

Preacher Jack looked at Wyatt, not at the man but at his internal conflicts, and felt a deep compassion. "Yes. You could say that, that we each need something or many things to believe in. But that doesn't necessitate a belief in God. It could be a belief in a better life, in the possibility of greater happiness, or in the basic goodness of mankind, as you stated earlier."

Wyatt raised his eyebrows in cautious humor. "Are you implying that I'm on a journey to the certainty of God's existence?"

Preacher Jack chuckled once then took on a sincere look. "I don't know where your journey will take you, how long it will last, or even if it will ever end. Only you can find the answer to those questions."

"Now we're sounding like Buddhists or Taoists. Or Scientologists."

Preacher Jack's eyes sparkled with affection. "We are, yes."

Wyatt wet his thumb and forefinger and squeezed out the glowing bud at the end of his cigarette, the momentary burn a kind of assurance. He put the butt in his cuff. "What if the journey to a divine certainty isn't completed before one dies?"

"Then we are comforted in the grace of God."

Wyatt looked at Preacher Jack with an easy expression. "Earlier, I said you were a good man, Preacher Jack. I believed it then but now I'm certain of it."

"And you, Wyatt, are indeed blessed. I was certain of it from the beginning." Preacher Jack sat up, prayed one more time, bid Wyatt goodnight, then ambled off to bed.

Wyatt sat for another half hour, smoked another cigarette, then got a few tools out of his fork bag. He carefully opened the door with the loose hinge and saw a hallway that led to the closed door of Preacher Jack's bedroom.

He placed a hymnal under the door so it would remain upright. The screws in the top hinge were so loose that he simply pulled them out. He got his big Swiss Army knife then went outside to the back of the church where found an old two-by-four. He shaved off a dozen slivers, each about an inch long.

When he got back inside, he pushed the wood slivers into the screw holes using a flat head screw driver, then used a small Phillips screwdriver to jam them farther in. The heads of the screws were worn so he got a rubber band out of the fork bag and cut a one-inch piece off of it. He placed the piece of rubber band over the head of the first screw and screwed it all the way in, then repeated the process for the remaining three screws. Last, he sprayed a small amount of WD-40 on each hinge. He closed and opened the door several times. It was quiet and held perfectly.

On the way to his room, he stopped before the altar and for some time looked at Jesus. The wretchedness and despair. He thought, I'm not convinced you are whom everyone says you are, but I'll take it as fact that you existed. And if, indeed, you died while nailed to a cross, I know that your greatest suffering was loneliness.

TWENTY-TWO

•••

SEVERAL DAYS AFTER LEAVING DALTON, BILLY ROLLED INTO TENNESSEE and pulled over at a mom and pop diner in Kingsport. He sat at the counter and ordered his usual: a plate of bacon and a tall glass of lemonade.

He had gotten there faster than I'd anticipated so I had to slip out of the back door.

Sitting next to a window was a man in a high-powered electric wheelchair, a nice one. Deep burgundy with white sidewall tires, internet radio, the works. He wore a soiled red baseball cap and a green camo army-issue jacket with the sleeves cut off.

When Billy's lunch arrived, he carried everything over to the man's table. "Mind if I join ya?" The man nodded at the chair across from him. Billy sat down and extended his hand. "Name's Billy."

"Wes." He shook Billy's hand then looked out the window. "Pretty day to be riding."

"It is that."

Wes was a large man. Thick arms softly curved with muscles that had once been chiseled. His face, rounded as well, was framed with an unkempt head of hair, a bushy moustache that sat like a crown, and a beard that reminded Billy of thick brambles in autumn.

He slowly scratched his neck in an upward motion. "I used to ride. When I was a youngster. Started with dirt bikes. Broke a few bones, but it was okay. Couldn't stay off of them. Bought a Gixxer when I was eighteen and got four speeding tickets in the first six months. Joined the army a year later."

Billy swallowed a mouthful of bacon. "I started out with dirt bikes, too, when I was six, and got a beat-up Kawasaki Eliminator when I started high school. When I got my license, I did what you did and got a used Ninja ZX-11. Got my share of tickets, too. Where was ya stationed at?"

"Fort Campbell. You?"

"Fort McPherson." Wes nodded twice. Billy asked, "Mind if I ask ya what happened?"

Wes gazed out the window, his eyes following an elderly lady pushing a baby carriage with a small white dog in it. He took a deep breath. "I's part of a sweep through a small settlement. Afghanistan. There was this building where eleven of them were hiding, waiting for us. When we got inside, they tried to set off an IED but it didn't do anything. There was some gunfire and I got hit twice in each leg.

"One of the other guys, Willmont, was helping me get out so's I could get to a doctor when we was ambushed by two more of 'em. He fell back on me – couldn't help it – and my legs got crushed between all the rubble. He killed one of them, stabbed him under the ribs, and a sniper got the other one. We had to wait two hours before the town was all clear and the docs could come. By then it was too late. The legs were gone."

Wes drew his fingers over the controls on the wheelchair's right armrest. "That fella, Willmont, became a sniper himself and later went on to work for the CIA. He reaches out a couple of times a year. Feels bad about what happened. I tell him he didn't do nothing wrong and that he saved my life, and he did, and that's what's important, but he still feels responsible."

Billy looked out the window. A cherry red '67 Camaro slowly rumbled by, its driver in a white tank top and there was a cigarette hanging out of his mouth. He looked back at Wes. "Think about it much?"

Wes cocked his head to the left. "Know what I think about the most?" Billy shook his head. "Beauty."

"Beauty?"

"Yeah, beauty. I find it everywhere. And you can, too. It all started this one time about six months before I got hurt. We was combing through another village looking for bad guys. Steel rods poking out the walls, rubble and dust everywhere, hiding places all over. So hot it felt like my skin was frying on a griddle. It was my first sweep and I was scared shitless.

"Walked up the stairs of this big building and in the room at the end of the hall was this Taliban guy playing a glockenspiel. Can you believe it? Just standing there trying to figure this melody out."

For a few moments, his attention went across the street to a shopkeeper who was sweeping the sidewalk. When he turned back to Billy, his eyes were closed, his voice distant. "I just stood there and listened. When he finally got the melody right, he started working on the rhythm. In his own world he was in another world, know what I mean? Shit. He knew he was gonna die and what's he do? Plays a goddamn glockenspiel. It was beautiful.

"At first I couldn't bring myself to shoot him. I just wanted him get that song right and when he finally did, I still didn't want to kill him." He opened his eyes and stared at his hands. "But then I started thinking about my buddies who lost all their blood in that fucking desert." He looked directly at Billy, his eyes glazed over like a frozen pond. "I shot him. In the back. Walked over and shot him upside his skull. Never did take a look at his face."

Wes took a deep breath and rubbed his neck on the collar of his jacket. "That's the only thing that's ever bothered me, that I never took a look at him. Killing him was one thing, a war thing, but not looking at his face was like I disrespected him, something he didn't deserve."

The two men sat in silence. Wes threw his head back and again closed his eyes. Billy gazed out the window, his eyes unfocused. A small flock of birds swooped down then up, a few of them chirped nonchalantly. After some minutes, Wes faced Billy with eyes from another world. "You believe in God?"

Billy stopped breathing for a few moments. "Yeah. Don't think I believe in Heaven and Hell, but I believe in God."

Wes stared at Billy then closed his eyes and slowly opened them. "Good way to look at it, I suppose."

Billy raised his eyebrows and nodded. "Hope so."

TWENTY-THREE

...

W YATT STOPPED BEFORE CROSSING THE MISSISSIPPI RIVER AND SAT next to the waters for a long while. He thought about its history and came to view it as a physical expression of the Dark Companion, bleak and inconsolable, and he wondered how many souls and dreams and passions lay inert in its depths. The mysteries hummed constant.

He would often look for the Dark Companion as he rode through the lush Ozarks and over the angled and richly foliated landscapes of the east- and west-running Ouachita Mountains, the curves taken quickly and without thought.

Bobcats, coyotes and badgers watched him from hidden nooks; hawks, crows and whip-poor-wills would fly away and mock the darkness that surrounded him. The few clouds followed. The people he passed viewed him as a loner who carried the darkness he chased.

A week later, he rode into the Kansas winds and the small, dry towns of Eastern Colorado. Still, the Dark Companion eluded him.

Wyatt was standing under the eave of a convenience store in Grand Junction smoking a cigarette. I didn't intend for him to see me but he did, so I kept looking straight ahead and quickly walked through the door. He threw down his cigarette and followed me.

When he got to the door, he stood face to face with a woman holding a large cloth bag with handles of duct tape and a sport biker's full-face helmet that was scratched with a furrowed scar on the right side. She wore a tan mechanic's shirt with the name tag ripped off, khaki Dickie pants, and new white tennis shoes with turquoise stripes and laces.

"You a biker?"

"Yes."

"Got yer bike with ya?"

"Yes."

"Hitch a ride?"

He looked at her, down and up. Though she was only thirty years old, there was a depression-era mustiness about her, desolate and brooding. Thickset, five feet nine inches tall with no curves on her sides, eyes like ancient bronze coins, lips curled down at the ends, and a hard face like the lift on the back of a moving van. Her short hair stood out in all directions, her skin was like medium-grit sandpaper, and her breasts were like cinderblocks. The impression was that she could live on a diet of broken bottles and used motor oil as easily as tiramisu and dry champagne. He said, "I'm headed southwest."

"Okay."

"All right." Wyatt walked through the doorway. "I need to eat. You hungry?" She shrugged. "Well, come on."

They went over to the deli counter and Wyatt ordered a double pastrami, fries and a large soda. He turned to the woman. "What'll you have?"

"Water's fine."

"Water?"

"Yeah."

"When was the last time you ate?" She stared at him, her eyes expressionless and distant. He turned to the girl behind the counter and said, "Double the order and add two pieces of cherry pie."

The woman first picked up the pie with her hands and ate it in three bites, ignoring the utensils the way a truck mechanic would ignore a Swiss watchmaker's tools. She devoured the fries like a wood chipper devouring a pine branch, and pounced on the pastrami like a junkyard dog on a steak. She drank the root beer in large gulps, belched after every gulp and refilled the cup four times. Wyatt admired her efficiency – she never even bothered to lick her fingers clean – because she finished before he was halfway through his pastrami.

"Want another piece of pie?" She stared at him. "Another pastrami?" She continued staring. "Both?"

"Okay."

When they were about done, Wyatt said, "Name's Wyatt." The woman swallowed the last of the pastrami, chased it with a last, long drink of root beer, then belched. "Cassie."

TWENTY-FOUR

...

IT WAS MID-AFTERNOON WHEN WYATT AND CASSIE ARRIVED IN MOAB, where Wyatt filled the gas tank and loaded the touring pack with provisions. They went back north then entered the rock-spired and inspiring Arches National Park. Wyatt turned on a macadam side road to the northwestern part of the park where he found a level place for their campsite.

He unpacked the little they needed for the evening, smoked a cigarette then did six sets of thirty pushups. Cassie stared at him the entire time like a carrion-eating animal looking at something it had never before seen. Wyatt unscrewed the top off a plastic water bottle and drank it in one gulp.

He held his hand in front of him, turned it sideways and it fit perfectly between the sun and the horizon. "An hour before sunset. Perfect time for a walk." He got up and walked west. After a dozen paces he turned around. Cassie, still staring at him, hadn't moved. He said, "Come on, Cassie, this is a magical place."

Cassie stayed a good distance behind Wyatt, his boots and her shoes squeezing out little puffs of reddish brown dust, some of which would lightly twirl and suspend in the dry air while the rest would settle back to the ground and look as if their new resting places had been theirs for millennia.

They meandered through pockets of pebbles and around rocks in patterns of incomprehensible geometries, boulders like felled and broken statues, and long-dead trees the color of bone. Yucca and blackbrush and rice grass and rockcress with flowers of washed out pink. A skunkbush with a plastic bag hanging from it that Wyatt put in his back pocket.

Insects ran or flew away and reptiles, possibly made grotesquely colorful by the proximity to uranium deposits that were carried away long ago, scurried out of their path then stopped and looked at the tall stranger and she who followed. In front of them the hoodoos were like Neolithic avatars.

The few other people around were walkers and hikers wearing high boots and shorts and wide brimmed hats to block out the sun, and most had two long walking sticks of gold or red or silver, and they would look ahead after several carefully placed steps as if to assure themselves that nothing had moved and that they still traveled in the best direction, like disciples drawn to shrines.

Wyatt climbed to the top of a small mound and looked around as if hoping for something, anything, answers to which he would later form questions. Cassie watched him, then after some minutes stood next to him. She said, "There ain't no magic here."

"Why do you say that?"

"'Cause you said it's a magical place."

"You're right, I did say that. But how do you know there's no magic here?"

"There just ain't."

They each stared silently in front of them, the air of the late summer's day hot, musty and still. She continued. "Y'see all there is, is what there is and if ya see something ya ain't seen before, that's all it is, something ya ain't seen before. Somebody else has seen it a bunch." Wyatt slowly turned toward her as she continued. "And if ya see something ya don't understand, somebody else probably does, and if nobody does, it still don't mean there's magic in it."

"Okay." Wyatt looked again at the view before them. "But this is really something, isn't it? The from-a-distance beauty of it all."

"Same thing with beauty and it don't matter if it's close by or way out there." Wyatt looked back at her. She went on. "See, you say it's beautiful but that's just you saying it's beautiful. Things ain't got no beauty in 'em 'cept for what people think is there."

"So you don't think an orange sunset is more beautiful than, say, the rotted carcass of a coyote."

"I do, but that's just me saying it is."

"So beauty is within us?"

Cassie voice was like an old and wearied philosopher, snubbed and forgotten. "No. That's just a different way of saying beauty is in something, which it's not."

"So we've created this concept of beauty and we label things with it."

"I guess."

Wyatt let his eyes scan over the hard and heated land, the drips of sweat on his face unmoving. He looked left to right then left again and farther beyond to a near vertical rock wall that seemed to have folded into itself, and the low tamarisk that grew at the bottom of it. The air shimmered as if the afternoon sunlight was angled through silk gauze, and it made the reds and browns bleed into one another as if they had been watercolored. He spotted a bobcat, low and stealthy.

When the sun first touched the top of the rock wall to their left, they headed back to their camp. Cassie asked Wyatt if he was going to make a fire and he said he would but only a small one for some coffee because they had no food that needed heating and there was nothing that indicated a particularly cold night.

Cassie kept her hand on her bag as she watched Wyatt gather wood, bundle it together and light it. He went to the bike, opened the touring pack, got out six water bottles, two packages of beef jerky and a large tin coffee cup that had a carrying handle made of several twisted layers of thin wire. Inside of it was a plastic food bag bound by a rubber band.

He unbound the bag and covered the bottom of the cup with coffee grounds, refastened the bag, put it in the touring pack and took out an old dishtowel. He secured the touring pack's latches then walked over to Cassie and handed her two bottles and one of the packages of jerky. He poured a half bottle of water into the coffee cup, slipped a twig under the handle and placed it on the fire.

Cassie quickly ate the jerky and drank both bottles. Wyatt drank slowly while eating small bites. He sat looking east. Cassie looked at him for a full minute then turned and faced the west, and they stayed thus, unmoving and quiet.

After the sun set and the gloaming had passed, Wyatt lay down and measured the passing of time by the movements of the stars against the ancient columns of rock. Cassie went back to studying him. She kept her hand on her bag.

A little while later, Wyatt slipped the twig under the handle of the coffee cup and lifted it from the fire. He added the other half bottle of water to cool it down and lessen the bitter taste. He wrapped it with the dishtowel, carefully took a sip then offered it to Cassie. "Nothing like cowboy coffee."

They passed it back and forth, each taking small sips. After a while, he said, "Had enough?" She nodded and he put the cup next to the fire.

Cassie studied Wyatt. "You think I'm ugly?"

"No."

"Yes you do."

"I do not think you're ugly."

"Then why ain't you making a move on me?"

Wyatt sighed. "First of all, you have knives and a gun. Second, and more importantly, our agreement was for a ride, not a ride and sex."

"How'd you know I had knives and a gun?"

"I saw them in your bag when you got on the bike."

She continued studying him, her eyes mere slits. "So you don't think I'm ugly."

"No, I do not."

"You a faggot?"

"No."

"I still think you think I'm ugly."

Wyatt breathed deeply. "I do not think you're ugly."

Wyatt got another package of jerky for each of them. They ate and had been silent for a long time when Wyatt got his sleeping bag and unrolled it. "Here. You get the penthouse."

"The what?"

Wyatt smiled. "The sleeping bag's yours. I'll sleep on the ground."

"Yer gonna get cold."

"I'll lie close to the fire. Besides, I'm good at bundling up."

Cassie scooted into the sleeping bag without removing her clothes or shoes. Wyatt laid out four t-shirts in a line next to the fire, put on a long sleeve undershirt, his leather jacket and his chaps, then rolled up his vest for a pillow.

Both stayed awake for a long time. Cassie watched the fire's smoke curl and lift and wondered about fine things she had heard about but had never touched, never experienced, what it must feel like to wear high-heeled shoes or a pearl necklace. Wyatt kept time with the revolving firmament.

They slept.

TWENTY-FIVE

• • •

*T*HERE WAS A MORE FRUITFUL PLACE FOR BILLY THAN MAINE, BUT HE
*can be, well, bull-headed about deciding his own routes, so I had to ride
by him three times before he decided to head into West Virginia. Three days
later, on a Thursday night, it was a relief to see him roll into the parking lot
of a bar in Welch. He saw me leave and started after me, but I hurried out
the door and disappeared into the night.*

The bar was large and served all sorts of fried food, including bacon,
which Billy thought was a blessed thing. For a while he played solids and
stripes on an old pool table that was slightly off-level and covered in green
felt that was so worn that the gray slate could be seen underneath. But no
one paid it any mind because the bet was only a dollar a ball and it was
much too hot to get angry.

Billy took a break from the game and looked around. The place was
over-furnished with creative wall lamps, framed posters and mirrors
advertising beer. Six TVs were scattered about, all with the sound off and
showing baseball games. Two couples were working an old pinball machine,
staring at the silver ball like they were following a hypnotizing watch. The
music coming out of hidden speakers blended with the drone of a dozen
conversations, the overall effect like a shopping mall a day before Christmas. There was one item, however, that didn't fit in and that's what fetched
his attention.

She was wearing ironed and creased light green slacks, black and polished
loafers, flowered socks, a beige blouse, a boa that was a mere wisp of green
and yellow and a pearl inlaid comb in her hair. She was sitting at the end
of the bar sipping a Tom Collins.

Billy sat next to her and struck up a conversation. Her name was Charlotte and she was pretty in a healthy, Midwestern type of way, and there

were lines on her face though none went deep. She was widowed and he guessed her to be in her late-forties or early fifties. She was an excellent conversationalist and they ended up talking quite a while.

They left around midnight and went back to her house, a large plantation-like structure with six high columns supporting a balcony that stretched its entire width. The tall wooden front doors had an intricate pastoral scene carved into them.

The floor of the entry way was wide slabs of heavily varnished, roughly hewn dark walnut with darker dowels. In the middle was a reflection of the large circular light fixture with dangling crystals that hung from the center of the domed ceiling. The walls were painted off-white and had wainscoting of a lighter wood Billy didn't recognize.

Charlotte led him to the parlor and told him to have a seat. The chairs were handcrafted and covered with a detailed brocade of flowers, foxes and multi-colored birds against a white background. He told her he didn't think his jeans were clean enough for them. She said not to worry, so he sat on one but couldn't bring himself to lean back because his vest was probably dirtier than his jeans. She asked what he wanted to drink and he said a beer was just fine.

She came back with a bottle and put it on a coaster on the teakwood table. In her other hand was some sort of mixed drink. She said she'd be back in a minute and walked down the long hall to the right. Billy finished his beer, threw the bottle into a lid-covered trashcan under the kitchen sink, then helped himself to another.

Charlotte returned wearing a short, transparent nightgown with a wide and ruffled blue hem, a dark blue lace bra and matching panties. She said that the night sky was pretty and asked Billy if he wanted to sit on the veranda and look at the stars. He figured she liked to have sex outside, something he enjoyed as well, so he said okay. It turned out she did like to have sex outside and came on to him so fast that he didn't have time finish his beer.

Afterward they walked back into the house and sat, naked, on the brocade chairs. She told him she was in four book clubs, each meeting once a month. Billy wanted to tell her how much he loved reading, but decided not to because he didn't want to encourage any long-range plans she might have, though she had made no indication that she had any.

She then told him she was sixty-seven years old and it was a surprising fact. In the light of the parlor he openly admired the fact that, other than the shallow wrinkles on her face, her skin was smooth, her muscles toned and her breasts still had a bit of an upward lift to them.

It was an easy conversation. Billy told her about riding around the country alone and she was honestly absorbed in his anecdotes. They traded stories for a while and within an hour, she was sipping on her third drink and was fairly drunk. Her vocabulary became a little gutter-like and out of the blue, in the middle of one of her own anecdotes, she told him that she goes to a bar once or twice a year and finds "a nice gentleman to fuck me until I'm so sore I can't walk." Billy took the cue, walked over, and they had another go at it.

There was a fourth and a fifth round of drinks and just after sitting down with her sixth drink, she leaned against the arm of her chair and closed her eyes. Billy barely caught her glass before any of it spilled.

He picked her up and carried her to her bedroom; pulled back the comforter, blanket and sheets with his right foot, then gently laid her down and tucked the covers all around her. She smiled. He went back to the kitchen, got one last beer and drank it while sitting on the veranda.

Afterward, he joined Charlotte in bed. She twice woke him up before dawn.

When Billy awoke in the late morning, he was alone. He rolled onto his back and stretched out with his hands as far back of his head as possible and pushed down the backs of his knees, and it felt so good that he stayed in that position for minutes.

He went to the bathroom, relieved himself and washed out his mouth. He looked at himself in the mirror, washed his face then gargled with the mouthwash that sat next to the water basin. His hangover was mild and he felt as good and relaxed as possible.

He didn't bother dressing and when he opened the bedroom door he smelled bacon frying. He walked into the kitchen and Charlotte was wearing nothing but a flowered pinafore apron. They kissed and groped and Billy lifted her onto the butcher's block and they went at it again.

Their conversations were lively and the subject matters ranged from movies to astrophysics to the paranormal. She talked about the freedoms of being elderly and said that because there was no boyfriend or husband in her future there was no need to look or hope for one and no need for romance and all the complications that accompanied it. Billy said it was pretty much the same with being an itinerant biker.

She told him that she could say whatever was on her mind in any way she wanted and that, because of her age, people might shake their heads in disapproval, but she never got any backlash. Billy told her that he was pretty much like that, too, but it sometimes resulted in a fracas.

Once, she asked him how he managed to stay on the road year round without a job. He told her about the million dollar out-of-court settlement he had gotten and that he figured he'd stay on the road until it got down to about two hundred thousand. Then he'd buy a small house in Georgia, get a job and get married.

She was incredulous. "You got a million dollars and didn't invest any of it?"

"Never thought to. Don't know about that kinda stuff."

"Oh heavens. How much do you have left?"

"Don't know exactly. Seven-fifty, eight hundred, something like that."

Charlotte gave him a stern look like an old schoolmarm disciplining a student. "Young man, this is what we're going to do. I'm going to give you a million dollars and you're going to give it to my investment banker to take care of. When your portfolio has grown to over one and a quarter million, you're going to pay me back. No interest. With the money you already have, you'll be back up to a million, which you're going to invest in an annuity that'll pay eight to twelve percent a year. That's enough to live on, right? Then you'll never have to work."

Billy looked at her like she was an angel. He finally shook his head and managed to say, "That's real kind of you, Charlotte. Don't know how to thank you."

She walked over, put her hand on his manhood and said, "Well, I can think of one way, darling."

On Monday morning, Charlotte transferred the million dollars into Billy's bank account and by the afternoon, her investment banker had found three lucrative construction projects.

As Billy was leaving Tuesday morning, he said, "I don't think I can ever thank you enough, Charlotte."

"Well, you've already done a fine job of thanking me, darling, but if you ever feel like thanking me more, you know where I live."

He headed west.

TWENTY-SIX

...

THE FOLLOWING DAY WYATT AND CASSIE SHARED THE REST OF THE coffee and each drank a bottle of water. Wyatt provisioned each of them with a bag of trail mix, a bag of dried apricots and another two bottles of water. They walked south.

Soon, Wyatt kneeled down and studied the red flowers of a Christmas cactus and another time did the same with the faded yellows of a biscuit-root. A large bird flew out of the mountains to the southwest, but it was too far away to tell if it was a peregrine falcon or an eagle. Cassie continued to follow from a distance and when he stopped she would stop, look at him, then glance at the highway.

They walked like that all day and arrived back at camp just after sunset. Wyatt again prepared coffee, smoked three cigarettes, did his one hundred and eighty pushups, then lay down and measured time with the stars.

Cassie again looked to the west catching glimpses of headlights. When Wyatt retrieved the coffee from the fire, she said, "So you really don't think I'm ugly?"

"No, I do not." Not wanting a repeat of the previous night's conversation, he asked, "Where'd you get that helmet?"

"Northern Colorado, east side of the Rockies. I's sleeping under this ledge below the road and woke up when there's a crash. Guy went over the edge and his helmet just flew off and I saw where it landed. Stayed hid while they took him away and cleaned everything up and when everybody was gone I went over and got it. Figured it'd be worth something."

Wyatt hadn't added any cool water to the coffee and when he took a sip, he grimaced as it scorched his tongue. "Where are you from?"

"Where I's born?"

"Yeah."

"San Francisco."

"San Francisco?" Wyatt was dumbfounded.

"Yeah. We white trash folks is all over but ya don't see us unless ya want to and most people don't want to."

He nodded. "Still have family in California?"

"I might, don't know. When I's three my daddy got into some trouble with some Mexicans and we hadda move so he robbed a liquor store and we took a bus to Kentucky. But then he got into trouble with the law and kept getting into trouble so we ended up living in both Carolinas and Georgia and Louisiana."

Wyatt blew on the coffee, cautiously slurped another sip then handed the cup to Cassie. "Are your parents still around?"

"Momma might be, daddy's gone."

"Have any other family?"

"I do, but I don't know where they's at. Don't wanna know, either."

"How long have you been running?"

Cassie choked on the coffee then hawked and spit. "I never said I's running."

"You're right, you didn't. How long have you been on the road?"

"Ten or eleven years, depending on where ya start counting from."

"Ten or eleven years."

"Yeah."

"Why did you leave?"

"Why'd I leave home?"

"Yeah."

Cassie gulped a mouthful of coffee and shuddered at the heat of it. "My daddy and step-daddy."

"Your daddy and step-daddy?"

"Yeah. My daddy started feeling me up when I's eight and by the time I's nine, he's making me fuck him regular. Kept going on for three more years then he got some lung disease. He'd just lay there in bed all day and night breathing funny and alls I could think of was killing him."

She swirled around the black liquid and a few drops fell onto her fingers. "One Sunday I pretended to be sick so my Momma went to church alone. While she's gone I got a old rag and stuffed it in his mouth and squeezed his nose shut. His eyes was wide open and he's shaking and staring at me all scared and I kept telling him he's going to Hell. Watched him die. Nobody ever thought it was me. They just figured it was all natural."

Wyatt watched the coffee on her fingers slowly reach for the earth. "What happened afterward?"

"I run away but they found me and brung me back. Momma got married a few months later and then my step-daddy started doing the same as my daddy'd done."

She took a sip then handed the cup back to Wyatt. He asked, "Then what?"

"I's having trouble in school so they thought I needed some outside interests so I got onto a softball team. One day I come home from practice, Momma was gone, and there's my step-daddy in the recliner just sleeping away, his belly sticking up like a revival tent. 'Bout as big, too. Anyways, I took my bat and hauled off and hit him a bunch."

She looked at the lights on the highway, which reminded her of lightning bugs in the Louisiana swamps. "Went to juvie a while then got set up with some foster parents. They's nice folks, treated me good, I liked 'em. Then one day I's walking home from school and my step-daddy drove up with a gun and told me to get in his truck. His dick was already out and hard and he made me suck him off right there. Ran away after that and they never done found me since."

Wyatt blew on the hot liquid then drank a small amount. "Where'd you go?"

She looked at Wyatt then the dirt in front of her. "Went west. Ended up in San Benito in Texas and hooked up with a Mexican family. They's nice, too, and I worked in their cafe for a bed and food and a little spending money.

"Then in just one day seems like, my tits started growing big and sticking out and all. Guys started saying stuff to me and I went with some of 'em and it was all right, so I figured I could make more money doing that stuff instead of cafe work and that's what I did."

She looked again at the lights on the highway. "Tried to get some jobs pole dancing and stripping but I wasn't pretty enough. Hooked up with a coupla pimpers but alls they did was steal my money and treat me like a cur dog so I left 'em."

She looked back at Wyatt as he handed her the cup. "How do you get around? You know, money and food."

She sipped twice while looking at the fire. "Blow jobs mostly. If they got the money I fuck 'em."

"Blow jobs and fucking."

"Yeah."

"Where?"

She handed the cup back to Wyatt. "Truck stops mainly. Bus stops sometimes. Churches, alleys, wherever they want."

He took another drink. "Truck stops, bus stops, churches and alleys."

"Yeah. Ain't that bad 'cept when they get crazy."

"Crazy?"

"Yeah. I's at a truck stop outside Philadelphia once and there's this guy said he's driving to Omaha and Topeka and Reno and San Diego, and San Diego sounded like a nice place and he seemed like a nice fella so I told him I'd do whatever he wanted all the way for two hundred bucks. He said okay and we had a time right there and then we took off."

Again she stared at the lights on the highway and Wyatt sensed a bit of sorrow as her shoulders slumped slightly. When she looked back at him, her face was dispassionate, lifeless, like a wax figure of a 17th century charwoman. "While I's sleeping, he'd drove into a forest somewheres and when I woke up, he hit me on the head and I's like to pass out. He took my clothes off, then wrapped duct tape around my wrists and hands and taped my ankles to the steering wheel. I tried to fight him but he hit me over the head again and I's like to pass out again."

Wyatt handed the cup to Cassie then opened a package of jerky while she continued. "He put me face down on the seat then he took a ball peen hammer outta the glovebox and said it'd look real nice sticking out my ass and he rams the handle in there, no grease or nothing, and it hurt like hell. He's grinning and laughing all the time."

Cassie put the cup on the ground and began opening her package of jerky. "He opened the door real wide and stood on the footstep and pulled his pants down in front of my face and when I got on his dick I bit down real hard and he fell over screaming. I's able to reach my bag and get my knife and cut myself loose. Then I took to cutting him up."

Cassie swallowed the jerky then took another bite. "I took his money and his bank card and walked on out to the road but there's nobody coming by 'cause we's way out in the middle of nowhere and I figured I's to walk a long ways to get to a town and I could use some food so I went back 'cause I remembered this little refrigerator he had. Good thing, too, 'cause he's still alive."

She took another bite. "So I got the hammer and hit him in the nose and said the same thing I told to my daddy, and then I hit him in the eyes and then I banged his skull wide open. Took the food and walked off. That bank card never did me no good 'cause I didn't know that PIN thing."

Wyatt reached for the coffee cup. "So you've killed two men."

"Killed more'n that."

"Like the Black Widow of La Porte."

"The what?"

Wyatt swished the coffee and jerky in his mouth and swallowed. "The Black Widow of La Porte. Just someone I read about."

"Ain't never heard of her. Now, I don't go around killing for no reason y'know. Only when they's getting real crazy. See like, I coulda killed you by now but I didn't 'cause you're a nice person and decent and stuff and even though I'm ugly you won't say it. So I ain't gonna kill you."

Wyatt parodied a joyous face. "What wonderful news, Cassie! I simply do not know how to thank you!"

She laughed and Wyatt could see several broken teeth. "Yer funny! You talk like a teacher or something."

"Yeah, I get that sometimes." He took another bite of jerky. "So, if it's okay to ask, how many people have you killed?"

"Sixteen all together, including my daddy. They's all men, too, and they all deserved it, too."

Wyatt stopped chewing. "So Cassie, you're telling me all this but, let's be honest, you don't really know me. Aren't you afraid I might go to the police?"

"I ain't afraid of nothing. Besides, I know you ain't going to the police 'cause I can tell you's a killer, too."

Wyatt was taken aback. "How?"

She looked at him in a knowing way, like an old rancher explaining the ways of horses and men. "Just know. Seen it in yer eyes. They got that killing thing in 'em. Yer not a mean type of killer, know that too, but once ya killed and no matter why, a black thing gets in yer soul and shows up in yer eyes. Ain't nothing you can do about it. A killer always knows a killer. You knew I's a killer when ya picked me up."

He grabbed a bottle of water and opened it. "Actually, I didn't. But I did know I wasn't going to mess with you."

She popped the last bit of jerky into her mouth. "That's 'cause yer smart. Maybe ya didn't know 'cause ya ain't been at it very long. I can tell that, too."

Wyatt pondered that while he swished the water in his mouth. "Well, since we're at a stage of full disclosure … "

She stopped chewing. "At a stage of what?"

"We're being honest, not holding back anything."

"Okay."

"I'll say this: I have no intention of killing again."

She shook her head as she struggled the last of the jerky down her throat. "Don't matter. I ain't never had no intentions of killing nobody and still don't. But when the time's there and ya ain't got no way out, you be killing again. It'll happen. You can go ahead and deny it but you will."

TWENTY-SEVEN

• • •

WYATT LAY FOR A LONG TIME LOOKING AT THE HEAVENS. IS SHE RIGHT? Will I kill again? I suppose that if some unavoidable, life-or-death situation arose I might. But damn, I hope not.

Cassie looked at the stars then at the few headlights on the highway then at the stars again. After a while she asked, "You believe in God?"

"I don't believe in anything."

"I do. I know I's going to Hell so it don't do me no good but I believe in him anyways."

Wyatt rose onto one elbow. "You don't know that."

"Don't know what?"

"That you're going to Hell, assuming it exists."

Cassie continued looking at the heavens. "Yeah, I do. I's born at the bottom of a stinking pile of white trash and been doing nothing but making it stink worse ever since." She lowered her head and took a deep breath. "Not saying all white trash is bad folks, most of 'em is good people, but in all my kin there ain't a good one and I'm the worst there is."

"Well, I truly hope things get better for you, Cassiopeia. A lot better. I really do."

She lowered her head and looked at Wyatt. "What'd you call me?"

"Cassiopeia. I figured Cassie was short for Cassiopeia."

She angled her head to the right. "It's not. I's born Cassie and as far as I know it ain't short for nothing. What's a Cassiopeia, anyways?"

Wyatt got up, took her hand, led her away from the fire and pointed at the night sky. "See those five bright stars that look like the letter W? They're spread out wide and angled down to the right." He traced the outline with his finger.

"Yeah, I see 'em."

"That's the constellation Cassiopeia." He waited. "Cassiopeia was an ancient queen." He felt the cooling night air mingle with the last of the heat from the ground. "It is said that she was the most beautiful woman of the ancient world."

Cassie, relaxed for the first time and continued looking, transfixed. "So yer saying I's named after a ancient queen and she's so beautiful they named a constellation after her?"

Wyatt looked at Cassie whose face had softened. "Yes."

Wyatt watched Cassie for a minute then went back to their camp and lay down again.

Cassie kept looking at the sky for a long time and when she came back to the camp, Wyatt was again following the stars. She crawled into the sleeping bag. "You awake?"

"Yes."

"Is there such a thing as making love?"

"Yes."

"And it's different than fucking?"

"Yes."

At 3 a.m., Wyatt went for his nightly stroll. The air was cool and wisps of wind tugged at him. He thought about beauty and white trash who were everywhere, about dead men and those who made them such. He thought about making love and wondered if he'd ever experienced it, and about love itself and wondered if he even knew what it was.

He looked at the darkness that surrounded Cassiopeia. He looked at the dark profiles of the hoodoos in the distance. He looked northeast and again wondered what was there. He looked at his bike, remembered the song he'd heard in Swannanoa, and thought that if a person lived with the abandon of a clean heart, any day would be a good day to die.

He went back to their camp, lay down and closed his eyes. Before he fell asleep, he could feel the earth rotate under the firmament.

He woke up a half hour before sunrise. He looked over and saw that the sleeping bag was empty and Cassie's bag and helmet were gone. He turned around and could barely make out her figure walking toward the highway. He ran to her and called her name. She turned around. "What are you doing?"

"Time for me to leave."

"Why?"

"It just is."

"Where are you going?"

"Walk a ways and when it gets light hitch a ride."

Wyatt reached into his left front jeans pocket and held out all his money. "Here. This will help you get by for a while." It was almost six hundred dollars. "Wish it were more."

"I don't wanna take your money. Didn't do nothing for it."

"You're not taking it, I'm giving it to you." Cassie was a bit startled. He said, "Just a friend helping a friend."

She looked at the money then at Wyatt. "It's okay? A friend helping a friend out like this?"

"Yes."

"Ain't never heard of such a thing."

He continued holding the money out to her. "Please."

"Well, okay." She took the money, turned to go then turned and faced Wyatt again. Around them were the faint sounds of the sparse traffic from the highway, the quiet night winds and the hushed revelations of the desert. "Y'know what I wish, Wyatt? I wish you hadda made a move on me. Maybe then I coulda known what it's like to make love."

TWENTY-EIGHT

•••

I T TOOK DAYS FOR BILLY TO FULLY COMPREHEND THE LARGESSE THAT Charlotte had laid upon him. He called her to say thank you again but she didn't answer and he didn't leave a message. Instead, he wrote an email and apologized for not thanking her enough and didn't know if he ever could. She replied telling him to stay safe and to make sure to visit again.

He rode north into Ohio in a state of increasing elation. When he was off the bike, he couldn't keep still; when he was on it, it was a constant, thrilling gush. He spent the night in Milan and after crossing over the glorious Mackinac Bridge, made his way west and spent the night in Houghton in Michigan's Upper Peninsula.

The following morning, he headed north and could not remember ever seeing so much luxuriance. He could sense the life in the trees and grasses – they actually spoke to him and wished him well – and it was as if he was being sucker punched over and over with life at its best. When he got to Copper Harbor, there was an arts and crafts festival in the park and every man, woman, child and beast was like a best friend.

He backtracked a ways, turned left onto Gay Lac La Belle until he was riding along the shore of Lake Superior. He saw a family picking around in the weeds alongside the road, then a young couple, then a mother and daughter. He stopped and asked what they were doing. The mother showed him three buckets full of wild blueberries.

"Well dang!" he said. "What y'all gonna do with 'em?"

"Make homemade pies. What else?"

"Now ain't that something."

"It is!"

He looked around. "You mean to tell me that all them blueberries was just sitting here waiting for you to pick?"

"Yes! And it's still legal to pick them!"

"Strike a blow for freedom!"

"And blueberry pies!"

"With ya on that!"

This time, with his mind mostly on what Charlotte had done for him, it was easy to get Billy to continue heading in a westerly direction.

After making his way down to the main body of Michigan, Billy went west across Wisconsin, Minnesota and South Dakota, and had just crossed the Wyoming border when he headed toward Colorado. During those days and miles, neither the expansive farmland nor the endless sky could hold his excitement and he felt as if he was blessed by every tree, bush and blade of grass, and he always returned the courtesy.

When he got to the Colorado Rockies, the sharply angled spires elicited a wonder and he kept pulling over to simply look at them and be them. The snow-capped fourteeners, the deep and lavishly colored valleys, the sky that stretched to heaven. He rode through the Arapaho and Medicine Bow-Routte National Forests, where the air tasted like life-giving herbs, and ended up in Craig, where he spent three days with a bartender named LeeLee.

In Dinosaur, he bought a fishing pole called a Shakespeare Ugly Stik, along with a bobber, some sinkers, and a tub of earthworms. He took a few smaller highways into the Ashley National Forest in Utah and spent the rest of the day fishing in the Green River. He threw back everything he caught and was so carefree that he didn't bother taking any photos.

As he headed northwest, the splendor and inspiration never diminished. In the mornings, it was as if he floated with the mist as it curled around the evergreens that stood above the rivers he followed, their purling waters like poetry; and he came to realize that riding a motorcycle is more than a freedom-creating activity, that it actually puts the rider into a different world, a parallel existence, that makes the trappings of society a two-dimensional parody of real life.

In Washington, he parked alongside Highway 20 and took his fishing pole down to the Skagit River. There, he sat on a small boulder just below a few gentle, rock-crested rapids. In front of him was a deep, swirling pool.

A half hour later, he landed a thirty-pound steelhead trout, dotted gray on top and rust-colored on the sides, all laid over undertones of pink. It was an older fish and before sending him back, Billy spoke to him. "Yer all right, my friend. Ya look good, too. Bet the ladies'll be happy to have ya back."

The following morning he went to the Pilot Travel Center in Ferndale for breakfast. Standing inside by the door were a mother and her two boys, anxiously looking out to the parking lot like they were waiting for the arrival of a special-delivery package.

Billy got his food, ate, went to the bathroom then walked outside. The mother and her two boys were now sitting on the curb to his right, staring at the asphalt like people who had just seen their house burn to the ground.

Billy rode to the exit, stopped, let out a quiet "Damn," made a U-turn and rode back to the family, cutting off his engine when he was in from of them. "Whatcha all so forlorn about?"

"Some peckerwood stole our money." It was the older boy, who was about ten years old. His mother elbowed him and said not to use that kind of language.

"Stole yer money?"

"Yeah. Twenty-eight bucks was mine and Danny had eleven. We worked hard for it, too."

Billy looked at the mother. "That right?"

"Yeah. We was sitting inside and I went to the washroom and then Danny had to go and he can't hold it none so Tommy took him to the boys room. When we all come back, somebody had took all our money. Left my purse and wallet and everything else, but the money's all gone. We called the police but they ain't come yet."

"How much all together?"

"A hundred and forty-seven. I promised the boys a nice day at the water park in Blaine if they'd work real hard for a month and save their money and not buy any candy and such, and that's what they did and now we can't go."

"Damn." Billy looked straight ahead for several seconds then put his bike down on the kickstand and dismounted. "Wait here."

He strode to the ATM in McDonald's, came back out with a wad of twenties and handed it to the mother. She counted them. "There's three hundred dollars here." She looked at Billy with her mouth open. He winked.

Billy looked at Tommy with a stern face and said, "Lookie here, here's a lesson ya need to learn. Don't ever, ever, ever let the bad guys win. Don't ever let 'em win. Got it?"

"Yessir!"

He looked at Danny. "Understand what I'm saying, little fella?" Danny nodded vigorously several times.

The mother said, "This is real nice of you but what's your name? I need to pay you back some time."

"Name's Billy and you don't need to pay me back. Someday you'll be able to help somebody else and you just go on and do that and we'll be good."

"Oh, thank you, thank you!" She got up and hugged him.

"Yeah, thanks mister," said Tommy, "and we'll remember what you said, ain't that right, Danny?" Danny nodded vigorously again. Billy gave them an approval nod, then continued north.

TWENTY-NINE

...

A FTER SAYING GOODBYE TO CASSIE, WYATT WAS ALONE, AN EVERY-where stranger, his emotions disconnected like old kitchen items strewn around a dump. Loneliness was his only companion. But the loneliness itself was something he simply observed rather than felt so it didn't bother him, but he did gradually come to worry about the fact that it didn't. He wondered if he was dying. Maybe. It didn't seem so, but still, maybe he was. Maybe he was already dead. That thought occurred to him, too.

Sometimes, he thought of the possibility that everything he was, was what he had himself created, and that the Dark Companion was an unsavory offering to himself for past sins. Whatever it was and however it came about, its existence was an unsolvable conundrum akin to the location of Cleopatra's tomb or who killed JFK.

Other times, he would think that neither the loneliness nor the Dark Companion mattered, that whatever was, was; that he was himself, nothing more, nothing less, and that was that. Fate, as it were. Then inevitably, he would wonder who he was exactly, what he had been, and what he would become, and that maybe what he had thought much of his life was true, that the Dark Companion wasn't a separate entity but a forever part of him.

For days he continued his solitary journey and it felt as if he had been forever riding a forever-changing road, and he thus came to view it as a river; and he thought that if he just kept riding, kept moving forward, he would find the beginning of it or the end of it or some kind of unalterable boundary or marker that would define it; something, anything, that would give it clarity, a forever static point from which he could align everything else, and he would then know all that had gone before and all that would be.

Some days later, he took off at sunrise in the Nevada desert. The sun shone weakly through the morning fog making the heat it promised seem

111

improbable, and for the time being, the frigid air clasped the skin on his face like a static-filled sheet of silk. In the lackluster winds, there was, however, a small measure of tranquility, being that he was far away from the pernicious sprawl of civilization.

Later, when the sun had traveled a quarter of its arc across the sky, he pulled over to remove a long-sleeved undershirt, stretch his legs and smoke a cigarette. He felt the inexorable encroachment of the coming heat like ocean tides rising against deserted beaches, so he put his jacket in the travel pack and replaced it with his vest. He lit another cigarette.

To his right, some tens of yards from the road, was a small cluster of rocks set in a crude circular pattern. Reaching up from the center of them, they were but three to five feet high, was a glow, unchanging, as if the source was a simple light bulb. He walked toward it but before entering, threw down his cigarette and crushed it in the dirt with the toe of his boot.

The source of the light was a single flame, about a foot high and hovering a half-foot above the ground, but it had none of the pulsations of a normal fire. Rather, it was a solid existence enclosed by nothing but the air around it, like a heart gone still yet still filled with blood. Through a small opening toward the back of the stones was a trail, barely visible, that led to a confusion of large rocks and a few boulders that lay in a ragged half-orb, like an ancient cairn to a fallen giant. Standing on the trail, facing Wyatt, was a woman.

Tall and full-bodied, she was quite pretty with high rounded cheeks and flawless ivory-white skin, eyes big and round and green like springtime grass. She wore a simple white cotton dress that gathered at her waist then pleated down to her ankles. Covering her head was a sheer, light pink scarf, which covered all but a wisp of golden blond hair, and it was tucked into the top of a bodice lined with knitted filigree.

Her arms were covered with puffy, darker pink tulle that ended at her wrists in long cuffs of burgundy Chantilly lace. She wore black, low-heeled boots with silver buckles that seemed to glow from within. Tight across her throat was a black choker, in the middle of which was a ruby in the shape of a heart.

She stared at Wyatt like a marble statue, austere, yet somehow friendly and welcoming, the draw from her powerful. Time slowed. The air became heavy and thick as if he gradually sank lower and lower into the ocean. He reached for her but the increasing pressure was such that the entire setting around him began to slowly tilt and swirl and roll as if he were in a gentle earthquake. Soon, he was unable to move.

I got there in time, stopped and cranked the throttle three times as loudly as possible, like grenades exploding. (Truly, to a man, a succubus is worse than death.) Wyatt emerged from his trance, threw his head back to me, then ran toward his bike. Just before taking off, he looked back at the woman and the circle of stones, but they were gone, the desert untouched as it had been for millennia. He took off in a cloud of sand and dust, sped up, then some more, but I was soon gone, swallowed up by the glare of the afternoon sun.

Wyatt gradually slowed to a respectable speed. The memory of the circle of stones and the woman were like a dream, the details clear yet unconnected to anything he'd ever seen or known or heard about. For many miles, he kept looking in his rearview mirrors half expecting to see her again.

With but an hour of daylight left, he realized that he hadn't thought about the Dark Companion for days, and for a short while fancied the notion that it was fading away, maybe gone and gone for good; that, perhaps, the loneliness he had felt for days had supplanted it. But he somehow knew that that wasn't the case. Maybe the loneliness was simply a facet of the Dark Companion that he hadn't noticed before. Or maybe it was its counterpart, a separate and brooding kinsman of sorts.

As the shadows grew, the mountains on his right were like monumental heaps of crumpled slate made indigo by the setting sun. The night's chill hadn't yet set in but the air was cooling and it felt good in his lungs. His sweat dried and the wind disconnected the t-shirt from his back. The peace he felt days before returned but, like the loneliness, it was something he observed rather than felt.

Whatever the Dark Companion was or wasn't, whatever his connection with it was, he decided to stop at the next town and get a room. A nice one. He smiled sardonically. *All these questions and mysteries swirling around and the only conclusion I can come up with is that I need a shower.*

Once in his room, he stripped off all his clothes, turned on the shower, and while he waited for the hot water to arrive, caught his reflection in the bathroom mirror. Long and tangled hair, a six-day beard, the scar on his left cheek like a thin strip of molten nickel. It was odd. The face was his, of course, but he was unable to connect himself to it or make a memory of it. Though he recognized himself, he didn't actually know what he looked like. It didn't make sense. But then, maybe it did.

He sat alone at a table in the diner next to the motel. When the waitress came over and he tried to tell her what he wanted, no words came out of his mouth, only a low-pitched wheeze. He hadn't said a word in six days and it was as if his vocal cords had become disconnected along with everything else in his life.

The waitress, Kylie, smiled. "It's real dry and dusty around here and lots of outsiders don't realize what it does to their voices. Sometimes takes a while to come back. You can just point at what ya want, if ya want."

Wyatt smiled, somewhat surprised. It was the first human contact he'd had in almost a week and, in a way, it made him hopeful. He drank some water and managed the words for his order, his voice like worn out axle bearings on an old pickup.

Kylie was tall, pretty, friendly and attentive, and they enjoyed several short conversations. During dessert, she sat across from him and said, "Seems like you could use some company."

While going to sleep that night, he decided that whatever became of him, he needed companionship, if only for a few minutes or a weekend, like it would be with Kylie, who was resting softly against him, her head on his shoulder.

On the following Monday, he rode through Carson City and wrapped around Lake Tahoe and over Echo Summit during the night. When he got to Sacramento, he jumped onto Interstate 5, heading north. After crossing over the Pit River Arm, the landscape began morphing into a dream-like wonderland. Crystalline air, a few puffy clouds, verdant mountains, the smell of pine.

After crossing the Sacramento River south of Redding, he turned left and followed two-lane and dirt roads to Whiskeytown Lake. He walked down to the shore, removed his boots and sat on a rock on a small strip of white sand with his feet in the cold water.

Around him were obtusely angled mountains and dull green trees, the sky unmolested except for a small white cloud to his right. There were a few birds, desultory in their flights, their songs lonely with a scant measure of optimism. He realized he hadn't done any thinking all day and it was a welcomed change. Without the mental machinations that had been plaguing him for weeks, for years, it was as if the day had passed without time.

Again, he felt an acceptance, a type of peace. The Dark Companion was still alive, he knew that, but for the time being, it didn't worry him.

He rode back to a main road going west through the mountains, and when he got to Highway 101, headed north, some time later taking a narrow, tree-crowded, one-lane road, which soon turned to dirt. He parked in a narrow turnout next to a mud puddle, walked to a deserted beach, stripped off his clothes, then swam in the ocean until sunset.

He continued into Oregon and Washington, riding along the coast as often as possible. To his left, small waves crashed on the shore and the air was alive on his skin. Again, he took solace in the fact that Mother Nature always reshaped herself, always moved forward, regardless of him or anyone else – the constant change – and he felt a deep respect for the earth.

The following morning, he would continue north, but that night, as he sat on a plastic chair outside his room smoking cigarettes, he realized for the first time that though freedom required truth, it did not require knowledge.

THIRTY

...

"**G**ODDAMMIT! WHAT DO I GOTTA DO TO GET RID OF YOU, YOU SUM-bitch!"

The over-crowded club in Vancouver, Canada's Granville District came to a silent halt. Wyatt, sitting at the bar, turned around and there was Billy with a smile as big as the Rockies. "Damn, is it good to see you!" They gave each other a long and strong guy-hug and the club slowly went back to its eardrum-depressing pandemonium.

Billy sat next to Wyatt and ordered a beer. The bartender was a slim metro-type in tight jeans. "We have over a hundred different brands, sir."

Billy thought about that for a few moments then shook his head. "Well dang, how 'bout a plain old PBR."

"I don't know that brand, sir."

"You don't know what a PBR is?"

"No, sir."

"And ya keep calling me 'sir.'"

"Yes, sir."

Billy paused with his mouth slightly open and stared at the bartender. After a few moments, he shook his head again and said, "Well okay. How 'bout one of them Mexican beers."

"We have La Lupulosa, Minerva, Calavera, Nocturna, Tempus Doble, La Migra..."

"Now hold on there. Ain't never heard of none of them. How 'bout a Modelo."

"Especial, Chelada or Negra?"

"Oh hell, I dunno! Just make it a Bud."

"Light, Light Platinum, Light Apple, Light Lime..."

"Dang it, man, just gimme a beer in a bottle, will ya? Any kind'll do. But not one of them light ones. And not one of them flavored ones, either."

"Yes, sir."

Billy looked around, stupefied. Twenty-somethings all dressed in a chic, uptown way, chattering to each other with no one listening, girls flashing cleavage trying to look like they were unaware of doing so, multi-colored lights strobing left and right, an enormous TV broken into twelve different screens, a DJ playing music with the volume at ten. "What kinda place you got me into, Wyatt?"

"What?"

Billy raised his voice. "What the hell is this place? Ain't never seen a bar like it."

"It's not a bar. It's a club filled with college students. Our leaders of tomorrow."

Billy got his bottle of beer, a Pabst Blue Ribbon. He thought about showing the bartender the initials, but decided it wasn't worth the effort.

The two men sat silently for some minutes, Wyatt staring straight ahead, Billy nervously looking around at the goings-on and tapping his foot. Some minutes later, Billy finished his beer, slammed the bottle on the bar and said, "Dammit, Wyatt. Know what we need?"

"What?"

"A coupla them sixty-forty chicks."

"Sixty-forty chicks?"

"That's what I'm saying."

"What's that?"

"Sixty percent muscle, flesh and bone, forty percent tit."

Wyatt scrunched his eyebrows. "Is that even possible?"

"Probably not, but it is interesting to think about. You pay for my beer. I'll let ya know when I find 'em."

Wyatt tipped his bottle and nodded. Thirty minutes later he got a text to meet Billy at another club a block away. Wyatt paid their tabs and walked there.

Thankfully, it was a much quieter place. He spotted Billy standing at the bar next to two slender twenty-something blonds with basketball-sized breasts sitting on stools. He laughed to himself and walked over.

"Here he is!" Billy announced. "This is that Yale professor I's telling ya 'bout. Wyatt, meet Tammy and Callista." Wyatt shook Callista's hand and nodded at Tammy, who was holding onto Billy's arm.

"Are you really a professor?" Callista asked.

"Yes, I am."

"Wow."

"Now, Wyatt," Billy said, "these two young ladies are here at this place 'cause they don't like mingling with them lame brains at that other place. No sirree, they's real serious 'bout their studies. Ain't that right, girls?" They giggled.

Wyatt, smiling, asked, "What are you studying?"

"Psychology," Tammy answered. "But it's really hard, isn't it, Callista?" Callista nodded.

"Well," Wyatt said, "that may be, but it is true that you can accomplish anything if you put your mind to it."

"Oh gawd, you're so smart!" Callista said.

"Well, thank you, but I learned that bit of wisdom from Billy. He may speak with a Southern accent but he's the wisest philosopher I know."

Tammy looked at Billy like she just met Jesus. "Really?"

"Well, I don't like talking 'bout it much," Billy said. Tammy laid her head on Billy's shoulder.

THIRTY-ONE
...

WYATT AND BILLY MET AT A DINER LATE THE FOLLOWING MORNING. They barely tasted their coffees, said nothing, looked at nothing and felt nothing, like mannequins left in a storage room. Finally, Billy broke the silence. "Now I'm just gonna say it, get it out in the open, 'cause it looks like you had the same kind of night I did and I'm thinking yer thinking the same thing I'm thinking."

"What's that?"

"That it is beyond all reckoning that women with bodies like that can be such prodigious bores in bed." Wyatt laughed, choked on his coffee and spit it out. Billy went on. "I mean, y'know, we coulda just got us a coupla them blow-up dolls."

Wyatt, smiling, settled down. "Thou speakest sooth, my friend."

"I know it."

The blond waitress, Darcy, walked over, wiped up the mess, filled their coffee cups and asked if they were sure they wanted nothing to eat. After a long gulp, Billy said, "Nah, and I know we're taking up a good table and all but don't y'all worry none, this one sitting over there tips real good."

She looked at Wyatt. "That right, sugar?"

Wyatt looked into her eyes for some seconds, smiling. "Yes."

She left. Wyatt took a long drink. "Why'd you put her attention on me? You have to be as horny as I am."

Billy took another drink. "She's tall and you like big tits more than me and she's got 'em."

"Oh that's right, you're drawn to the tight ass, aren't you?"

"Got that right. I'm not saying I don't like a healthy rack, I do, but a man's got his priorities."

121

"That is true." Wyatt took another long drink. "How about that brunette switching out the coffee pots?"

Billy turned around. "Damn!" He poured the rest of his coffee into Wyatt's cup. "I do believe my cup needs refilling."

Darcy brought Wyatt a piece of pecan pie. "Couldn't stand seeing you sitting here at breakfast time and not eating anything."

"What a sweetheart you are, Darcy, thank you."

She snickered. "You an English teacher or something like that?"

"I have been so accused. What do you do, Darcy? I'm interested."

"Well genius, if you haven't noticed, I'm a waitress."

Wyatt laughed. "I did notice that but what I meant is what do you really do? Paint with watercolors, design clothes, illustrate children's books?"

"Oh, that kind of thing." She blushed. "I used to think I wanted to be a writer but could never finish anything but a paragraph or two."

"Is that right?"

"Yeah. Can't spell, either. I'm so bad at it that my English teacher at the community college told me I misspell words when I talk."

"That's a good line."

"Made me laugh."

Wyatt cocked his head to the right. "The thing is, spelling is just spelling. It really has nothing to do with writing."

"Well, I'm glad to hear you say that, uh … "

"Wyatt. My name's Wyatt."

"Wyatt, huh? I won't mention Wyatt Earp because you probably get that all the time."

He bowed elegantly, like an 18th century Spanish aristocrat. "Muchísimas gracias, señorita hermosa de la bella sonrisa."

Darcy smiled and looked away for a moment, blushing again. "Now Wyatt, I do like being called pretty as much as the next girl, and my daddy would be happy to know all the money he spent on braces meets with your approval, but there's no need to go overboard with the compliments."

"Disculpe mi torpeza, señorita linda."

"Apology accepted, but you're anything but awkward, big fella."

Wyatt smiled. "Say, do you have an aversion to motorcycles or bikers?"

"If I did I wouldn't be here talking to you, now would I?"

"I guess not. Did you know that the sun sets around seven-thirty this time of year?"

"I'd've guessed it'd be around that, yeah."

"What time do you get off work?"

Darcy smiled coquettishly. "Five-thirty then another twenty minutes to cash out."

"Then I propose this: I pick you up at your place at six-thirty, we ride for an hour while you show me all the prettiness around here, we watch a sure-to-be gorgeous sunset, then go back to your place, order take-out, and I help you with your writing."

She took a deep, sultry breath. "Wyatt, if I ride on the back of your bike for an hour, we're not getting any writing done when we get back to my place."

Wyatt smiled again. "All right. But I just want to be clear. Did you say wri*ting* or ri*ding*?"

"Oh sugar, you won't have any problem figuring that one out."

The next morning, Wyatt and Billy contentedly sipped coffee at a Coffee Bean and Tea Leaf. Billy spoke up first. "I can see from the look on yer face that you had the same kind of night I did, so I'm just gonna say it out loud. That there are some real women, ain't they? Know when to go at it like a warrior queen, know when to hold back and be all kitten-like shy. Damn!"

"Got that right."

"Thinking we oughta stay another day or two."

"Now that is something I'm in favor of."

Startled, Billy said, "Wait a second. Did you just end a sentence with a preposition?"

"I did."

"Dang, I just might make a regular guy outta you yet."

The following morning they were again at the Coffee Bean and Tea Leaf. And again, Billy was the first to break the silence. "This coffee's a lot better than Starbucks."

"It is that."

"I mean, you can actually taste the beans and they taste goo-ood, the aroma and all that."

"It is remarkable."

On the third morning, they were packed up and ready to head back to the states.

Billy was the first to spot me at a gas station cater-corner from their motel. Then Wyatt saw me. I could tell they wanted to talk so I scooted out of there as fast as I could, but they began to follow and were gaining on me as we worked our way through the city traffic. Once we got into the countryside, they were only sixty yards behind me. I rounded a blind corner and when they got there, I was a half-mile away, sitting on my bike, smoking a cigarette.

The two men pulled to the side of the road and cut off their engines. Billy said, "How the hell he do that?"

"I don't know. It's impossible. We were going close to ninety."

"I know. He covered a half mile in like five seconds."

"And had time to stop and light up."

"Damn."

I finished my cigarette, smiled and nodded to the men, then took off. In reality, it was all a simple trick I learned from an old vaquero in Argentina many, many years ago.

After standing in silence for a while Billy said, "You know what we oughta do?"

"What's that?"

"We oughta go up and ride that Alcan thing."

Wyatt looked at Billy disapprovingly. "The Alaska Highway? Are you crazy?"

"Probably. But it is a good idea."

"I don't know. Isn't it covered with mud?"

"Might be, don't know. But think about it, it'd really be something, wouldn't it?"

Wyatt did think about it for a bit then looked at Billy with big smile. "Well, if you're game, I am.

THIRTY-TWO
• • •

THE RIDE TO THE BEGINNING OF THE ALASKA HIGHWAY IN DAWSON
Creek was uneventful, as was the ride to Wonowon, where they topped
off their tanks. The short stretch to Pink Mountain had two narrow strips
of half-dried mud but Wyatt and Billy just slowed down a little and didn't
worry about them. There were three more such strips before they got to
Fort Nelson, which is where they ended the day.

They were waiting for their dinner when Billy said, "Shit, this don't seem
so bad. What's all the fuss about all the mud about?"

"I've no idea."

"Me, neither. Maybe they make all them white-knuckle stories up just to
keep people from coming up here. Don't blame 'em. It sure is something-else
beautiful, ain't it? And not enough people to fuck it up. Not a McDonald's
or a Starbuck's to be seen."

Wyatt had an amazed look on his face. "I've never seen anything like
it. I mean, it's enormous and drop-dead gorgeous. Can't wait to see more."

"Me, too."

The following morning, they took off without a care into temperatures
in the fifties. Thirty miles later, they came upon a line of twenty or so cars,
rode to the front and saw something that stopped their hearts. A long, foot-
deep stretch covered with mud. Deep mud that looked like the bottom of
an ancient cesspool. And it had begun raining and the temperature was
dropping.

After some minutes, Billy walked over to the stop-sign girl. "Uh, I's just
wondering. What happened to this here road?"

She smiled. "Oh, they're just fixing it up."

"Fixing it up?"

"Yeah."

"Okay. How long is it gonna take?"

"Oh, the road won't be done for a week or so, but the pilot car will be here in about fifteen minutes."

Billy scrunched his eyebrows. "Pilot car?"

"Yeah."

"And what's it do?"

"Just follow it through the mud, stay in its tire tracks."

"Well, okay." He turned to go then looked back at her. "How long is it like this?"

"About eight kilometers."

"Okay. How many miles is that?"

"About five."

Billy nodded slowly and walked back to Wyatt. "Wyatt, we're fucked. That mud there goes on fer five miles."

"Seriously?"

"Kid ya not."

"Shit."

A few minutes later a group of four riders joined them. "Damn!" one of them said, "looks like we got us some baby shit mud!" They all laughed. Wyatt and Billy looked at them like they were nuts. Another one said, "Jackie Girl, you get to go first."

"Why me?"

"That Goldwing of yours has the fattest tires."

"Shit."

It was colder and raining harder when the pilot car showed up. It turned around and they all followed, Wyatt and Billy inviting the other bikers to go first.

It was brutal. Even in the path left by the pilot car, the mud was three inches deep and there were rocks the size of fists. Their feet were off the pegs much of the time and they never got above fifteen miles-per-hour. After fifteen minutes of being in shock, both Wyatt and Billy's backs were tightening up, so they tried to relax, but neither could ever get there. And the cold rain kept coming down.

A half hour later, they emerged at the other end and pulled over. They stood, rigid, for a long time. Finally, Wyatt said, "Fuck me."

"Yeah. Me, too."

"So glad that's over."

"I hear ya."

They spent a half hour stretching and sheltering their cigarettes from the rain. After taking off, they came across several slippery slimy spots and even though they slowed down, their tires would momentarily lose their grip and their hearts would skip a beat. As the miles went slowly by, however, they became somewhat accustomed to them.

One time, they pulled into a turnout that overlooked an enormous V-shaped valley that stretched for miles. Steeply angled and hard cut mountains on the right, pine-covered mountains on the left. Through it ran a river that was fragmented into a myriad of small streams that glistened in the sun like liquid platinum.

A number of ewe were standing on the steep embankment and a few came over to the guardrail. Billy tried talking with them but they just listened passively with faces like aliens from a 60s sci-fi flick.

They stopped at the Toad River Lodge and ordered a late lunch. Afterward, they walked around looking at the thousands of hats hanging from the ceiling and browsing a small souvenir section. Billy bought a t-shirt that said "Alaska Highway Survivor," and they each bought a book on the history of its construction.

They decided to spend the night. After dinner, they were outside sitting under an overhang smoking cigarettes when Billy said, "Y'know, Wyatt, after that five-mile stretch and getting a little used to those slippery spots, this is getting to be fun again."

"Yeah. I do believe I'm getting used to it. Definitely the craziest adventure I've ever been on."

"But them five miles of mud was crazy, wasn't it? Glad it's behind us."

"I never want to see anything like it again."

THIRTY-THREE

...

WHEN THEY TOOK OFF THE NEXT MORNING, THE RAIN CAME DOWN hard but their spirits were high. The slippery-slimy spots were even more slippery and slimy, and it seemed like they could never go more than a mile without coming across one, and no matter how slowly they went, their bikes would always start sliding to the side of the road. But that's when the magic of the Alcan came over them.

The magnitude of the mountains and sky filled them with a heartiness such that the two good men felt they could handle anything, road-wise or weather-wise.

Now they were really able to enjoy the undiluted beauty of the Northern Rockies, the way it stretches into savage mysteries and you want to go there, the way the blues and grays and browns create an untamed patina, the way the occasional moose and bear and wolf refuse to let you dominate the land.

The combination of beauty and physical exertion was a sort of yin and yang. On the one hand, they were exhausted, yet they kept going and going, always wanting to see the other side of the next curve.

When they came to the turquoise-colored Muncho Lake, they stood for the longest time and marveled at how it sat undisturbed, its water glistening in the sun like a million diamonds, and how it stretched to a mist-shrouded forever. Even Billy had no words to describe the magnificence of it.

About forty-five miles later, they turned a corner and their elation quickly turned to dread. It was another stretch of deep mud and rocks, this one about ten miles long.

For a full hour, they never got out of second gear and there was no way to relax, physically or mentally. Even with the temperature in the forties, their bikes were overheating. Their backs ached, their heads ached, and their hands were cramping. When they got to the end, they again took a half hour to stretch and get the kinks out. Not far after that, they stopped at the Liard River Lodge and decided to call it a day.

The interior was made out of lacquered wood, clean and, in an Alcan way, rather upscale. The two teenaged girls manning the desk smiled knowingly at the two whacked-out riders. One of them said, "Why don't you stay for two nights and go over to the hot springs tomorrow."

Billy asked, "How far away are they?"

"Not too far, but you'll want to ride there, probably."

Wyatt asked, "Are they really hot or just warm?"

"Depends on where you sit. At the kids' end, it's just warm, but the farther away you go, the hotter it is."

"Sounds good to me. How about you, Billy?"

"Oh, I'm all in."

They unloaded into their rooms, which were clean and newly furnished, and came down to the dining room for dinner, moving like stop-action Claymation figures. They were silent until dessert arrived. Billy said, "Wyatt. What the hell are we doing?"

"I don't know. I was just getting used to the cold weather and the rain and those small mud spots, even started enjoying myself, and then we passed through the gates of purgatory."

"I know. It's like one of them levels in Dante's Inferno. Don't know which one, though."

"Don't recall myself, but it has to be in there."

The next day, incredibly sore and stiff, they managed to get dressed and ride to the hot springs. They parked at the beginning of a wooden walkway then walked along it like old, arthritic men. They passed a park ranger who smiled.

The hot springs were cleverly designed and clean and larger than they expected. They stripped down to their bathing trunks, slipped into the warm water and promptly fell asleep. Every fifteen minutes they would wake up and move farther and farther into the hot end.

An hour later, Billy said, "I'm getting all wrinkled like one of them wrinkly dogs. What're they called?"

"Shar-pei?"

"That's it. I feel like a Sharpie."

"So do I. But damn, does this feel good. I don't want to get out."

"With ya on that, my friend. Getting hungry, though."

"Me, too. Let's give it another fifteen minutes,"

"Good with that."

An hour later, they got out, dried off, got dressed and went back to the lodge, where they ate a huge lunch. It had stopped raining and, smiling and contented, they sat outside smoking cigars that Billy had bought in Vancouver.

Wyatt said, "You know something, Billy, this really is an awesome thing we're doing. I mean, yeah, all that mud knocked us senseless, but you know what? We're doing this road. We're fucking doing it."

Billy thought about it for a few moments. "Ya got something there, Wyatt. We sure as hell went through hell and here we are, all relaxed and smoking and lounging around like there ain't nothing wrong in the world. Fucking A is all I can say."

Both Wyatt and Billy were fully refreshed the next morning, and they attacked the rest of the Alcan with unabated verve. They spent a few hours reading some of the hundreds of thousand signs in the signpost forest in Watson Lake, and later remarked how the evergreen-covered island in the middle of the Rancheria River was like a hand-knitted scarf made for a giant.

As the miles passed, both men felt a growing awareness. Colors became more vivid, the air more fresh, the oneness with their bikes more definite. Life itself became more alive and they were indestructible.

They spent over an hour on the shores of Kluane Lake. The sky was streaked with white clouds in an infinite parallax, the mountains were perfectly reflected in the waters, and the island in the middle of it was colored like a centuries-old Flemish painting.

Destruction Bay lay at the end of Kluane Lake and that's where they decided to spend the night. While waiting for their dinner, Billy went out to have a talk with the ravens. They had been seeing them all along and often remarked about their intelligence and how they always operated in pairs. Unlike the ewe several days before, the ravens were talkative, and Billy enjoyed a long conversation.

At dinner, he told Wyatt about them, that they welcome two-legged travelers into their world except for the very few who abuse it. With those, the ravens laughed at how their vehicles were always somehow covered with raven shit. "Tell ya what, Wyatt, ya don't ever wanna piss off a raven."

"I have no intention of ever doing that. Besides, they're beautiful birds."

"They are that. All shiny black and all-seeing, too."

"And their slightly hooked beaks give them a noble and sage-like visage."

"The philosophers of the animal kingdom."

When they made it to the end of the Alaska Highway in Delta Junction, they celebrated for two days and nights, getting passed-out drunk. On the third morning, both men were feeling damn miserable. Billy, weaving left, right and around in his chair, said, "Dang it, Wyatt, only two days of drinking and I'm all done in. I must be getting old."

Wyatt looked at his friend out of one eye and said, "Maybe so. But you're doing better than I am."

"Don't think that's possible, amigo."

They drank little on the third night and were feeling almost okay the following morning.

This time, it was easy to slip by unnoticed.

They were having breakfast when Billy said, "Ya ever go to a place just 'cause of the name?"

"Oh yeah."

"Me, too."

"I know what you're thinking."

"Ya do not."

"Yes, I do."

Billy put his arms on the table and leaned toward Wyatt. "No way. Ya cain't know what I'm thinking."

"I know exactly what you're thinking." Wyatt looked straight into Billy's eyes. "Ketchikan."

"Sheeit. How'd ya know?"

"I've been thinking about it, too. Always wondered what it's like."

"Me, too. Wanna go?"

"Why the hell not."

THIRTY-FOUR

...

THE FIVE-HOUR FERRY FROM HAINES TO JUNEAU AND THE SEVEN-teen-hour ferry from Juneau to Ketchikan were bliss. Sipping brews, smelling the salt air, watching imposing mountains rise on either side, all the fried food they could eat, surprisingly comfortable cabins. The only regret was not seeing any killer whales but Billy put it in perspective when he said, "They probably regret not seeing me, too."

When they rode out of the ferry's hull and onto the dock in Ketchikan, both stopped for a minute to take in the town. The colorful buildings, the hearty breeze, the working men and women. Wyatt said, "This is perfect."

Billy looked around and said, "I think I belong here."

They rode around for a while and ended up on Creek Street, the original home of the Ketchikan brothels. The many walkabout tourists, however, were bothersome, so they went south to Saxman, where they enjoyed the dozens of totem poles in relative tranquility.

They continued around the cape past clean homes with steeply angled roofs, a few children walking home from school, and several neighborhood marinas.

They took small side roads, many of them dirt, and stopped often to walk down to the rocky shore and to the small, brown-sand beaches. On the mainland, the mountains were covered with hemlock and spruce and cedar; across the ocean they were like sleeping leviathans shrouded in mist.

They arrived back in Ketchikan around nine o' clock, got rooms, and sat down for dinner, both still dazzled beyond words. They ate like they'd been gone for three years and just got home to some of grandma's stew. Afterward, they sat outside smoking cigars, drinking brandy, and engaged in two-sentence, aimless conversations.

The following day, they took a cruise tour of the Misty Fiord National Monument. All day, they marveled at the sharply angled mountains that cut into the clouds like battle axes, at the mesmerizing sapphire-colored waters, at the pods of sea lions and seals that chattered in mysterious languages; and once, an elegance of porpoises arched through the ocean's surface, staggered and perfectly timed; and sometimes birds they knew not the names of would soar and circle, then continue migrating toward unknown destinations.

The majesty of it all, the overwhelming grandeur, quelled both men into a serene elation that neither had ever imagined possible. When they got back to their motel, they sat on the veranda for the longest time, silent, looking not at what was in front of them, rather the memories of that day and their ride on the Alcan.

They didn't settle in for a meal until just before midnight. They were sitting next to a window in a diner at the southern end of the town. Wyatt excused himself to go wash his hands. Billy remained where he was, looking at the waning lights and the gradually diminishing number of pedestrians.

It was a Friday night and soon, a group of revelers came dancing down the middle of the street, shouting and laughing and singing. At first, Billy smiled, thinking it was some sort of local festival.

He then noticed that one young man had a handful of a woman's hair who was topless, and another was dragging a woman who was totally nude. Still others were pushing nude or half-nude women, laughing and kicking them when they fell. Something snapped in Billy and he got up so quickly that his chair fell down with a crash.

He ran outside and belted the first man in the face, breaking his nose. He pounced on the second man, then a third. By then, the others converged on him, taking hard swings, and wrestled him to the ground. Billy fought back but blood was pouring and most of it was his.

Wyatt came out of the bathroom, saw what was happening, ran out with a vehemence born of the Dark Companion, then flew into the group of young men like a whirling madman. Several fell and he continued beating whomever was in front of him, not noticing that he, too, was becoming bloody.

He saw a large man sitting on Billy's chest, his arm arched back, ready to smash a broken bottle into his face. Wyatt ran over and his size twelve, steel-toed boot sent the man into unconsciousness.

By then, others had come out of the saloons and diners, brawny fishermen and dockworkers all, and in fewer than two minutes, all of the young men were immobile or unconscious.

The locals hurried back to their drinks. The women, crying, bent down to succor Billy and to look after Wyatt. A middle-aged woman and her son hobbled all of them into an alley, down a dirt road, into another alley and across a field to an old Victorian-styled house.

Billy was in and out of consciousness. Disconsolate, Wyatt said, "He needs a doctor."

The middle-aged woman said, "Can't do that."

"Dammit, he needs a doctor!"

"We'll fix him up."

"What the hell? He's lost half his blood and is still bleeding! He's got to go to a hospital!"

The woman got in Wyatt's face. "I said we can't do that. Do you know who those guys are? They're football players from a university in Washington. If we take him to the hospital, the police will find out, we'll all be in jail in less than an hour, and your friend will be there for a year at least."

"What?"

"Rich lawyers get a hold of this and in a week he'll be guilty of assault and what kind of medical treatment you think he'd get in jail?

"But he didn't do anything wrong!"

"Oh, really? And who does he have for witnesses bearing that fact? A bunch of whores, that's who." She stood back with her hands on her hips. "And whores are such reliable witnesses, aren't they?"

"What the hell are you talking about?"

"Look around, smarty pants. Where do you think you are? This is a goddam whorehouse."

"Oh, good Lord. What about Billy?"

"James already radioed Tingly. She'll be here in a couple of hours."

Wyatt got a suspicious look and lowered his voice. "Who the hell is James and who the hell is Tingly?"

"James is my son. Ever since my husband died he's had to help me run this place. Tingly's an Eskimo, a Tlingit. She lives alone on a small island about six miles west. She'll get him right, better than any doctor could. Now it's time for you to shut up and get those wounds mended."

Wyatt first helped clean and bandage Billy, pushed in his dislocated shoulder and three dislocated fingers, then he and the girls bandaged up each other.

A couple of hours later, Tingly arrived. She was a couple of inches under five feet, looked to be over a hundred years old, and carried an old sealskin bag. She ignored Wyatt and didn't bother arousing Billy but spent a few minutes checking him out.

Lucy, the woman Wyatt had been talking with, brought in a teapot full of boiling water. Tingly made a horribly smelling concoction and coaxed it down Billy's throat. She took off his bandages and put compresses on his wounds that smelled like week-old mackerel left in vomit. She then sat back in a rocking chair, mumbling invocations to once powerful gods.

THIRTY-FIVE

• • •

ONCE THE EMERGENCY WAS OVER, WYATT AND LUCY GOT ONTO GOOD terms. Wyatt gave money to James to pay for their motel rooms along with the keys to their bikes, which he hid in the shed at the back of the brothel. Now all there was to do was wait for Billy to come around.

For the next two days, Billy looked worse than death. Tingly continued with her potions and prayers and the most consciousness Billy exhibited was to moan and mumble for a minute every now and again. Wyatt would visit every hour and even considered joining in Tingly's prayers. Anything that would help.

By the third day, Billy was feeling better. He looked at Wyatt and asked what had happened. "You came to the rescue of some ladies."

"Damn. All I remember is a motorcycle boot saving my life. Where are we, anyways?"

"A fine establishment for ladies of the night."

"Is that right? Well, I guess there are worse places." He fell asleep.

On the next day, Billy was sitting up in bed talking with Tingly, who couldn't understand a word but was laughing hysterically. Wyatt walked in. "Wyatt, meet my fiancé, Tingly. We's gonna get married soon as my shoulder heals up, ain't that right, Tingly?" Wyatt smiled and thought how good it was to see Billy becoming his old self. "Tingly, meet my good buddy, Wyatt."

Tingly spoke incomprehensible monotones and made angular arm motions at Wyatt. Billy said, "That was either a blessing or a curse. Whatever it was, yer life's gonna change." Wyatt laughed. "So tell me, Wyatt, have ya fucked all of 'em yet or just the tall ones with big tits?"

Wyatt was still laughing. "Well, it would be unforgivably impolite to deny a lady from expressing her gratitude, wouldn't it?"

"Dang it, Wyatt, you're as big a whore as there is!"

The police, knowing what actually happened, hadn't really been search-ing for Billy and Wyatt. However, when the university's lawyers and public relations ladies showed up, they got into hyper-action, fearing a rash of bad press. So on the fifth day, Billy woke up from a nap and standing at the foot of his bed was the chief of police. He had just shooed Tingly out of the room.

Chief Marquette had a permanent scowl on his face and gave the impres-sion of a man who was as willing to screw someone's eyelids open as eat a piece of cherry pie. He stared at Billy for some minutes. Finally, he asked, "What happened?"

Billy instinctively knew he was the kind of man who wanted straight answers and hated listening to extenuating circumstances. So he told him everything he remembered in the sequence it happened without elaboration. Chief Marquette stared unflinchingly, waiting for some sort of excuse, but Billy offered none. He then went to the other side of the room and stared out the window.

Without turning around, he said, "The PR ladies and lawyers from the university showed up itching to make a big stink about how two bikers rab-ble-roused some locals into beating up their upstanding football students. They don't give a damn about truth, only the reputation of their school. Hate people like that. Bad as politicians." He leaned back and stared at the ceiling. "So I either arrest you for assault or they'll make up stories about how dangerous it is here. Get that stuff on the evening news and the tourist business dries up. Folks here depend on that." Billy said nothing.

Chief Marquette waited some moments. "I already got the story from your friend and the two of you mostly agree, which makes me think you're telling the truth." He waited some more. "Fact is, I talked with some locals and I know you are."

He turned to Billy. "I'm going to go to the local paper and tell them everything. Truth and facts. We'll spread the story around, make some bad publicity for the university ladies to handle, and with some luck, Ketchikan will be fine."

He walked over to Billy's side. "Get a hold of Fatso down on the docks. He leaves every morning at three. Give him six hundred dollars and he'll take you to Prince Rupert. They may be looking for you at the border in British Columbia so ride into Alberta before going back to the states. Your friend is leaving tomorrow, you leave three days from now. That'll give you enough time to heal that shoulder. In the meantime, you don't leave this room." Chief Marquette turned to go then stopped at the door. "You're lucky to have Tingly."

Wyatt came into Billy's room after midnight. For a long time, the two looked at each other without speaking. Finally, Wyatt said, "There is no man I'd rather ride behind, next to, or in front of than you, Billy Balcomb."

"Same here, Wyatt Youngblood, same here."

Wyatt looked around the room. "Helluva ride, wasn't it?"

"The best. Wouldn't trade it for all the others combined." Billy stared at the floor. "We'll meet up again. No need for phone calls or texts or emails or any of that social media shit. We'll meet up again. Destiny. Destiny of the road."

Wyatt took a long, deep breath. "It is thus."

THIRTY-SIX

...

FOR SIX YEARS THEY RODE.
Endless miles of mountain and river and ravine, of cloud and rain and cloudless sky, of dirt and broken roads and pelting sand. Routes with sentries of prongbuck and coyote and deer and bear, of eagle and hawk and flock of sparrow, of armadillo and skunk pig, vole and fox.

They stayed in rundown motels, or off the roads in fields of cabbage or potato or soy bean, or next to small streams where they watched the stars follow their chosen paths and imagined them as portals of freedom anchored upon the earth.

They became bearded. Wyatt's hair grew even longer and Billy's curled in unkempt designs. They hiked and climbed and walked and ran. Wyatt did one hundred eighty pushups a day and Billy did planks and isometrics every morning and evening.

Their skins darkened in exposed places and their faces and necks and hands became hard against the wind. Their skins further transformed with the etchings of dark tattoos the meanings of which only they knew, but with some they came to not know or they changed the meanings thereof.

Billy, as usual, made friends wherever he went. Blue collar, white collar, no collar, it mattered not. Wyatt was friendly to those he met but always stopped short of making an actual friend, not from a lack of desire for camaraderie, but from being on guard about the Dark Companion.

And there were women. Those who cried after sex and said, "You probably think I'm crazy" and then snuggled and groped until they were again grinding in sex-sweat; those who told them how they were going to go back to school and "start my own business;" those who said that someday they'd find "the right guy" and have kids and be a wife and mother, "and I know how to be good at it, too;" those who talked of nothing but other lovers they

141

had had; those who told them they were scared because "my man's getting out of prison in a few days."

There were those from upper and upper-middle class homes who told them that "just once" they wanted "an outlaw biker," and they led them to believe they were such; those who asked for money, "I'm not a whore, I just need to get by for a few days;" those who pleaded with guttural undertones and clenched teeth for a hard pounding against grease-slicked walls in the back of old cafes; and the very few who reciprocated the lust of every stroke and grasped and moaned as if they fulfilled a destiny.

Billy read novels and poetry, and recalled the lines and poems he had memorized before and newly memorized lines of prose and rhyme, and these he reveled in and repeated over and over as he rode, like mantras or prayers. Sage proverbs from ancient minds.

Too, Wyatt read, but he sequestered memorized lines in the core of his heart until he felt he warranted them, until he was released from the Dark Companion and its dark intentions, which forewarned that he may in some future time become that which is without emotion, without empathy, without reason, without remorse or pity, without hope, without sense of accomplishment, without wonder or beauty.

They rode.

PART II

I did not die,
And yet I lost life's breath.

—Dante's The Divine Comedy

THIRTY-SEVEN
...

THE SUN SHINED BRIGHTLY, THE WAY IT DOES ONLY IN EARLY SPRING. Gleaming shards like mirrors exploded outward promising warmer days and softer nights, the rolling back of winter's silent sheath of white and gray, and the thawing of lakes and mountaintops. Too, people came out of their solitary confinements and greeted neighbors and strangers alike with friendly inclinations. Spring: the new and the hearty and the unsullied.

During the three years after Ketchikan, Wyatt and Billy did cross paths three times, once in Ohio. Unbeknownst to each other, they'd each chosen the same day to ride the Triple Nickel. Billy had taken off a half hour before Wyatt and while riding, they each had similar thoughts about what a fine American road it was. The gentle hills, the small farms, the sun-speckled shadows, and every now and again a right-angled turn that seemed to serve no purpose whatsoever.

It was mid-afternoon when they met at the Smiling Skull in Athens. They immediately started talking and drinking and didn't quit the place until it closed. Before leaving, they each bought a bottle of cheap whiskey then found a motel a mile away where they continued talking and drinking until sunup. When they woke up in the early afternoon, they went back to the Smiling Skull and continued where they left off.

On the third day, Billy was weaving in a chair and said, "Wyatt. I do believe I'm getting old. Only two days of drinking and I'm all done in."

"Seems like I've heard that before."

"Well then, it must be true."

Another time was in Massachusetts at Bill Ash's Lounge in Revere. Wyatt was at the bar, drinking his gin and tonics, and a hooker or a waitress, he

145

couldn't figure out which, kept coming by, stroking his arm and leaning into him and talking about something or some things he couldn't hear because of the loud music.

He smiled and nodded now and again, but despite his scant attention, she was rather taken with him. As soon as Billy walked in, however, he forgot about her and the two bikers went out back. The talking didn't stop for another three days. Neither did the drinking. They were sitting on old plastic chairs in front of their motel rooms on the third day and as before, each was heavy with a hangover. Billy said, "Wyatt ... " and his head involuntary fell forward.

Wyatt looked over. "I do believe you're getting old, Billy. Only two days of drinking and you're all done in."

"How'd ya know I was gonna say that?"

"An elevated aptitude for observation, my friend."

"Sheeit."

Their third meeting took a while for me to set up. I had been leading them, one then the other, for several weeks when they finally converged at the same time at the County Line Barbecue in northeast Albuquerque, Wyatt from the north, Billy from the south.

After lunch, they were standing in the parking lot when Billy noticed a white pickup with a camper and one of those old, silver teardrop trailers parked on the hillside. He said, "Seems like an odd place to park a pickup and a trailer."

Wyatt looked up. "Sure does. What do you think he's up to?"

"No idea."

A slender middle-aged man wearing a black Area 51 t-shirt walked out of the restaurant. Billy asked him, "Is there anything of interest up on that there hill?"

The man looked. "Nah. Just a bunch of dirt."

"No hunting or fishing?"

The man smiled, "Well, if you're looking for ground squirrels, you might find one or two."

After the man left, they looked back at the pickup and trailer. Wyatt said, "Maybe he's new to the area and didn't know there was nothing up there to hunt."

"Maybe. But if he's hunting, why'd he take the trailer?"

"Good point."

They stared a bit longer. Billy said, "I say we go take a look."

"Right behind you."

Just as they started to leave, the pickup descended the dirt road. They watched it go past them into town.

They made their way up the dirt road, which was surprisingly in decent shape, and parked in front of the trailer. The door was padlocked so Billy pounded on it. Then again. Then a third time. "Hello! Is somebody in there?"

"Yes." It was a child's voice.

"Would ya like to get outta there?"

"Yes."

While looking around for a way to get in, neither Billy nor Wyatt noticed the pickup making its way back. The man stopped twenty yards away and yelled, "Get the fuck away from there!"

Billy and Wyatt started toward the man. He panicked, pulled out his keys, unlocked the camper, and his three Rottweilers attacked.

The dogs were vicious, strong and relentless. Both Billy and Wyatt were on the ground, getting bloodier by the moment. Simultaneously, they pulled out their guns and killed the dogs. By then, the pickup was disappearing down the hill.

They lay on the ground for a few minutes, moaning and covered with patches of blood mud. When they got upright, Billy looked at Wyatt and said, "Ya look like shit."

Wyatt shook his head. "Fuck me."

They hobbled over to the trailer and looked for a way in, but it was tightly sealed up. Billy walked to the door again, said, "Fuck it," and shot off the lock. The door squeaked open and two girls and a woman stepped out.

The youngest, the one who had answered, was four or five years old and had an innocent and interested look. Her sister was eleven and looked at Billy with no expression whatsoever. The mother, like the two girls, was haggard, underfed and dirty. All three were covered with bruises.

Wyatt rode down the hill to get into cell phone coverage and call 9-1-1. Billy looked at the three of them and said, "Y'all look hungry. Got some trail mix and water. Interested?" The younger girl nodded, the other two just stared, though the mother had begun mumbling and every now and again would become startled, as if a swarm of wasps had just appeared.

For a while, Billy watched the three of them eat and drink, not knowing what to say or do. When he heard the ambulance's siren, he said, "Don't y'all worry none. Help is coming. Y'all'll be just fine."

The little girl said, "What about the lady?"

"The lady? What lady?"

"The one in the box."

"There's a lady in a box?" The girl nodded.

Billy, thinking it was a doll, got his flashlight and went inside the trailer. It was hot, dark and overstuffed with junk. A rusted propane stove, filthy blankets, empty jars and cans. He had been looking around for a couple of minutes when he saw a green eye staring at him. He froze, momentarily frightened, then went over to take a look. It was at the top corner of a large ice chest, the lid of which was broken off, and surrounding the eye itself was a crusty, black substance.

Billy thought it was the eye of a doll until, under the glare of his flashlight, it closed then opened. A tear formed. Billy shuddered and carried the ice chest outside.

What he saw in the sunlight made him alternately horrified and enraged. "Who is that?"

The younger girl answered. "It's the lady."

"What's this black stuff?"

"Dog poop. Daddy told her that's what she had to eat. He peed on her when she was thirsty."

"Fuck, fuck, fuck!" Billy fell to his knees and began frantically scraping away the dog shit.

"How long has she been in there?"

"Five weeks."

Billy's breaths became rapid and short, sweat dripped off his face. "Gotta get her out of there, gotta get her out!"

The ambulance and Wyatt arrived. Wyatt asked, "What the hell is going on?"

"She's been in there for five weeks!" Billy was crying, desperately scraping, and started pulling on her arm. "Gotta get her out."

One of the paramedics said, "Sir! Don't! You could damage her spine!"

Billy screamed, dirty tears covering his cheeks. "Gotta get her out!"

The two paramedics tried unsuccessfully to hold him back. "Sir! Stop! You could kill her!"

Finally, Wyatt tackled Billy and kept him pinned to the ground.

The paramedics quickly took the woman away then, several minutes later, the mother was taken to a hospital and the two girls were taken to social services. Wyatt stood silently on the hillside and watched a photographer take pictures of the items in the trailer. The police put them into boxes and took them away. Billy stared at the ground and every now and again would tremble in a quiet rage.

A woman detective questioned the two men and wrote down all the details, all of which she got from Wyatt. She kept glancing at Billy then at Wyatt as if to ask, "Is he going to be okay?" Wyatt looked at her in a non-committal way simply because he didn't know.

The fact was that Wyatt was worried. He'd never before seen his friend like this or in any way close to it. It was as if something had broken in Billy, something at his core. After the detective left, Wyatt looked at his friend and said, "She'll be okay, Billy. Don't worry." Billy didn't answer. Instead, he continued to look at the ground, seething, as if he was staring into an evil pit.

The two men stayed on the hillside while a man in blue overalls disposed of the dogs and a man in white overalls hitched the trailer to a pickup and took it down the hill.

Billy continued looking at the ground like he was ready to pounce on anything that moved. Wyatt, said, "Where do you think you'll be headed next?"

"Los Angeles. The fucked up part."

"Los Angeles?" He was incredulous. "You'll hate it."

"Good. I'm in the mood to hate."

THIRTY-EIGHT
...

Worried about Billy, Wyatt insisted they go back to the city for a good dinner. Billy said nothing during the entire meal and ate little of it. When Wyatt attempted to start a conversation, he would just nod once or twice and keep staring at something that was not in front of him.

Billy's demeanor stayed the same as they later sat in a saloon. He didn't even finish one beer. Around ten o'clock he said, "I gotta get moving." Wyatt watched him walk like a dead man to his bike then take off into the moonless night.

I tried my best but I had no influence on Billy whatsoever.

Billy, oblivious to his surroundings, rode without purpose, his thoughts a shambles. The wind ripped the tears from his cheeks. He rode through the night and ended up west of Tucson the next morning. At Three Points, he turned south. Twenty minutes later, he rode over a cattle guard and onto a dirt road and took no notice of the wobbling of his bike from the uneven surface.

He rode as far as he could then walked to the western base of Baboquivari Peak where he sat staring at the dirt. When the sun became visible, he walked to the eastern side and sat in its shadow.

Late that night, a wrinkled and bent old man, who seemed to have emerged from the mountain itself, sat next to him. Billy didn't even bother to turn his eyes.

For a long time, the two sat in silence then, almost imperceptibly, the old man began humming in quiet, guttural tones that slowly rose in volume, morphing into different pitches and timbres, the sounds chorusing with the desert winds. Then silence once again.

After some time, the old man began describing ancient battles. The blood and the screams of the cut and felled. The triumphant songs of the victors.

151

The aftermath when the victors dismembered the male children and sexually defiled the women and girls. The prolonged agony of the defeated men being tortured. The more he droned on, the more Billy became transfixed, hypnotized into a strangling horror. Eventually, all he could envision was a world wrapped in evil.

Billy awoke with the sun, went back to Three Points and continued west. He tasted nothing of a breakfast in Gila Bend and afterward jumped onto the interstate, riding like a furious, swirling wind. Ten minutes later he got a citation for speeding and reckless driving. He said nothing to the officer and when he crossed the border into California, threw the ticket into the desert.

Later that day, he got a cheap motel room in El Centro then went to a nearby dive bar. The first thing he saw was a man berating his wife. Billy punched him out then left.

He wandered into a liquor store where the X-rated magazines taunted him with gleeful malevolence. He bought as many bottles as he could carry and when he got back to his room, began a drinking binge intermixed with fits of weeping that lasted for four days. All the while, he clutched the two steel vials on his keychain as if they contained the essence of life itself. And that's when the nightmares began.

Swirling images from his childhood knotted with the scene in Albuquerque. Truthfully, he had been a good kid, but in his drunken state, even the smallest transgression took on hellish proportions. Pushing a girl into the dirt became beating a child, kissing his best friend's girlfriend on the cheek became sexually abusing an eleven year old, forgetting to feed his new puppy became killing two Rottweilers. Each sin the sum of all sins.

There were times when he would snap out of his grief-filled torpor and rage at whatever was around him. One night, he went to another dive bar and got into a fight with four locals. He was badly busted up and ended up with a five hundred dollar fine and two nights in jail.

After getting out, he went to a Harley dealership and while waiting for an oil change, got into an argument with two customers. When the owner asked him to leave, he kicked over a brand new Street 500. The police arrested him. The fine was twelve hundred dollars, another two nights in jail, and he had to pay for the damage to the bike.

He headed north, carrying his nightmares like growing millstones. He continued drinking, was losing weight and slept in fits and starts. Soon, the horrors of the nightmares overtook his thoughts when he was awake as well. Every bump in the road became a rebuke, every breeze an indictment, every gear shift an admission of guilt. Every transgression, both real and not, mocked him and grew into fantastic images that howled incessantly. All evils, imagined and not, were like a festering and ever-growing wound.

Throughout all of this, the one constant image was the woman trapped in the ice chest. Her green eye watched him always, asking for help he could not give, for relief he could not offer. He would fixate on the tear that flowed from it, and would watch it transform into a crystal, infinitely-faceted, reflecting memories of childhood joys and friendships and aspirations that he could see but not feel or touch. The crystal would grow and grow until it was a pool of fire that burned away all that had been good. It would then burst into a raging river that flowed in all directions, destroying everything in its path.

Billy rode around the Los Angeles area for two days before finding what he was looking for: a squalid, two-floor hotel that smelled like a mixture of vomit, mildew and insecticide. His sleep continued to be filled with battered children, screams, bloody dogs, and visions of torture. A green eye floating in space.

He woke up late every morning and drank cheap whiskey, rum, vodka, anything. During the first week of walking around the area, he had a few physical confrontations and many verbal ones. On the second Friday night he saw a hooker getting kicked out of a car. She fell to the sidewalk. He looked at the two men inside the car and said, "We got a problem here?"

The passenger said, "Fuck you."

"Well, why doncha come on out and try it?"

As he was stepping out of the car, Billy smashed his head into the door-frame then kicked him in the face. The driver backed off, but Billy ran after him and pummeled him unconscious. He went back to the hooker and said, "Keys are still in the car. Why doncha drive around for a while and dump it in the ocean? Or sell it. Or whatever." She drove off without a word.

Soon, word got out about an out-of-control redneck, a drunk with a deadly right hook. People, good and bad, religious and criminal, would stop and stare as he walked by. No one spoke to him, prostitutes avoided him, the hotel owner wanted him to leave but was afraid to say anything. And he continued getting into verbal and physical confrontations, gathering scars like a whipping post.

Mostly, however, he drank. And wept. He simply didn't know what else to do. For some reason, he felt he had failed, that he was somehow responsible for the woman in the ice chest, that her nightmare had been made possible by his carelessness. It didn't make sense, of course, but the drinking and his misplaced accountability became a growing maelstrom of self-loathing.

He often held the two steel vials, would close his eyes and cry "Ten minutes" over and over.

After a month, Billy again took to the road, looking for cities that had long since lost hope, cities where the refuse of life gathered like vultures on carrion, where death and the stench of it sat like the walls of a prison. Oakland, San Bernardino, National City, Commerce, Richmond, Sacramento, Westmont.

He sought out neighborhoods that offered a familiarity with his nightmares, a kinship of degradation, the faux peace of apathy. Hookers, pimps, pickpockets and grifters. The smell of urine in doorways and steamed garbage in alleyways. Places where arguments and fistfights formed a normalcy.

One morning in South Stockton, he woke up to find his bike had been stolen. He immediately went to a bank and withdrew two thousand dollars. He then went to all the vagrants in the area and offered the money to anyone who would bring it back.

An hour later, a lanky, disjointed man wearing a red baseball cap knocked on his door. Billy let him in and had him sit down. The man said he knew where the bike was and that his friend would be happy to return it for the two thousand dollars. Billy took out his Colt, pointed it at the man's crotch and said, "Call yer buddy and have him bring the bike here. In perfect condition."

"Whoa," the man said, "no need to get all jungle on me!"

"You heard what I said. Do it. Do it now."

A half hour later, his bike was parked in front of his room. Billy spread out the twenty one-hundred-dollar bills on a table, urinated on them, then handed ten to the man in the red cap and the other ten to his partner.

Billy left that afternoon and rode to San Francisco. By then, he had a feel for the worst parts of a city, like a witching rod pointing to water, and he ended up in another dump of a motel in Hunters Point. He parked his bike inside his room.

During the day, he would sit in his room and drink. At night, he would walk around the neighborhoods, an ever-present bottle in his hand. He got

154

into four or five fights a week, some being only scuffles, others where the pounding and cutting were a bloodletting.

He'd been there for a little over a month when one night he was especially inebriated. He weaved left, right and backwards bumping into people and through small crowds, sometimes would break out into half a melody from some old Country song, and would randomly shout insults to ghosts and living people alike.

He wandered into one of those makeshift clubs that the enterprising young set up for one night only, brushing past the bouncer and the doorman who asked for ten dollars. It was crowded and loud with Hip-Hop. He went to the middle of the room and began dancing. At first, the people laughed but it soon became apparent that he was like a mad bull, bumping into people then pushing them out of the way. When he started with the insults, it got ugly.

He screamed invectives at everyone. Some screamed back. He threw a beer bottle into the crowd and it glanced off a woman's head then clanged against the wall. He then walked up to an especially large-breasted young woman and ripped off the top of her dress.

Immediately, thirty people pounced on him. It was over quickly, lasting only long enough for each person to get in a couple of punches, kicks, deep fingernail scratches, or a knife wound. They dumped him on the sidewalk a block away.

THIRTY-NINE

...

AFTER PARTING WAYS WITH BILLY, WYATT RODE WEST TO ANDRADE, just over the border in California. There, he emptied a few personal items, including his .357 and Ruger, into a storage locker and paid for three months. He texted Billy for the fifth time. As he had come to expect, he didn't get a reply.

It was with a premonition that I watched him head toward Mexico.

As he was waiting at the border checkpoint, he turned around and faced northeast and, again, wondered why.

He rode into Los Algodones, ate a late lunch and found a room at the south side of town. He hailed a cab, sat in the front seat and told the driver to just drive around, which he did as Wyatt engaged him in conversation.

Twenty minutes later, the driver parked in an alley, got out and knocked on a door that was recessed into the wall on the left. A large man with a folded slab of carne asada in his left hand opened the door. The driver said something, pointed at Wyatt, then the man in the doorway shrugged and disappeared. The driver waved to Wyatt, who got out and followed him through the doorway.

Wyatt chose two worn but clean Glocks and said he needed to test fire them. The three walked into the alley. Wyatt emptied two clips into a large mound of trash, first using two hands, then one.

Wyatt paid for both Glocks, two hundred rounds, four clips, a shoulder holster, and a muslin sack with the items to clean the guns. That night, he took them apart, cleaned and oiled them. He filled all four clips, jammed one in each handle, placed one gun in his shoulder holster and one of the extra clips in the left inside pocket of his vest. He put the other gun and clip into the right glove compartment of his bike.

157

The following morning he bought a metal gas can, a small tube of Gorilla Glue and several cheap wallets. He tore off the Velcro from each wallet, glued the strips to the top of the right glove compartment and made loops to hold the second Glock and clip. He then filled the gas can and the bike's tank.

He rode south and had an early lunch in Estación, where he also bought some dried fruit, nuts and water bottles. He stopped for a while to admire the turquoise and deep blue waters of the Sea of Cortez. Peaceful. He then kept on the most southern route he could until he ended up at a small, family-run motel on the beach of Puerto Peñasco.

The next day, he found a nameless trace that paralleled the coast. The crashing waves on his right that rippled the sand, the caw of sea gulls and the smell of salt and sun-rotted seaweed. The sound of his engine. It all combined into a vast existence.

For many days, he continued south. At night, he would settle down next to an ancient fig tree or between a gathering of boulders and have a dinner of sunflower seeds, wild persimmon and coffee. He continued southwest or southeast but always south, and stopped only for food and rest and gasoline when it was available.

One day, he had been riding on a narrow dirt road when he stopped at the top of a small rise. A quarter mile to his left was a stream. He turned around, found a footpath, then rode down it past ocotillo, yucca and saguaro and parked in the latticed shade of three mesquite trees.

He got out a set of Allen wrenches, unscrewed the air filter cover, then removed the air filter itself. He stripped off all his clothes, walked naked to the stream carrying everything in his arms, and washed himself, his clothes and the air filter in the cold water. When he was done, he wrung the water out of his clothes and laid them atop some boulders. He shook the water from the air filter then set it next to his boots. He smoked a cigarette then slept.

The sun had traveled an hour when he awoke. He checked the air filter and it was dry. He put on his jeans, socks and boots then retrieved a plastic canister of oil from a saddlebag. He poured small droplets of oil onto the filter screen then turned it and watched the oil seep into the aligned holes, helping the flow with his left forefinger. He then inspected the entire unit to make sure it was completely covered, set it back on the boulder, smoked another cigarette, slept for thirty more minutes then smoked another.

The filter left a dark, round ring that glistened green with the sunlight. He gently shook off the excess oil, attached it and the air filter to the bike and put away the Allen wrenches. He checked the oil level, added a quarter of a quart and put the oil canister away. He put on his t-shirt and vest, rolled up the rest of his clothes and put them in the touring pack, then rode back up to the dirt road.

To avoid Acapulco, Wyatt turned inland onto a pretty and sparsely traveled route and soon began riding on smaller dirt roads. Late that afternoon, he stopped in a small settlement outside of Atrixco. He parked his bike some yards away from a cantina so as not to spook the horses that were tied to a railing that looked as if had been fashioned by an axe decades before.

Inside, he ordered a beer and a plate of beans and rice with corn tortillas. A large silent woman in a smudged white dress brought him his meal, left, then came back with a jar of dark red hot sauce, thick like cold blood.

A man wearing two side arms, his chest crisscrossed with half-filled gun belts, walked over. He wore a star. He asked Wyatt if he was there for the Festival of the Virgin and Salvation. Wyatt said he wasn't aware of such a thing and was just riding through, going nowhere and everywhere. The man looked him down and up as if he were a strange species, then turned and left. Wyatt paid for his meal and when he left, the man who wore a star was sitting in a jeep watching him.

Wyatt stopped at the edge of the village to allow a group of children to cross the dirt road. The girls wore pink, white and green dresses with crocheted flowers on them, the boys wore suits and ties and polished black shoes that had become covered with dust.

When the children had passed, he rode on and a quarter mile later was hailed over by a pre-teenaged girl wearing blue jeans and a Hornitos Agave Tequila t-shirt. She stood in front of a folding table that sagged in the middle from age. He took no notice of the man who wore a star as he drove past, accompanied by four others.

He got off his bike and looked at the merchandise. Glittering jewelry. Hand-knitted dolls and crude leather items. Plastic crucifixes. Photos of drawings of the Virgin Mary, Jesus, and Jesus being crucified.

The girl's grandmother sat, toothless and grave, on a bleached wicker rocking chair to the left and behind the table, staring at memories of what was and what had never become.

He bought a pair of gray leather fringes, paid the girl twice what she asked, attached the fringes to his handlebars, then continued riding.

Some minutes later, he came upon a bridge that spanned a narrow river north of Marquelia. The man who wore a star hailed him to stop by waving his hands.

Wyatt turned off his engine and had just glanced to his right at the disappearing sun when a teenaged boy swung a two-by-four that glanced off the bottom of his helmet and smashed onto the top of his backbone. He fell to the ground and narrowly avoided the second swing, which struck the ground with a thud. He threw dirt into the boy's eyes then ripped off half his right ear and the boy screamed in agony. The four other men converged on Wyatt kicking him in the head and ribs, one of them whipping him with a chain.

Despite the beating, Wyatt stood up and blindly pummeled whomever was in reach. He cracked open one man's skull and he fell to the ground unconscious. He smashed the jaw of another one who also fell, screaming like a wounded wild boar. Blood was everywhere. Wyatt managed to get out his Glock but the man wielding a chain knocked it out of his hand. The man wearing a star picked it up.

I rode as fast as I could and got there just as the man who wore a star pointed the gun at Wyatt. I drifted through a large patch, spraying the men with sand and gravel. Those still on their feet turned their backs and covered their ears as I cranked the throttle, the roar like that of a prehistoric beast in the throes of death. Wyatt, covered with blood and filled with broken bones, rolled down the grass-covered embankment and disappeared into the weeds lining the river.

FORTY

...

IT HAD TAKEN THE REST OF THE NIGHT FOR BILLY TO MAKE IT BACK TO his room. For what seemed an eternity, but in fact was only two days, he lay on his bed barely conscious, the pain of the cuts, bruises and broken bones like a steel trap, his nightmares like a constant weight. He also suffered from the withdrawals of not having anything to drink, and he couldn't believe that anyone could feel as miserable as he. Clutched in his hand were the two steel vials. Often, he would mutter "Ten minutes" under his breath.

On the afternoon of the third day, he woke up and saw me sitting on a chair next to his bed. He looked at me for a long time and finally said, "I'd offer ya a beer but I done run out." I smiled. He looked at the patch on the left side of my vest and said, "So what do I owe the honor of the presence of the Poet to?"

"I was just in the neighborhood, señor, and thought I'd stop in for a visit."

"Well sheeit, that's right neighborly of ya."

I washed out an empty whisky bottle then filled it with water. He struggled onto one elbow, drank all of it in one swallow, then fell back onto the bed, breathing heavily. I asked about his injuries and he told me what they were and how he got them. I admitted he looked thoroughly beaten and unhealthy, and the stench coming off him was powerful.

He lay in silence for some time. "Well, if yer a poet, ya got any wisdom in rhyme to impart? Something to make sense out of the mess I'm in?"

"Well, I'm not a poet in such a sense, more of a teller of tales. I bought the vest some years ago in a thrift store in Davenport. A month later I bought the patch at a bike rally in Indianola. The lady selling it sewed it on for me."

"So you ain't a poet but ya like telling stories?"

"That is true, señor."

161

"Well hell, if ya don't mind, I could use a good story, something to take my mind off the misery I'm in." He was silent for a few moments. "But I suppose I ought to take a shower first."

"An excellent idea, señor. Allow me help you."

It was a slow trip to the bathtub. I turned on the water then opened the shower nozzle. After the hot water arrived, I added some cold water to make the temperature tolerable. I wasn't inclined to help him wash off the stench and, fortunately for me, he said he could manage it himself, so I left him to it.

I got a set of clean sheets from the motel manager, made the bed, then got out some clean clothes. When Billy was clean and dried off, he managed to put on a pair of underwear then slowly eased himself onto the bed. He looked at me and said, "Thank you for that, Poet."

"El placer es mío, Billy Balcomb. "

"Well, that's right nice of ya. So, do ya got a story all wound up for me?"

"I have many, amigo mío."

He looked at his bike then back at me. "Ya got one that don't have nothing to do with the world I'm living in?"

"Ah, sí señor. One from long ago then?"

"Sounds good."

"Very well." I let him take some moments to get more comfortable.

"Many, many years ago, there lived a man, a gentleman, who owned a large hacienda. He was wealthy but humble and it was said that his wife was the most beautiful in all of Mexico. Too, he had many other loves in his life: his two children and the men who worked for him and their families.

"He also had a vast love for horses and one day, he and his caballeros set out to find a passel of wild ones. They had been gone for a week and when they returned, they stopped, as they always did, atop a ridge to admire his ranch. But what they saw horrified them.

"Except for Our Friend's wife and two children, all of the women and their children were lying on the ground, shot to death. Our Friend's wife was on her knees begging for mercy. They were surrounded by a dozen and a half men on horses and one driving a wagon filled with all of his precious belongings. The leader listened for several seconds then shot and killed his two children.

"His wife continued begging, but Our Friend, being a mile away, could not hear what she was saying. Soon the leader smiled and nodded, and his wife jumped onto the back of his horse. They rode for only a few yards before they stopped and his wife dismounted. She ran back into the house, jumping over their dead children as if they were scraps of junk. When she came back out, she had her pearl-studded bag filled with all of her priceless jewelry.

"For days, Our Friend and his caballeros buried their loved ones, mourned their deaths and prayed for their safe passage to Heaven. Afterward, Our Friend visited his neighbor, a good man, told him what had happened, then sold him his hacienda. He split the money and all the rest of his belongings with his caballeros then began walking west."

Billy became restless. "Liking this story a lot, Poet, but my eyes are getting tired. Mind if I rest a bit before ya finish?"

"Not at all, Señor."

Billy awoke three hours later and looked at me with disbelief, as if he thought I had been an apparition who would have vanished. He swirled around the steel vials in his hand, the sound like the distant song of sirens. Eventually, he nodded slightly. "Glad you're still here."

"Of course, amigo mío."

"Been dreaming about yer story. Wondering what happened to that guy."

"Ah yes. Our Wandering Friend." I waited for Billy to get more settled in.

"After saying goodbye to his caballeros, Our Friend roamed on foot all over Northern Mexico for three years. He was a man with no home, no friends or family, no name and no future. He eventually came to a village on the coast. As he walked on the dirt street between the few wooden buildings, he noticed two things. The first was that everyone smiled but they were false smiles, the smiles of those who are afraid. The second was that all the men were old and bent from age."

Billy closed his eyes so as to listen more acutely. "He walked between an old cantina and a vacant building toward the ocean. To his left he saw a large, two-story house surrounded with gardens. To his right was a new, wooden platform that was covered with a wooden roof. Sitting there were a man wearing only swim trunks and a woman in a white dress. Between them was a table and on it were two bottles of tequila and below the table was a chest filled with beer.

"Our Friend walked around to the front of the man and the woman, pulled out a gun and shot the man in the stomach. The woman was shocked and unable to scream. She did not recognize her husband."

At this, Billy stared at me with laser-like eyes.

"Our Friend told his wife to take off the outer part of her dress and this he tore into many strips. He tied the strips together into larger strips then used them to fasten the man's arms and legs to the posts holding up the wooden covering. With the last strip he gagged the man then covered him with tequila.

"He then took his wife to her house and together they walked upstairs to her bedroom. He told her to bring in all the guards and tell them that he was her husband's brother and was to be treated with respect and courtesy. When this had been done, the guards relaxed and that is when he killed them.

"He asked his wife where the younger village men were and she said in a jail one mile south. It was then that he told her who he was.

"She dropped to her knees crying and told him what a blessing it was that he came to rescue her and how horrible it was to watch her children, the children she loved with all her heart, be murdered. All the other children, too, and all of the wives of the caballeros because she loved everyone of them, and she told him how she had been plotting revenge ever since she had been abducted.

"When she had finished, our Friend stared at her without emotion for many minutes. He shot her in the right eye but angled the gun so that the bullet went out of her temple and not into her brain. For many more minutes, he watched her slowly die, then shot her in the middle of her forehead."

I could feel Billy's imagination fire with justice as he looked at me with eyes like arrows shot by a Sioux chief. "Retribution's a bitch, ain't it."

"Sí, it is indeed." He closed his eyes once more and I continued. "Our Friend went down to the kitchen and told the cooks to prepare as much food as possible because they were going to feed the entire village.

"He then went to the barn, hitched two horses to a wagon and drove to the jail. He killed the sleeping guard then let out all the prisoners and drove several of them back to the village. One man was skilled in the art of handling horses and to this man he said to go back to the prison and get the rest of the men.

"When they had all arrived, he told them to dress with whatever clothes they chose from the closets, then eat however much food they wanted.

"He then walked out to the wooded platform and watched the man who had killed his children. The man, speaking in a tongue only those being tortured know, was hopelessly trying to shake the fire ants out of his eyes and ears and mouth. It took another hour for him to die.

"He went back to the bedroom, wrapped all the money and jewelry he could find in a quilt then carried it downstairs where the entire village was eating and celebrating. He ate in silence with them and when he was done, he told them that the money and jewelry were theirs to share. He then walked out the front door and disappeared into the twilight."

Billy looked at me for a long time. "Was that man you?"

"No. Not me, señor. Only someone I met. I knew him for but one day."

"Well, that is one helluva story, I gotta admit. I'll have to ponder on it for a while." He stared at the ceiling for a short time. "I do believe I have to close my eyes again, Poet, maybe sleep a little more, if you don't mind."

"Please, señor, I shall wait."

When Billy awoke, he said, "Damn. I can barely move."

I smiled. "Well, I have something that will help." I opened a small, leather satchel and pulled out an old bottle of tequila.

"Where'd you get that?" Billy asked.

"The tequila? I've been carrying it around for some time."

"No. That leather bag. Where'd it come from? Didn't see it before."

I smiled again. "It is a small one, easy to miss."

Billy took the bottle and inspected the label. "Don Julio, 1948. Was that a good year fer tequila?"

"The best, amigo mío. It was the finest year for Don Julio for it was then that he finalized his brewing process and married his lovely and faithful wife, Dorothea Garcia. El tequila de ese año contiene magia."

"What's magical about it?"

"Drink it, all of it, and you shall be renewed."

"Renewed?"

"Sí."

"Well, if you say so." Billy took a long drink then laid back his head in dreamlike ecstasy. "Now that's nice. Real nice. Smooth, like it's wrapping ya in a blanket." He looked at the bottle and frowned. "How come there ain't no worm in the bottom?"

"The worm is but a gimmick, a way to sell cheaper tequila."

"Sounds like something somebody'd do to make a buck. Was never partial to the idea myself. So you say that if I drink this whole bottle, I'll be all new, maybe even be able to walk to the bathroom by myself?"

"Sí, amigo mío. But you will be able to do much more than that."

"Well good, I hope yer right. I do thank you for this, Mr. Poet, and I thank you again for that fine story. It's something I'll be thinking about fer some time. Now if ya don't mind, I need to close my eyes again."

FORTY-ONE

...

WYATT LAY HIDDEN AND WOKE UP AT DAWN. A SMALL FLOCK OF BIRDS flew right to left but he was unable to focus on them, unable to focus on anything. He soon closed his eyes and dropped back into a dreamless sleep and for the rest of the day, he would sleep and awaken in erratic rhythms.

The five men who had beaten him were, as well, fairly beaten themselves. The man who wore a star figured Wyatt would soon die so he hadn't bothered looking for him.

The next morning, Wyatt's senses began to come back. He heard things. Cars passing on the road sixty yards to his left, one of them with damaged valves, another seeming to be without suspension. He heard a bus, a school bus probably, and wondered if one of the students on it would ever imagine a bloodied man lying in the weeds fifty yards away and would someday write a story about it.

His eyes focused more and more. He was able to move them left and right but only enough to see the tall grasses that surrounded him and the top of a dead tree. He could feel the pressure of pebbles on the back of his head but when he tried to lift his head in order to move them, a severe pain shot through his fractured clavicle.

Soon, he could feel the wetness of his sweat and the blood that covered his back and the pressure of the ground on his legs. He could smell the hot and fetid mud, and a stale stench laid on him like the stone lid of a sarcophagus. By mid afternoon, the pain and pressure from his injuries were as if a separate life form had been born inside of him and was growing.

When he opened his eyes on the morning of the second day, there were two children, a girl and a boy, staring at him and not moving, their eyes like those who have become hypnotized by a waterfall or a campfire. Wyatt tried to speak but his vocal cords had become rigid and his tongue was like a bag of rosin.

After several minutes, he fell asleep then awoke three hours later. The children were gone. On the low rock to his left was a tortilla covered with dried and cracked refried beans. Next to it was a two-liter plastic milk jug filled with water. His left hand and arm were mobile so he drank and ate and drank again, then removed the pebbles from under his head and the pain spread out and settled in different places.

At dusk, he drank the rest of the water and gazed at the sky as the pale blue turned to indigo. Insects buzzed around him and when they alighted on his face, their buzzing stopped. In his peripheral vision he would sometimes see birds in flight. The blood on his clothes had crusted and dried a blackish-brown.

On the third day, Wyatt awoke at noon and saw me sitting on the higher rock to his right. He tightly closed his eyes then opened them, as if expecting me to be a hallucination that would disappear. He even squinted his eyes but still I remained. He said, "So. You finally caught up with me."

I smiled and nodded to the rock on the other side. "You should eat your breakfast before the ants do."

Wyatt did eat and drink and afterward said, "I have to close my eyes."

Just before sunset, Wyatt woke up again and took a deep breath but halfway through it, the pain from his cracked ribs paralyzed his whole body. He slowly settled into a tenuous relaxation then looked at me. "You're still here."

"Sí, amigo mío."

"Hmph. You get around a lot."

I nodded once. "Like you."

He looked away and said, mostly to himself, "Wish it was my bike that was leaning against that rock instead of you."

"Entiendo, mi errante amigo."

"Yeah, I guess you would understand that, being a helluva traveller yourself."

"Gracias."

"I don't suppose you know where my bike is."

"Lo sé y a ciencia cierta. It is past the bridge on the southeast side of Marquelia. The house is a white one with blue trim and belongs to the man who wears a star. He is to give it to his nephew, who is hoping he will someday get another ear. Your bike is in the shed behind the house, a little scratched but in good shape."

Wyatt nodded slightly. "Thank you for that. So what are you doing here, anyway?"

"Oh, I just thought I'd stop by and see if I could help."

He looked at my patch. "Poet to the rescue."

"Sí."

Wyatt looked at the weeds to his left then scanned the sky, left to right and left again, his head following in half-measure. He looked back at me. "I'm afraid I haven't been much of a host, perhaps even a bit ill-mannered so, please, forgive me."

"No os preocupéis, amigo mío. Uno debe cuidar de sus necesidades antes de poder ser galante con los demás."

"Thank you for understanding, but I don't believe my travails prohibit me from being polite. And if I could minister to myself, I would have already done so." He opened his nostrils and smelled the hot and foul air. "Without those two silent children, I'm afraid I'd be shaking hands with Mictlantecuhtli by now."

"Ah! The Angel of Death. An often mischaracterized god."

He raised an eyebrow and looked at me. "How so?"

"Despite the many tales, most who die are ready to do so, some even eager, and it is Mictlantecuhtli who eases the transition. Those who die before they are ready are made so by others, but even then, Mictlantecuhtli does what he can to soften the injustice and quell the grief."

Wyatt's eyes took on a kind look. "Now you sound more like a philosopher than a poet."

"Perhaps. ¿Puedo tomar lo dicho como un cumplido?"

"It was, indeed, a compliment. So Mictlantecuhtli is compassionate then."

"Sí. Only those who are not ready for death fear or revile it. Truly, only those who are prepared for death understand it. Some say death is part of life but, perhaps, it is the other way around. Perhaps it is both."

"Sounds like the basis for a religion."

"Perhaps."

"How did you come upon this?"

"I once met a man many years ago who was, I believe, already dead. A man with no name, no home, no hope, no future. However, he did have memories of a fine life, loving children and a beautiful wife. One day, as he watched from a hilltop a mile away, his wife willingly left with the man who had just murdered his children."

"What a vile thing to have witnessed. What did he do?"

"He wandered around, alone, for years until he found his wife living in luxury with that man. He killed them without emotion or remorse. He told me that at first he wished he himself had died right after that, that that's what he deserved. But as the days and years passed, he realized that he was fortunate because he was close to discovering the true relationship between life and death, something that perhaps only Mictlantecuhtli understands."

Two birds chittered and swirled around the branches of the tree to our left. "I asked if he could explain it but he said it was an understanding too fundamental for words, that words are paltry translations for truths such as life and death. Other things, too, such as beauty and friendship. And that those who claim to understand life by words alone are like those who see only the entrance to a cave yet claim to know the mazes that form its construction and the treasures that lie within."

Wyatt slightly nodded. "I like that, Poet. I do." He thought for some moments. "I suppose it's like that with people as well. That you can talk with them, sometimes for years, but until you see them act, maybe even become them, even for a short while, you will never know their inner construction nor their true treasures."

He half closed his eyes and stared at the rock to his left. "Too, that would apply to ourselves, would it not? That if we look inward with only labels and prior explanations, we will never know by which designs we are made nor our true worth."

I looked at him with admiration. "Now it is you who is the philosopher, Wyatt Hazel Youngblood."

He laughed lightly. "I'll take it, I guess. As long as I don't become some sort of priest. What else did you learn from this man?"

"I learned that only through such things as beauty and fidelity and friendship can one truly know the blessings that living can be."

I could see that Wyatt thought of the Dark Companion. "But there are things, appendages, that can follow one around, no?"

"Sí, sí. And we all have them. Insignificant ones like a lucky number as well as onerous ones like guilt. The mechanism by which they attach to us are the same. And the way we rid ourselves of them are the same as well."

"How is that done?"

"Perhaps by simply saying 'be gone.' Perhaps by delving deeply into one's soul. Perhaps by praying to one's gods. It is different from person to person but the same for each person."

"Hmph. Well, with me being in this condition, I don't suppose I'll ever find out."

"Perhaps I can help, amigo mío."

He looked at me with a wry smile. "You say 'perhaps' a lot."

"I do, sí."

"Perhaps because you know things?"

I opened my hands unassumingly. "Perhaps."

Wyatt continued smiling. "So you say you can help me. How?"

As I did with Billy, I took an old bottle of tequila out of my satchel. Wyatt looked at it, then at me, then at my satchel again. "Where'd that come from?"

"The bottle? I bought it at an estate sale not too long ago."

"No, I mean the satchel. I hadn't seen it before."

"Ah. It is small and easily concealed." I smiled and handed him the bottle.

"Don Julio, 1948. If I remember correctly, that was his first excellent year."

"Sí. It took him six years to perfect the finest liquid ever devised by man. Ese año fue mágico."

"Magical? What's magical about it?"

"Drink it, all of it, and you will be well. Sore and stiff for a while, but physically you will be whole."

"Well, I don't know if I believe that, but it's worth a shot, pun intended." He swirled around the tequila. "Thank goodness there's no worm in the bottom." He took a long drink, then closed his eyes and looked like a man who just found love. "Now that is the finest elixir I have ever imbibed." He looked up at me with a peaceful smile. "I dislike being rude, my Poet friend, but I'm afraid I must close my eyes again."

"Por favor, amigo mío."

FORTY-TWO

...

WYATT AWOKE SEVERAL TIMES THROUGHOUT THE NIGHT, EACH TIME taking a small sip of tequila. He finished the bottle the next evening then slept twelve hours straight. When he woke up, two things were missing. One was pain and it took several minutes for him to realize it. He sat up and checked out his ribs and arms and clavicle. Except for a profound stiffness, they were all as they should be.

The second thing missing was me, but he wasn't surprised. In fact, he would have thought he'd only imagined our conversation if it weren't for the empty bottle.

He got up, brushed himself off, stretched, then washed himself and his clothes in the river. Before walking to Marquelia, he left all of his money, twelve thousand pesos, under a stone for the two children.

On the surface, Marquelia itself seemed somewhat prosperous, but underneath was a brooding malevolence, like a partially buried serpent. Throughout the day, Wyatt stayed in the shadows except for one time to get cash from an ATM and buy some trail mix and water. He waited until after sundown to find his motorcycle.

The house was maybe forty years old but in decent shape, the blue trim having been painted a few years earlier. He took a wide arc around it to the shed, which was unlocked. He walked in and his bike was indeed a little scratched but looked to be in good working order. He checked the right glove compartment and both the Glock and the extra clip were still there. He chambered a round and pocketed them.

He sneaked to the back of the house and looked through a window, past the kitchen and into the living room. The nephew had a bandage on his ear and was sitting on a wooden chair with a lime green cushion on it. Standing in the middle of the room was a heavyset woman, the housekeeper, who was being crudely railed by the man who wore a star. She was crying.

"¡Ya tiene edad para coger y lo necesita! Hazle un favor, dásela a Pablo y a sus amigos. ¡Se va a divertir!" He looked at his nephew and they laughed.

The housekeeper was crying profusely. "¡Por favor, señor! ¡Solo tiene catorce años!"

Good lord, Wyatt thought. What kind of depraved trash would force a woman to whore out her own fourteen-year-old daughter?

A car drove up and the man who had wielded a chain at the bridge walked in carrying a rifle. When he heard what was going on, he backslapped the woman and she fell to her knees crying. He screamed at her to do what her boss said. "¡Obedece a tu jefe!"

The door to the kitchen was unlocked. Wyatt walked in and crept to the living room doorway. The man with the rifle kicked the woman and spat on her. The man with the star and his nephew laughed again.

Wyatt flew into the living room like a cataclysm. He first bull rushed the man with the rifle, then smashed him three times in the face.

He turned around and saw the man who wore a star getting a pistol out of the drawer of a side table. Wyatt kicked the drawer shut on his wrist. The man screamed with pain, then Wyatt made a bloody mess of his face.

The nephew was cowering in his chair, shouting that he was going to kill Wyatt. Wyatt calmly walked over to him, leaned down so they were face-to-face, and stared at him for some moments before ripping off the rest of his ear.

The man who had wielded a chain fired his rifle, missing Wyatt by inches. Wyatt pulled out his Glock and shot him three times in the chest. The nephew pulled out a large knife and lunged at Wyatt, cutting his left shoulder. Wyatt shot him in the stomach and his neck, and blood spouted out of his left carotid artery.

Wyatt then walked over to the man who wore a star. He watched him as he fumbled with the pistol and when he finally got a grip, Wyatt placed his gun barrel against his forehead. The man dropped the gun. He was crying. "¡Por favor, señor, agarre lo que quiera! Dinero, tengo dinero. Lo que sea. ¡Por favor!" Wyatt waited a full minute while the man continued to sob and plead and offer money. Finally, he grew silent and looked into Wyatt's steady and merciless eyes. Wyatt shot him in the middle of his forehead.

During all of this, the housekeeper was hiding behind a chair, terrified. He told her to stay where she was. He searched the bedrooms and came back with a handful of cash then rifled through all the men's pockets. He gave her six hundred thousand pesos then told her to never say a word to anyone about what just happened.

She looked up at him. Tears coursed down her cheeks, clutching the money as if praying. "Muchísimas gracias, señor. Dios lo bendiga."

―∽―

Wyatt went straight to the shed, got his bike, rode through Marquelia then continued north without stopping for anything but snacks and gas until he got to El Rosario. He got a room, but before going to sleep, thought of that time in Arches National Park when he was camping with Cassie. She had been right. He did kill again, and he felt the vice-like grip of his fate with the Dark Companion.

He awoke six hours later and spent the day doing nothing but riding, snacking and filling his tank. The following morning, he headed toward Nogales. It took just fifteen minutes to pass through the DeConcini Port of Entry into Arizona, the border guard only making sure the name on his passport matched the one on his driver's license.

He rested for three days in Tucson and during that time, reflected on his time on the road. The thrills of riding, the scenery, the women, the killings. He often asked himself, "What the hell am I doing?" but it wasn't a serious question because it led to no revelations. The fact was, he knew why he was riding, why he had no home, and why he was almost always alone.

One night, during his nightly sojourn, I rode by a block away. By now he had learned the sound of my bike but rather than trying to find me, he simply looked up at the heavens and stared at the stars and the darkness that surrounded them.

A few minutes later, as it had happened many times before, his attention was again pulled to the northeast, somewhere in Michigan it seemed like. And as always he wondered why he often looked in that direction. What's there? Something lost or something to discover?

FORTY-THREE

...

THE NEXT DAY, BETWEEN LONG STRETCHES OF SLEEPING, BILLY FINISHED the entire bottle of tequila. When he awoke the following morning, he looked around his room. The cracked ceiling and walls, the lamp next to his bed, the flimsy and mucked-up curtains. His bike, neglected and quiet. He was oddly relaxed and it was some minutes before he realized that for the first time in over a year, he was not surrounded by hostility.

He got up, relieved himself in the bathroom then looked in the mirror at the few scars on his face. He examined the scars on his chest and stomach then the ones on his arms and legs. He flexed and turned them. The movements were natural and full and unobstructed save for a stiffness like that of wearing a heavily starched overcoat. There was no pain. He looked back into the mirror and said, "Well, don't that beat all."

Billy left Hunters Point in the late morning and arrived in Albuquerque two days later. It had been a year since he found the woman in the box.

He first talked with the woman detective who had investigated the scene. The crime was still an open investigation and she told him the data she could, which included the hospital where the lady with green eyes was undergoing physical therapy. Billy was relieved but somehow not surprised that the lady had survived. She also told him the father's name, Harvey Smith, and the location of his children. His wife was in psychiatric care and unavailable.

He told the woman detective that he'd like to visit the lady with green eyes and the girls, so she gave him the address of the hospital and told him the girls were living at the Albuquerque Christian Children's Home. She then called the administrator and let her know he was coming to visit.

He first went to the hospital and walked into the rehab area on the first floor. He sat on a chair next to the door and for an hour watched the patients go through their routines, but he did not see the woman with green eyes.

He went to the children's home after lunch. The administrator said she was expecting him and thought his visit would be good for the girls. They walked through double glass doors and into a yard that was mostly covered with dirt. She pointed out the girls, who were sitting at a wooden picnic table in the shade of a walnut tree. He walked over.

The younger one looked up and with no surprise in her voice said, "You're the man who broke our trailer door."

"Yes, I am." He smiled, sat down and said, "You know, I never got yer names."

"I'm Mary, that's Mona. She's my sister but she doesn't like to talk. What's your name?"

"Name's Billy, pleased to meet both of ya."

Both girls were dressed in plain jeans, worn out tennis shoes and button-up, long-sleeved flannel shirts. Mary, the five-year-old, was precocious and the conversation with her was easy and delightful, and he took an instant liking to her.

Mona, on the other hand, would only nod or shake her head or shrug her shoulders to Billy's questions, and he felt she held inside a deep injustice and he wanted to hug her and make it all go away.

The three of them laughed and played with dolls and Billy told silly kid jokes. Time slipped away and it was around sundown when he got up to leave, jokingly saying he didn't like to be out after dark. It was then that Mary said, "After daddy sold his business, he always stayed up all night."

"Is that right?"

"That's when he became MasterBlood."

"MasterBlood?"

"That was his name when he went to the no-no places on the internet. I saw him type it once and he got really mad and hit me and told me to never say the word or he'd send me to one of those places."

"But you just said it to me."

"That's because you're nice. Besides, he's all gone."

"Well, he is that, ain't he."

Late morning the next day, Billy went back to the hospital and sat in the same chair as before. The room itself was like a gymnasium but with chiropractor's tables, fitness balls, pedal exercisers, hand and leg extenders, and a slew of other equipment he'd never before seen.

Against the back wall and to the right, a short, slender and somewhat frail woman slowly walked along parallel bars, doing knee bends and such. Her back was to him. Her hair was short and gray at the ends but red at the roots. When she got to the end of her walk and turned around, she saw him, stared for some seconds, then broke into a relaxed smile. Billy didn't know how to react. Finally, he waved.

When she finished her session, she walked over, lightly leaning on a cane. Billy stood up and when she got to him, they looked into each other's eyes for the longest time. She smiled and broke the silence. "My name's Katy."

"Katy. Why, that's a right fine name."

"Thank you." She continued smiling. "And yours?"

"Oh, it's Billy. Just, ya know, Billy."

"Ah. And a right fine name that is as well."

She held out her hand and when Billy took it, a flush and rush went through both of them, like going over the first hill of a tall roller coaster. When they let go, Billy, out of breath, said, "So uh, I guess yer getting ready to head on home?"

"Yes. What there is of it, anyway."

"Well uh, do ya think it'd be okay if I, ya know, accompanied you? Maybe get something to eat? I mean, ya gotta be hungry after all that working out and stuff."

Katy's smile reached through her eyes and into the air. Billy had never experienced such wonderment. "I'd like that, Billy." They walked out but instead of going to the parking structure, Katy headed to a bus stop.

"What're we doing here?" Billy asked.

She looked at him with a droll smile and a twinkle in her eyes. "This is where my limo picks me up."

Billy chuckled once, looked around and said, "Is that right? Well, we could wait for yer limo or we could take my bike. Get a nice breeze on yer face to cool ya down."

"I haven't been on the back of a motorcycle in years. I might fall off."

"Won't happen. Guaranteed." Seeing that Katy was a little weak and not wanting her to walk more than necessary, he said, "Why doncha wait right here while I fetch my bike. Won't be long, I promise."

Katy's smile made Billy lose his breath again. After some moments, he recovered and scurried off. Katy watched him disappear into the shadows of the parking structure with a hopefulness she hadn't felt for a long time, perhaps never.

Wary of bringing up a disagreeable past, lunch was a mostly quiet one consisting of intermittent small talk. Nevertheless, it was a pleasant, floating time. The kind of time where the rush of wanting to say everything kept both of them from saying anything, a time where each wished that all of it had been said long ago, and they were already amid the thrills of living which, to Katy, was fairytale-like. Billy was simply wonderstruck.

The deepest conversation started when Billy said, "Noticed ya got a few tattoos."

"Yeah, six of them. They've been coming back lately as I'm filling out. You have quite a few yourself."

"Yeah, I forget how many. I like 'em. I mean, I like tattoos in general, if they're done right, that is, like yers are."

"Why, thank you." She paused a moment. "You gentleman, you."

Billy turned red with embarrassment.

FORTY-FOUR

•••

W YATT, AT LAST, DID RIDE NORTHEAST TO MICHIGAN AND ENDED UP in Lansing. Though the traffic wasn't as compressed as he'd experienced in other big cities, the drivers drove with big city personalities, like uncontrolled robots whose batteries were running low. The only relief from the heat was the brief and slight wind on his face as he rode from stoplight to stoplight.

He left the metropolitan area riding west then south. He passed by lush trees of medium height, dark green grasses and clumps of light green weeds, a small corn field, a used car lot, a two-story apartment building that looked more like a medium-priced hotel, and all the while the parallel telephone lines drooped between wooden telephone poles that leaned as if they hadn't been buried deeply enough.

He parked at the far edge of the parking lot of a water park, the shrieks of excitement passing by like bullet trains. Across the street was a split rail fence and there was a dog trotting alongside it, its tongue hanging out. A bland sunset was beginning.

Whatever had been grabbing his attention for years was now closer than it had ever been, and as he looked west and a little to the north, he felt like a deep-sea diver on the verge of finding an old Spanish galleon laden with gold.

I chuckled when he turned around to see if I was there.

He got a bottom floor room at the Royal Castle Arms, an old and almost deserted two-story hotel in the gray western outskirts of Lansing. The heat of the late afternoon was hard, constant and vertical, as if invisible columns of rock cut short the intermittent breezes. The hotel's pool, surrounded by a chainlink fence, was dry and baked and there were dusty-gray and brown weeds growing through the cracks. At the bottom of the fence, clumps of weeds sat still.

Nothing in the area had any personality, which was pretty much the way he felt. He was hot, sweaty, smelly, tired and wanted a drink. He lay on the thin, bumpy mattress, slept for three hours, woke up, took a shower then dressed with his last clean t-shirt and last clean pairs of socks and underwear.

The only place he could see that was open for business was called the Satin Pillow, which was a half-mile away. He decided to walk and soon wished he hadn't. Even though it was nighttime, it was still baking hot.

Once inside the door, he paused to let his eyes adjust to the dark interior. Cool and sterilized air came out of the air conditioner vents, music was blasting, and down two steps to his right was a carpet covered floor where about two dozen men were watching a writhing dancer who seemed to be magnetically connected to a brass pole.

He didn't see me as I walked out.

Wyatt walked to the farthest end of the bar where the music was more like background noise and sat down facing the rows of bottles set in front of a mirror painted with gold fleurs-de-lis and chubby cherubs nestled in repeated patterns of gaudy scrolling.

He watched the bartender shaking a margarita, her back to him. Tight jeans, a conch covered belt with a black and red braid down her right side that ended at her knee, tight short-sleeved white top, arms softly sculpted, long black hair that weaved and waved like wheat in a light wind. She was maybe an inch above five feet, her back and hips were perfectly curved and he figured she weighed a tad over a hundred pounds.

Wyatt looked to his left at the eight other patrons sitting at the bar. There was one old drunk whose shaking chin almost rested on the bar between his two arms that were awkwardly angled, his arthritic fingers flayed out in different directions. Another man with short hair wore a cheap but clean and pressed light green suit and he sat perfectly upright with his back to the bar, staring woodenly at the stage. The other bartender, a young and good-looking man, flipped bottles like a juggler. The barback carried in a tray of freshly washed glasses.

The woman bartender came over. "What'll I getcha, big fella?"

Wyatt turned to her, blinked three times and felt as if he had backed out of his head, sucker punched with aesthetics. For the first time in his life, a sight perfectly slotted into his ideal of feminine beauty. The alluring

Aphrodite. He breathed deeply and slowly exhaled. "If I may, I'd like a gin and tonic, please. Beefeater."

The bartender stood still for several seconds, slowly closed her eyes then opened them. She thought to herself. *A tall, ruggedly handsome stranger walks in and perfectly orders the perfect drink. It's like I'm in a Raymond Chandler novel.* She left to make his drink. There was no bottle of Beefeater on the mirror-backed shelf so she went into the storage room.

When she got inside the door, she put her hands on a shelf and took rapid and shallow breaths. *God, he's gorgeous. Should I? I want to. I need it. It's been how long since that oafish liquor store owner bought me a cut glass bracelet and earrings and wanted them back when I broke up with him? Six months?* She backtracked along her memories. *No, it was a year and a half ago. And two years before that. And I can't remember how long it was before that.*

I deserve this, right? I'm forty-two years old and I still have needs, right? Besides, my plane leaves tomorrow and he'll be long gone and I'll be in Florida and it'll all be just a memory. A good one of an orgasm or two. But then, with a guy like him it could be a night of nothing but. Wouldn't that be something. A first-ever. She looked along the shelves of bottles. *Fuck it, I'm going for him, full tilt. Slam-bam-thank-you-ma'am, I'm good with that.*

She walked back to Wyatt. "Sorry, we're out of Beefeater but we have Bombay and Tanqueray."

"Ah. I'll just have a PBR."

"You want Professional Bull Riding?"

Wyatt chuckled. "Just a beer. Pabst Blue Ribbon if you have it. If not, a Corona or Dos Equis."

"So let me get this straight. You want a PBR and tonic?" Wyatt laughed out loud. She put out her hands, palms up. "I just want to give you what you want."

Wyatt exhaled with a big smile. "You are a something else, uh ... "

"Maddy."

"Short for Madeleine?"

She gave him a kitten-like look. "Yes."

(*God, what a name!*) "Well, you are a delight, Madeleine." He looked kindly into her deep blue, crystalline eyes and wondered who she really was, her story. "Just a PBR, straight and neat."

"We have it on tap."

"I prefer a bottle."

"No glass?"

"No glass."

"You got it, big fella."

Madeleine went to get his beer and thought that "big hunk" is more like it. "Big hunky sexual animal who'll fuck me like I'm an obsessed wench and give me orgasms all night long" is what I really meant. She brought back the beer. "So what's a guy like you doing in a place like this?"

"Funny, I was about to ask you the same question."

Madeleine angled her head to the left, pouted, and pushed out her breasts. "But I'm not a guy. You didn't notice?"

(She has wit!) "I did happily notice that, but I do appreciate the reminder."

"Any time."

"I might take you up on that."

They held each other's gaze for some moments then Madeleine said, "So I'm going to go out on a limb here and guess that you're a biker."

"Thou art wise and perceptive."

(Oh God yes, he's intelligent.) "The personification of freedom with wings for the wind."

(Oh thank you. She's literate.) "Yeah, that's about it these days."

"Really? Nothing else?"

"I'm afraid that's all I've been doing for seven years."

Madeleine stared at him for several moments, her mouth slightly open. "That sounds, oh my, amazing!"

Wyatt smiled modestly. "It is."

"So what's your name?"

"Wyatt."

(Of course. He has the perfect name.) "Wyatt. I like that. It's strong."

He bowed his head slightly. "Thank you, m'lady."

And manners. He has manners. I am so going to enjoy this.

One of the waitresses walked up to the waitress station with an order for four drinks. Madeleine looked at her, turned to Wyatt, curtsied and winked, then walked over to fulfill the order.

Madeleine's mind was rapidly turning over. Did I come on too strong? Doesn't matter. Just one night, right? Slam-bam-thank-you-ma'am, that's all, right? I hope he likes me. Out of the corner of her eye she could see that he was looking at her. God, I wish I wasn't so fat.

She continued secretly looking at him while mixing the drinks. That sexy half-smile is driving me crazy, and that scar on his cheek alone is enough to seduce any woman. He hasn't even turned around to watch Chelsie dancing to some Hip-Hop whatever. She looked at the stage with an experienced eye. She's good, moves well for a girl her size. She finished the drink order and came back to Wyatt.

"So of all the gin joints in all the towns in all the world, how'd you end up here?"

(She quotes a classic film. Correctly. Awesome.) "Oh, it was the end of a long, hot day of riding so I pulled in to the closest place, the only place actually, that had beds for rent. It's always a good idea to rest up before taking another long, hot ride."

(Oh, the literate way he implies!) "Where's that?"

"The Whatever-It's-Called Castle Arms down the street."

"They're still open for business? That place should have been condemned years ago."

"I'll say. It's not the Taj Majal but more like the Taj M'Hell. Not only that, getting here was a much longer walk than I expected."

Madeleine stuck out her lower lip. "Oh you poor boy. If you turn around and watch Chelsie and Her Chunky Cha-Chas, maybe it'll perk you up a bit."

(Perk me up. Good Lord, she's in a league of her own.) "If I get any more perked up, I won't be able to walk straight."

Madeleine giggled. "But you're missing the show."

He waited, not moving, and looked deeply into her eyes. "Am I?"

She replaced her kitten look with a sultry one, slowly closing her eyes then opening them. "I should get back to work, but if you wait until I get off, maybe I'll give you a ride to your Taj Majal."

More implications. God, this woman is pure electricity. He smiled.

FORTY-FIVE

• • •

A FTER LUNCH, BILLY LIFTED KATY ONTO THE BACK OF HIS BIKE THEN they rode a mile to her apartment house, a four-story building of cinderblocks painted a drab white. She unlocked the front door and as soon as she opened it, they heard a woman screaming profanities and another pounding the walls. A glass vase shattered somewhere. Katy was nonchalant about it all but Billy was a bit perturbed and asked, "What the hell's going on?"

"Oh, just another day in paradise."

They walked up a few stairs then turned right. Her apartment was the third on the left and just as they got there, a short old woman came out of the apartment across from hers and began screaming at Katy, telling her she was a lazy whore and to stop having men over at all hours, that she needed to stop making so much racket and get a real job. Katy, unruffled, ignored her, but Billy became incensed. In the middle of the woman's diatribe he got into her face.

She stopped shouting in the middle of a word, froze, and stared at him with an open mouth. He said, "Now lookie here. Yer bat-shit crazy, I know it and you know it, so this is what ya need to do: never say another word to my good friend here. Never. Not one word. And if ya do, you'll hafta answer to me, and I'm crazier than you are. Do we have an understanding?" The woman remained frozen. "I said, do we have an understanding?" The woman, terrified, nodded twice then backed into her apartment without taking her eyes off of him.

Katy's apartment had only one room and like the outside of the building, it was non-sparkly with age. There was a small window covered with a flimsy and torn curtain, a small refrigerator, a hot plate, a sink, eating utensils for one, a small and round table, one wire chair with a beige pad on it, and a coffee table with a lamp and a three-year-old Architectural Digest magazine on it. In one corner was a nearly empty clothes rack without wheels and a mattress on the floor in another.

There were no books, no TV, no computer, and no source for music. Katy opened her arms and said, "Welcome to my Taj Mahal."

Billy, frowning, looked around. "So this is where ya live?"

"Courtesy of the New Mexico state government."

Billy looked around again. "So, where's the bathroom? Where do ya take a shower?"

"Down the hall to the left for the girls, to the right for the boys."

Billy paused. "Well, I don't mean no disrespect but this just ain't right. Not fer you, anyways."

(Could he be my rescue-knight?) "Well, considering I have no money and I'm presently unemployable, it's not bad."

"It may not be bad, but it still ain't right." Katy sat on her bed with a weary look. Billy paced around, tapping his hand against his leg. After some minutes, he said, "Y'all look tired. Do ya normally rest when ya get back from working out?"

"Mostly I just sit and stare at the walls. But that was the best meal I've had in over a year and, yes, it got me sleepy."

"Okay, tell ya what. Y'all rest and sleep and stuff and I'll be back in a coupla hours and treat ya to a nice dinner. Okay?"

"That would be lovely, Billy."

"All right, then that's what we'll do." A smile crept across his face. "Now, don't y'all sneak out and go drinking and dancing and such and getting all tired and worn out. Promise?"

Katy smiled. (Oh god, he is a knight. A fine one.) "Promise."

When he got to the door she called to him and curled her finger. He walked over then bent down. She kissed him on the cheek. Billy, transfixed, thought she couldn't be more perfect.

Three hours later, Katy answered the ringer in her room to unlock the front door of the building, and when she opened the door to her apartment, Billy slowly looked her down and up, gawp-jawed. She wore a simple purple blouse, black slacks, and black sandals with purple socks. She had on a bit of makeup. To him, she was as fresh and as bright as Spring itself.

She smiled. "You're welcome to come in, you know."

"Oh. Right. Okay." Billy walked in, took another long look at Katy, then grabbed his composure and said, "Ya need to pack up. Found ya a nice place to live."

"What?"

"They got a diner, a heated pool, a workout room, vending machines, yer own bathroom, a nice comfy bed, and maid service every day."

"What?"

"Okay okay, it's just a medium-priced hotel. But it's clean and it's got all the stuff I just said."

Katy had a look of disbelief. "But how? I mean, who is ... where's the money coming from, Billy? Did you pay for all this?"

"Oh, ya don't gotta worry about that none. Ya just gotta get packed. We'll get a cab."

Katy stared at him for a long time. Is this possible? Does he actually care for me? And where does he get his money? And how can I pay him back? But he doesn't seem to care about that, so maybe he actually does care about me. Is that even possible? Who is this man?

Billy held her gaze. Did I overdo it here, overstep my bounds? I mean, this woman is the most I could ask for. The scars and the tattoos, damn! Her hair is wacky but it's growing back, but even with the way it is, she's just beautiful. And those eyes. Man, I could look at them forever.

Finally, Katy said, "I, uh, don't know when I'll be able to pay you back."

"Like I said, ya don't gotta worry about that none. We're all good."

"Where are you going to be?" (Please don't leave me.)

"I'll be around, don't ya worry. Got a cheaper place a block away." (How could I ever leave this woman?)

"I ... I don't know what to say, Billy."

"Well, ya don't gotta say nothing. But ya do gotta get packed."

"Oh. Okay. But all I have are my rehab clothes, some bathroom stuff and what I'm wearing."

Billy looked around the room. "That's it? No closet full of clothes and shoes and stuff?"

"That's it. It's all I have."

"Well then, I guess I'll save some money on a cab. I'll take ya out tomorrow and you can buy whatever ya want." Then he added, mostly to himself, "We'll definitely need a cab then."

"Billy…" She looked at him with those eyes, eyes that made him feel something deep, something he'd never before felt. "This is like a dream." (Oh thank you, I didn't screw up.) "Well, I don't know about that. But I do know ya gotta get packed. We gotta get ya moved and then get some dinner. You hungry?"

She had a look that would make a hardened longshoreman fall to his knees in thankful prayer. "Yes." She continued looking at him then fluttered her eyelids in disbelief. "Just give me a minute." She grabbed her toiletries and wrapped them in her workout clothes. "Thank you, Billy. Thank you."

He smiled. Anything, Katy. Anything.

They checked into the hotel and when they got to the room, Katy was thrilled. She plopped on the bed, stretched full length and started laughing. Then she started crying. Billy sat next to her, the most fulfilled he could remember being.

FORTY-SIX

...

WYATT CLIMBED INTO THE PASSENGER SIDE OF MADELEINE'S OLD, faded red Toyota. They were silent during the short drive. She parked in front of the hotel but Wyatt didn't get out.

She smiled in an honest way. "What did you do before you became a nomadic biker?"

"It was another life. Trying to forget about it."

"You must have had a good career if you can afford to do nothing but ride a motorcycle. Stocks? Tech? Real Estate? What?"

"I was a teacher."

"Teachers don't make that kind of money."

Wyatt sighed. (Someday I'll get to a point where I don't have to think or talk about that past life.) "I was a professor of literature at Yale."

Madeleine looked at him with her mouth half open. (That's an unbelievable scenario: professor of literature to full-time biker-stud.) "Really? That's wonderful!"

"Thank you, but honestly, I am so glad to be done with it."

"Why? What could possibly be wrong with talking about Jane Austen all day long?"

(A bartender in a strip joint mentions Jane Austen. What are the chances?) "Well, if that was how it was it would have been wonderful. In seventeen years, I had maybe a half dozen students who were interested in reading Sense and Sensibility."

Affronted, Madeleine replied, "What! How could anyone not love that book!"

"I don't know! I love Jane Austen and I love that book. The way Elinor so closely observes Marianne and is always there for her but never intrudes into her life or her decisions."

191

"She let her be." Madeleine hit the side of her fist on her knee emphasizing the word "be."

Wyatt gestured almost violently pointing a finger straight up. "Yes!"

"So many miss the exquisite simplicity of that."

Wyatt shook his head in disgust. "And start rambling on with intellectual absurdities. Politics, misguided manners."

Madeleine's nostrils flared. "Jealousy on Elinor's part."

From his gesticulations, Wyatt's hair had become even more unkempt than usual and he had the look of a wild man. "When it's really just about two sisters."

"One who is free and idealistic."

"And one who admires that freedom and idealism."

Madeleine threw up her hands in a religious-like reverence. "And the writing!"

Wyatt's voice lowered into a deep admiration. "Perfect sentence after perfect sentence."

Tears formed at the bottom of Madeleine's eyes. "Like a child waving a dandelion in a breeze."

"Like the breeze itself."

"Like the poetry of a breeze."

Too, Wyatt's eyes were now filled with moisture. "Yes, the poetry."

Wyatt and Madeleine looked at each other for a long time, each wondering about the other, who he really was, who she really was, what they were possibly becoming, each afraid that any movement, even a breath, would cloud over the crystalline honesty and they would lose the moment, lose the timelessness, lose the hold each had upon the other.

A limousine with bar patrons and a few of the dancers went weaving by. The driver honked the horn. They were both jolted out of their reverie and followed the car with their eyes until it was out of sight. Their breathing had returned to normal when Wyatt broke the silence. "I'm hungry. Any decent places around that are still open?"

"No, not really. I have a little food at my place. We could go there."

(The perfect invitation.) "Are you sure?"

(Oh god, yes!) "Sure!" She started the engine then turned it off.

Wyatt was afraid to look at her. (Please don't change your mind. Please.) "Yes?"

"Wyatt, I have a plane to catch tomorrow around noon and I still haven't packed. Would you mind following me on your bike?"

Twenty minutes later they arrived at Madeleine's small house in Grand Ledge. She waited while Wyatt backed his bike next to her car and removed his helmet. Together they walked to the porch.

Madeleine paused just after putting her key into the lock. She looked up at Wyatt, her beauty ineffable in the starlight. He put his arm around her waist, pulled her to him then paused when their lips were within an inch. He kissed her deeply and she returned the kiss and he held her as if to bring her into him. It was the first time they had touched. Wyatt looked into her eyes then kissed her softly, lightly breathing in her breath as if it was her soul.

His voice was deep, husky with desire, his smell masculine, his muscles taut yet comforting. "I want you."

"Oh yes. Oh yes."

FORTY-SEVEN

•••

AFTER GETTING A BOOTH AT A DECENT RESTAURANT, BILLY AND KATY couldn't stop talking. Katy was impressed, thrilled, that Billy lived on the road. He told her some stories, mostly funny stuff, and even mentioned Wyatt and their ride on the Alcan, though he left out the part about the fight. In fact, he didn't tell her about any of the fights he'd been in, thinking she might think of him as some sort of thug.

Billy was equally impressed at how she had managed on her own after her parents had died in an automobile accident when she was fifteen. How she had always made a go of it, though she didn't mention the escort service she used to work for because she was afraid to scare him off.

While they were eating, Billy looked at her for some seconds and said, "Ya remind of a woman I once read about."

"Who's that?"

"Lily Bart."

Katy gasped and put her hand to her heart. "The House of Mirth? You've read The House of Mirth?"

"Twice. Been in love with Wharton ever since I first read her."

"Really? Me, too!" They stared, each a bit confounded. To be truthful, Billy was already unnerved, perhaps overwhelmed, by her combination of strength and beauty, but the revelation of her having read Edith Wharton, and most likely many others, sent him into a sort of fevered wanting.

Katy struggled with hope, the hope that he, of all the men she'd ever known, would actually want her and not some image she projected. She quoted the Old Testament line that Wharton used for the title: The heart of the wise is in the house of mourning, but the heart of fools is in the house of mirth.

"Something to dwell upon, ain't it?" Billy paused a few moments. "Y'know, I ought to start calling you Lily."

Katy broke into a big smile. "If you start calling me Lily, I'm calling you Mr. Selden."

"I might go for that. But then, Katy is a damn cute name." Billy thought for a few seconds. "Now, I don't know about me being Mr. Selden, but I'll tell ya this, though: I ain't no lawyer but I sure would have been smart enough to stay away from that Bertha bitch."

"I bet you would have. But would you have been able to stay away from Lily?" (Are you going to stay away from me, Billy?) "Break their lunch engagement and travel to Europe instead?" (Are you going to leave me, Billy?) Billy held her eyes. "No."

Oh god, what have I done, Katy thought. Comparing myself to Lily Bart. Even at her poorest, she had more than me. And she was never less than perfectly beautiful, and my hair looks like a straggly dog's and I'm still ten pounds underweight. But I'm coming back, right? That's the plan, right? Sure, I'll still have all these scars, but they don't seem to bother him. Yeah, I'll be back, but will he still be here when I have?

Too, Billy's thoughts were dizzying. Damn, this is the most amazing woman I've ever met. Going through what she went through and now she's fighting back, not feeling all sorry for herself. She hasn't even filled out yet and she's already the most beautiful woman I've ever seen. But when she does get back to what she once was, will she want me? I'm just a biker. Don't even own a home. Either way, it don't matter because she deserves everything I can do for her, everything I can give her.

He said, "On second thought, I don't think calling you Lily is a good idea. She did come to a grievous end, ya know."

"Yes, she did. It was so sad. And Mr. Selden felt awful, probably for the rest of his life. So I'll keep calling you Billy. Deal?"

"Deal. And you'll be Katy from now on. Okay?"

"Deal."

After dinner, they continued with their non-stop conversation as they walked into the cooling night air. Katy had a bounce in her step Billy hadn't seen before and she was delighted that Billy remained a gentleman. After several blocks, Billy noticed Katy was tiring a bit so he stopped and looked around. "Where the hell are we?"

"Oh! I don't know. We just kept talking and started walking. I totally forgot about your bike."

"Me, too, which is weird because I never forget about my bike. The thing is, I'm lost. You know which way the restaurant is?"

(Oh God, this man is so cute. I just want to hug him.) "Yeah, it's back that way. Make a left at the drug store."

"Right. Good thing ya came along. I mighta been walking around here fer hours."

Katy laughed. They turned around and walked back, she with her arm inside of his.

Katy, after enjoying the most exciting time she could remember, was too tired to do any shopping the following day, so she and Billy stayed in her room and continued the conversations from the night before. Their first loves as pre-teens, getting in trouble in high school, their first jobs. However, as they continued talking, they each began to feel that there was more to the other than was being revealed.

Billy wasn't bothered by anything it could be – he'd already imagined the worst – and was ready to accept and forgive any of her past. As far as he was concerned, whatever sins and indiscretions she may have committed, she had paid for them far too dearly.

Katy, on the other hand, sensed a mysteriousness about Billy. Where did he get his money? What does he normally do? What has he done, other than ride a motorcycle? Despite the questions and any possible unsavory answers, there was a far-away romanticism about him, an intangible something that drew her into him, made her want to be carried away.

They immediately settled into a schedule. Katy began going to her workouts during the afternoons so Billy could visit the girls while she was rehabbing. Katy's improvements were remarkable. She gained weight and strength and flexibility every day and by the end of the first week, no longer needed her cane.

Mary and Mona looked forward more and more to Billy's visits. He'd talk with their dolls, play house and hopscotch with them, help with their homework, and he managed to always come up with a new silly kid joke or two. And although Mona joined in the gaiety, she was still silent most of the time.

On the third Friday, after he said goodbye to the girls, Billy asked the administrator if he could bring Katy with him the next time he visited. On the one hand, she thought it would be good for the girls to interact with a safe and sane couple. On the other hand, seeing Katy might bring back damaging memories. She told him she'd think about it over the weekend.

On that weekend, Billy and Katy went for a ride. As they were going east on the interstate, Billy looked in his rearview mirrors and watched Katy – head flung back, eyes closed, a contented smile – and wondered, as he often did, what more he could do to deserve her. He'd come to grips with the fact that he loved her, but was that enough? He didn't know. He wanted to live his life with her, to be with her always, but was that enough?

What else he didn't know was that when Katy closed her eyes, she was wishing he would remain with her, for she, too, had come to realize that she loved him.

They turned right onto a state highway and ended up at the Oak Parks Picnic Area. Though the mileage wasn't great, to Katy it felt like the world because it was the first time in over a year that she'd been outside the one-mile radius of the hospital.

They placed a blanket under an apache pine and after munching on trail mix and dried fruit, they lay next to each other for hours, hardly talking. The filtering of the blue sky and the ambling white clouds through the pine needles gave them a weightless sensation, like floating. Timeless.

The administrator of the children's home decided to let Katy visit the girls, so on one fine, mid-spring Tuesday afternoon, she did just that, arm in arm with Billy. When they walked into the yard, Mona stared wide-eyed, but Mary looked at Katy as if she were expecting her, and in her matter-of-fact way said, "You were the lady in the box."

"Yes, I was."

"Your hair looks funny."

"I know. I laugh every time I look in the mirror."

"That's cool."

Katy looked at Mona and there was an instant and deep connection, which made sense, being that they each had suffered similar fates. "Hi Mona."

"Hi."

"How are you doing?"

"Fine. How are you?"

"I'm doing well, thank you. Want to go for a walk?"

"Okay."

As the visits continued, a natural and deep camaraderie formed among the four of them. Billy would spend most of the time with Mary, while Katy and Mona would go for a walk then sit under a tree and talk.

Soon, a remarkable change came over Mona. She became talkative, though never as much as Mary, and would smile and laugh as easily as a cocker spaniel wagging its tail. Too, Katy began to flesh out in ways more than just the physical.

I'll admit I looked in on them more than I needed to. Actually, to be honest, I didn't need to look in on them at all, but it was such a fine sight to see those two girls, especially Mona, come into themselves. And to see Billy and Katy continue to grow together. My, oh my.

FORTY-EIGHT

...

W YATT GOT UP EARLY THE NEXT MORNING, PULLED ON HIS BOXERS then went out to the small back porch where there were two un-matched wooden chairs, weather-beaten and splinter-ridden. He carefully sat on the one without armrests.

The wooden fence along the back of the yard bent under large-leafed ivy like an arthritic old man. There was a row of small houses, all painted a drab green, on the other side of it. The grass covered only half the yard, and what there was of it lay low as if afraid to look at the very sun it needed for growth. Birds chirped half-heartedly. The trees, oppressed from age and neglect, labored under their own weight, their dusty green leaves huddled together like children afraid of the dark.

Wyatt tried unsuccessfully to grab hold of the myriad of emotions that swirled through him. I should be getting ready to leave, he thought. Hell, I should already have left but there's just something about that woman. A lot of somethings. He shook his head, confused.

He thought about her body. Beautiful face and eyes that change from blue to green and back. Jet-black hair, long like I like it. Sultry contralto voice. I've always preferred taller women and I'm more than a foot taller than she is, but for some reason it's okay. Feels right. She has a body made for sex, the way she welcomes it, takes it in like an addictive drug.

He imagined her twenty years younger. Large and firm breasts, perfect smile, not an ounce of fat, curves to die for, expertly coiffed hair, designer fingernails, long and unique. Vivacious, seductive.

He compared that to the way she is now. A face still beautiful but with the beginnings of wrinkles, a body that's maybe five to ten pounds over that of a runway model. Nails done by herself, hair done by friends. Breasts bigger but softer and lower with their weight. The now version is so much more appealing. But all that isn't what's holding me here. Part of the draw, yes, but there is so much more.

Madeleine came out onto the porch wearing a plain muslin shift down to her knees. She sat on the other chair, looking beyond the obvious neglect. "I kept waiting to hear your bike fire up. That's something you would normally do, right? Leave early the next morning."

"Pretty much."

She still hadn't looked at him. "But you didn't. Why?"

Wyatt paused and looked at the gray-blue sky as if for an answer. "Trying to figure that out myself."

Madeleine looked at Wyatt, her eyes squinting against the morning sun. Wyatt looked back at her, at her neck, how it twisted and curved, and her throat, how it seemed sculpted, and thought, she's more beautiful now than last night.

She smiled. "I guess I should make some breakfast."

He smiled. "Sure."

Madeleine went inside, Wyatt stayed outside and smoked a cigarette. Soon, he could smell coffee and hear the sizzle when Madeleine poured the scrambled eggs into a frying pan. He went inside, sat at the small wooden kitchen table and watched her and wondered again, why am I still here?

The light coming through the kitchen window filtered through old cotton curtains. He could see she was wearing nothing underneath her shift but there was nothing indecent about her comportment, no pretense. She was nothing more than someone making breakfast. Madeleine. A lovely name.

Madeleine brought over forks and butter and butter knives and plates and napkins and two coffee cups. Nothing matched. Wyatt stood up and wrapped his arms around her waist. They waited to kiss, then kissed hard and deeply, breathing the fevers of the other.

He lifted her onto the table and the sex was aching and hard and immediate and equal. Within minutes, it was done, but Wyatt continued to hold her and she, quivering, held him. They were each afraid to look at the other, again afraid of the naked honesty, afraid of what it might mean. They finally gazed into each other's eyes, their lips close, fulfilled yet still afraid.

Wyatt saw smoke rising from the stovetop and broke the spell. "Uh, breakfast is burning."

During breakfast, Wyatt and Madeleine were each lost in thought and fantasy, each wondering about the other, about themselves. When they were done eating, Madeleine smiled shyly and said, "Sorry for the burnt eggs."

Wyatt astutely looked at her. "It was worth it." Then he said as if pontificating a newly found religious wisdom, "In fact, I do believe that from this moment forward I shall prefer them as such." Madeleine giggled.

Damn, he thought, was that implying a future with her? Was it too presumptive? Do I want a future with her? True, if I were to have a future with a woman, it would be someone like her. But no, don't think like that. That's not what you'd planned for your life. God she's beautiful, but there's more, but don't think of that, either. It's just great sex. That's all she is, a great fuck. But that's not right. There's much more to her than that. The literate wit for one thing. Did she notice the implication of a future? God, I hope not, but yes I do. Damn, I want her again. I want her now. And the fevers rose up the back of his neck.

Madeleine thought that for a woman who has decided to stay single the rest of her life, Wyatt is a dangerous man. Charming, gorgeous, rugged, strong, easily the best lover I've ever had. Oh god, what am I thinking! Why did I come on to him? Okay, I just wanted sex, and why not? It'd been a year and a half and two years before that. Sex, that's all, right? But I had to choose him. The one man who ... oh god ....

"Wyatt, you're a good guy."

Am I a good guy? No, I'm a bastard. A fucked up bastard who wants only sex. But with her ....

She went on. "But um, I need to catch that plane and I still need to pack."

A reprieve, he thought, I can leave without guilt. But I don't want to leave. Don't want her to leave.

She continued, "My daughter and her husband are having a baby and I'll be gone for six weeks."

Wyatt's eyes drooped slightly. (Six weeks! God, that's an eternity. But no, don't think that, don't put her in your future. After six weeks she won't even be a memory. But she will, I won't forget her. I can't. But I have to. Or do I?) "You have a daughter?"

"Yeah. We're close. Well, not physically close – Brandy and Brock live on the outskirts of Pensacola – but we're emotionally close. Spiritually connected. She teaches kindergarten, he teaches high school chemistry."

"And they're having a baby."

"Yeah! We each married when we were twenty. Perfect age for her but too young for me." She said the last part mostly to herself and Wyatt leaned toward her, wanting to know the backstory.

His thoughts swirled frantically. Dammit, you'd better watch it. You're getting too close. But I want to get close, all the way in. But I can't. That's not the life I set out to live. But what if it could work? It can't. She could but I can't. I'm itinerant, don't even own a house or a car.

Out of the blue, he asked, "What's your last name?"

"Marks. I went back to my maiden name after the divorce."

"Middle name?"

"Merry, but it's spelled M-e-r-r-y."

(How wonderful can wonderful be?) Wyatt spoke slowly. "Madeleine Merry Marks."

Madeleine giggled again. "Yeah. What's your last name?"

"Youngblood."

(Another perfect name.) "Middle?"

"Hazel."

Madeleine cocked her head in mild disbelief. "Hazel?"

"Mother's maiden name."

"Ah. So your initials are WHY."

"And yours are Mmm Mmm Mmm."

She smiled. (He may be dangerous but he's deliciously dangerous.) "Anyway, I'd better start packing."

(Why am I disappointed? Damn, what the hell is going on?) "Okay, I'll clean up in here."

FORTY-NINE

...

A FTER DINNER ONE NIGHT, BILLY AND KATY WERE IN HER ROOM, BILLY sitting on a chair, Katy on the bed. Earlier that afternoon, they had finished their third shopping trip for clothes and shoes and toiletries and various little accouterments. Katy felt she was the most pampered woman in the world.

They'd been sitting in silence for a while when Billy looked at her like he had the worst news in the world. "Y'know, we've been talking a lot about all sorts of stuff. Found out a lot about each other. But, I dunno, I think it's time we told the worst. Get it all out in the open. Truth and nothing but. And uh, I'll go first if it's easier for ya."

Katy looked at him with a mixture of fear and honesty. "Okay."

He told her about the time in the army when he beat up his commanding officer for having sex with a five-year-old boy, about being in the brig for nine months, and how the officer's father paid him a million dollars to keep quiet.

"After I got out of the army, one of the first things I did with that million was to buy a motorcycle. Didn't need to work, so I started riding. First for a day, then two, then three, and within a month, figured it was all I wanted to do. So that's what I did."

"How long have you been on the road?

"Guess it's coming up to nine years."

Katy bit her lip. "And there've been women, right?" (Oh god, is that any of my business?)

"Yeah, that's what I was gonna get to next." Billy took on a resigned and somewhat embarrassed look. "I'd been out for a couple of months when I went to a coffee shop. There was this gal sitting at a small table all alone, so I asked her if I could sit there with her. She said it was okay and we started talking about this and that and she kept giving me that eye that girls do when they're interested. Anyways, long story short, I spent two days and three nights with her, fucking my brains out. The weird thing about it, weird for me, anyways, was when I left."

Billy took a deep breath and looked around the room. "Y'see, from the way I's raised and having my momma and daddy as an example, I'd always figured that in life, you have some fun for a while, then you fall in love, get married, and that's end of your freewheeling ways. But with that chick, she not only expected me to leave, she actually said that's what she wanted because she didn't like to fuck strangers for more than a day or two so's she wouldn't get attached."

Billy shook his head in disbelief. "Anyways, as I was riding away, I got to thinking there might be other women like that, and sure enough there are. It didn't take long for me to be able to spot 'em and so it became a normal routine. Go to a new town, a new bar, a new coffee shop, whatever, and that night I'd be in some gal's bed, fucking like it was the most natural thing. And if I didn't find anyone, there was always a hooker or two around. So for years, I looked forward to only two things: riding and getting my dick wet. And reading. Always made sure to get my reading in."

Billy intertwined his fingers. "Now, there's one gal in particular I need to tell ya about. Her name was Charlotte." He then told her about their time together and how she set him up with an annuity that made it possible to live on the road.

Katy was trembling inside and not doing a good job of hiding it. "Do you still see her?"

"I did once. Right after I paid her back. Then right after that, she got sick and died. Went to the funeral but there was so many rich and important people there, politicians and such, that I just stayed over by some trees. She was a good woman."

Katy apprehensively asked, "Is that everything?"

"Well, as far as the sex goes, yeah."

"How many?"

"Oh dang, I don't know. Twenty to thirty a year, I guess. Sometimes more, maybe less sometimes."

Katy relaxed a bit and smiled wisely. "You must be one helluva stud."

Billy turned red. "Oh hell, I don't know about that."

She laughed. "You said that was it about the sex. What else?"

"Well, that might be the worst of it, I don't know. Anyways, as the years rolled by, I'd get into a fight every now and then, but I's pretty drunk every time. So there's that." He told her about Wyatt and the fight in Ketchikan, then closed his eyes and breathed deeply. "There is one other thing, though."

Billy looked to his left, gathering courage. "After I found you on that hillside, I couldn't take it. It cut me deep. Real deep. Deeper than I ever thought possible. I took off afterwards and started drinking all the time and having the worst nightmares ever. Got into a lot of fights, too. Busted up a lot of people, some of 'em permanently probably. Got busted up myself a bunch, too. That's how I got all these scars. Spent a year doing nothing but drinking and fighting and fighting off the nightmares."

His eyes took on a different color, as if he was looking into her. "Ya see, I got to hating everybody and everything for what had been done to you, Katy. Eventually got to believing it was all my fault and got to hating myself the most."

He continued looking at her, intense and imploring. "One night in San Francisco, I made a fool of myself and got pounced on by twenty or thirty people. Broken bones, knife cuts, everything."

He slightly shook his head. "Looking back, I don't blame 'em. Had it coming. Finally made it to my motel room and had the worst three days of my life. Couldn't think straight, couldn't move, either. Ending up lying in my own shit. Thought I was gonna die and hoping I was."

Katy was amazed. Here was this well-mannered, cute-as-a-panda-bear man, magnanimous to a fault, yet he had been a bruising alcoholic just two months before. And all because of what had happened to her. She asked with a compassion held by only those who have known the worst. "How'd you get out of that?"

"Well, I got a visit from this guy. An old school biker. Calls himself the Poet."

"Is he an old friend?"

"Nope. Seen him a few times before riding an old rat bike but never spoke a word to him. Wanted to, but he was always going off somewheres.

"Anyways, I woke up and there he was sitting by my bed. Don't know how he knew where I was. So I got myself washed up a bit and he tells me a story. Crazy story, too, about this rich Mexican guy hundreds of years ago who saw his kids get murdered and his wife run off with the guy who did it.

He wanders around on foot for a couple of years and eventually finds them, kills 'em both, and goes off walking into the night, never to be seen again."

Katy interrupted him. "Wait a second. This Poet person. He's an old guy riding an old motorcycle? Long silver hair, brown leather vest?"

"Yep."

"Oh god! I saw him a day before you showed up. I was waiting for the bus to go to the hospital and he was just sitting there on his bike, smiling at me. I remember thinking it was odd because you'd think that'd creep me out, but it didn't. It made me feel safe somehow."

Billy, thinking about the impossibility of it being a coincidence, said, "Damn. Now ain't that something."

"So go on. What about your broken bones and the knife cuts and everything?"

"Well see now, that there is the weirdest part. This Poet guy pulls out this round leather bag that I swear wasn't there before. It was like he pulled it out of the air. He opens it, hands me a bottle of tequila and tells me that if I drink all of it, I'll be all 'renewed.' So I take a swig and, tell ya what, it was the smoothest alcohol I ever tasted.

"I told him I needed to rest a bit and he said okay and when I woke up, he was gone. Spent the rest of the day finishing up the bottle, and the next morning, everything was all good. Everything. Like nothing ever happened. Except for the scars and being a little stiff. Then I came straight here."

Katy grew soft and timid. "To me?"

Billy smiled. "Yep. Right to you, Katy."

FIFTY

...

MADELEINE WENT TO THE BEDROOM AND AFTER GETTING OUT HER clothes and toiletries, called the airline, the shuttle service, and her daughter. Wyatt washed and dried all the dishes, put them away, then went back out to the porch and lit a cigarette. Madeleine joined him. "Already packed? That was fast."

"No, I changed the reservation to a later flight." (Oh what have I done? Why did I make him think I'm interested? Because I am. But I shouldn't be. He's just a nomadic biker, a one-night stand, nothing more. But he is more, so much more. The intelligence and the education.)

Wyatt remained self-possessed on the outside but inside he was elated. Madeleine broke the silence. "Tell me about yourself, Wyatt Hazel Youngblood."

"What do you want to know?"

"Everything." (There. I'm committed. Now he knows I'm interested.)

"Everything? That could take a lot of months. A lot of boring months."

Madeleine giggled. "Okay, how about telling me how you came to be an itinerant biker."

Wyatt told her about his first and only wife and how they fell in love, or thought they did, and how they had dreams of artistic finery. He told her about getting professorships at Yale, about his affairs with students, about the books he never finished writing and those he never started. About one day waking up without a soul. He told her about their divorce and the selling of their house and stocks, and how he now lives off the annuity from a mutual fund.

"And now it's your turn, Madeleine Merry Marks. Tell me about thee." (Shit, why did I say thee? That's a term of love, isn't it?)

"Well, okay." Her eyes nervously darted back and forth. "But I should make a pot of coffee first."

Wyatt stayed outside and smoked another cigarette. Madeleine stayed inside while the coffee brewed. Do I really want to tell him about me? No. But I have to. It'll be the end of any possible relationship. I mean, he's an Ivy League professor for crissakes! She looked out the window at his profile. But not any more, right? Now he's just an itinerant biker, right?

God, I hope he understands. If there's going to be something between us, he deserves to know the truth. Damn, this is tough! And exciting and mind-bending and scary and dizzying and everything love should be. Love. There, I said it. Well, if my past is a deal breaker, I need to tell him now and get it over with.

She looked around her small, outdated kitchen. What can I offer him other than a romp in the sack? A lot of romps, sure, but that's about it, really. And I'm fat. And no matter what I do the wrinkles are coming. She looked at her diaphanous reflection in the window of the oven. Shit, I gotta lose weight.

On the other hand, I can give him things his wife never did, that no one ever did. I can believe in him, trust him, love him, let him be Wyatt Hazel Youngblood. Love. That's twice now that I've thought of love. She poured the coffee into two cups, walked out to the porch, handed Wyatt a cup and sat down. "So. What do you want to know?"

"Everything." (There, I did it. Now she knows I'm interested.)

"Well, my months of storytelling would be a lot more boring than yours." Their laugh was gentle but nervous.

Madeleine couldn't remember ever fretting this much. (Can I even do this? Okay. I just need to start slowly, see where it goes.) "Well, I grew up in Indianola. Had a good and wholesome childhood. Wonderful! Everything was going along fine until my parents got an ugly divorce when I was in my mid-teens and that's when my life started going downhill."

"How?"

"Oh Wyatt, I wanted it all. I wanted to be an actress, a model, famous, oodles of money, the works. But every time I hooked up with someone who said they would help, it wouldn't go anywhere. Every agent I signed with either wanted me to pose nude or do porn. I mean, Christ!, I wasn't even eighteen for the first year and a half. In five years, I had only four magazine shoots modeling t-shirts and underwear and got paid a total of three hundred dollars.

"My love life, if you could call it that, was one disaster after another. I never had a boyfriend who was faithful and my ex-husband was a total loser. The only thing I did right was raising Brandy."

She looked at him for some moments. "This is going nowhere, Wyatt. I mean, how boring can boring be?"

"I'm not bored at all."

"Well, I don't want to tell you all that, I don't know, depressing stuff. Can we just leave it that my life was, and still is, one disappointment after another?"

Wyatt gave her a kind and understanding smile. "Okay. How about telling me how you came to tend bar in a strip club."

FIFTY-ONE

...

WITH HER PAST FLASHING BEFORE HER, MADELEINE WAVERED BE-tween wanting to leave, wanting to make love again, and wanting to hide. (Well, here it goes, the proverbial all or nothing.) "Oh, the strip club gig started years ago. I worked for Al, the owner, in my twenties." Wyatt looked at her, interested, but said nothing. (Why does he have to be so damn hot!)

She took a deep breath. "Okay, I was newly divorced, a good move on my part, a single mom working at a Denny's. Al came in one day and said he had this strip club and I could make more money waiting tables there. I did start out as a waitress but the tips were shit so I went to bartending because the base pay was two dollars more an hour. The tips were still shit because, well, the men, patrons, whatever, give most of their money to the dancers."

"Pole dancers?"

"Yeah, and strippers. Anyway, it wasn't long before Al convinced me to give it a shot. I wasn't very good at first but there was this lady, Carla. She used to strip but got too old for it so she took care of our outfits and helped with our make-up. She taught me everything."

"Like what? What did she teach you?"

Madeleine raised an eyebrow and gave him a playful smile. "You really want to know? Thinking of a career as a stripper?"

Wyatt laughed. "Yes and no, in that order."

"Well okay. There's 'point don't look'; point your eyes at the creeps but don't look at them. They'll think it's exotic. And 'flat smile, good smile', never let the smile go past your teeth. Then there're the three Ts: technique, technique, technique. When you're dancing, concentrate on your technique because you don't want to pull a muscle or anything. And don't worry about not looking sexy enough, their feeble imaginations take care of that." She raised one side of her lips. "Go to strip clubs much?"

"I have a few times but no, generally I don't. Not to offend, but to me they are, to quote our favorite word of the past fifteen minutes, rather boring."

"Even a filthy lap dance?"

"Well, I've never had one but was never interested."

She leaned toward him with a mischievous smile and winked. "Even one from me?"

"Dear woman, I have been persuaded!"

"Yeah, right."

"It's the truth, I swear. I want one."

She leaned back and crossed her legs. "Maybe later. If you're a good boy. Anyway, the last thing was to leave some money on the stage, never take all of it."

"I never imagined. Then what happened?"

(Oh God, should I be telling him all this? He's going to hate me, I know it.) She took another deep breath. "So I was making more money but there were some girls who made so much more than me. By then I was sleeping with Al, the little shit, and one night I asked him about it and that was the beginning of the worst."

"How?"

"Oh Wyatt, I slipped down that slope so fast I didn't have time to be scared. Within a week I had a cute little Louis Vuitton leather bag full of coke and was taking bumps all day long. Within another week I had three regulars and by the end of the first month, Al was hiring me out to any of a half dozen others when I wasn't with my regulars."

She stared emotionless at the splintered wooden porch between her feet. "Once he hired me and the rest of the girls out to a frat party. I must have had sex with ten or twenty of those little shit-brats but all I remember is snorting coke and meth. And the money, that's what I wanted the most. And I was making a lot of it. Bought a new car, jewelry, expensive make-up, new clothes, a lot of things for Brandy."

Madeleine looked at the trees in her pathetic backyard, the rustle from the leaves like an indictment of failure. She looked back at Wyatt, docile and worldly. Fatalistic. "It went on for about four or five months until one morning Brandy asked me what was wrong. I didn't think anything was, but after I got home from taking her to school, she was five, I looked at myself in the mirror and it was so fucked up weird. I didn't even recognize myself but it was more like I couldn't even see myself."

214

Madeleine slumped then looked at Wyatt, expecting the worst. "So now you know. I was a fucking coke whore."

Wyatt held her gaze. "It's okay."

"No it wasn't! I had a little girl who depended on me and here I am snorting coke all day long and fucking strangers for money and that's supposed to be okay? What the fuck's the matter with you?"

Wyatt didn't take his eyes off her and quietly said, "I meant that it was okay for you to tell me and I don't think badly of you."

Madeleine closed her eyes. "Oh. Sorry."

"It's fine."

(What is it with him? Why is he so ... oh I don't know.) "Anyway, I came straight home after work that night and the next, but that Friday I left with this slick turd from Lansing. Asshole son of a big drug money asshole. I kept thinking about Brandy and didn't want to go but Al insisted and convinced me with a bag of meth. So I went. The guy was young and dressed like a dandy in a silent film and smelled like he thought layers of cologne were a better alternative to a shower.

"Right after we took off in his limo, he pulled my top down and wanted me to blow him in the back seat while the driver watched in the rear view mirror. I started thinking about what a fucked up life I was giving Brandy and I couldn't do it. Tried everything to avoid it.

"He kept getting more and more pissed and finally he grabbed my hair and started pounding my face. I was bleeding all over. I dug my nails into his nuts as hard as I could. He screamed like a little girl and kicked me out of the car and wouldn't give me my purse. Said I owed him all my money and the meth. I had to walk home."

Wyatt felt a depth of compassion and, oddly, wished the rustle from the leaves would go away. "What did Al do?"

"Oh, he was pissed. Punched me in the stomach, pushed me down and kicked me over and over. Ripped my clothes off and told me to get out. Had to drive home in nothing but a thong. Lied to Brandy about how I got hurt."

"Did you ever tell her the truth?"

"Oh yeah. She was sixteen and ran into some trouble with some high school gangsters. Sex and drugs trouble. She got beat up and lied about how it happened. I didn't buy any of it but she still wouldn't fess up, so I did. Told her everything, even all the details. After she heard what I'd done, she told me everything she'd done." Madeleine half-smiled with satisfaction. "It was the best thing we ever did together."

"Can't beat the truth. Ever get married again?"

She shook her head. "No. I wanted a decent life and figured I had to go it alone because no decent guy would ever marry a whore."

"That was a long time ago."

"Was it? Just last night I fucked a stranger in my own bed."

"Don't forget the bathroom."

"Or the shower."

"Or the living room floor."

"Or the kitchen table."

"Fun, wasn't it?"

Wyatt was experiencing unusual feelings and when the word love crept into his thoughts he couldn't push it away. It can't be, he thought. I'm not good for love, I'm not ready or not capable or not worthy of it or whatever. I'm a wanderer who fucks women whenever and wherever. I don't even know what love is, do I? No I don't. When it comes to love, I'm ignorant.

But maybe there's a chance. Maybe. God, the thought of it is driving me nuts. What if I just went for it. The love, a relationship, the works. The worst that could happen is that I'd go back to being what I am now. Is it worth the gamble?

Madeleine was lost in her own thoughts as well. Is he thinking anything close to what I'm thinking. God, I hope so. But what if he's not? Then I've made a fool of myself. I've done it before. He'll leave and no one will be the wiser, right? But I don't want him to leave me. I want him to wait for me for six weeks. That's asking a lot, probably too much, but it's a gamble I want to take, have to take. Oh, what should I do? What can I do?

"Wyatt, these chairs are uncomfortable. Let's go inside."

FIFTY-TWO

...

KATY'S HEART WAS POUNDING. (GOD, THIS IS GOING TO BE HARD. I DON'T want him to know everything. But then I do. It'll bring us closer. At least I hope it will. I have to tell him everything, right? He told me everything, right? My god, how many women has he been with? Two hundred? Three hundred? I never ....) "So. I guess it's my turn."

"Yeah, it is. But don't y'all worry none. It's all good."

She closed her eyes. (God, I wish I could just tell him I love him and have it be over with.) "Okay. Here goes."

"I was an only child, had a good home, really good, the best parents ever. We lived in Davenport and I did well in school and had a lot of friends, and everything was, you know, all-American, Boy Scout, Girl Scout.

"Then a few weeks after my fifteenth birthday, my parents were killed in a car accident. I already mentioned that, right? Anyway, for a while, life was a black and gray blur. I didn't know what to do or say or how to act. I ended up shutting out the world and it was weird because I didn't want to, but it was like I had no choice."

Katy looked to the side then wiped a tear from her left cheek. "Anyway, my uncle in Harrisburg was an alcoholic and womanizer and just your basic jerk, so my high school English teacher took me in to live with her. She was wonderful. I loved her totally and she was exactly what I needed. But then, after a half a year, she got some weird disease and died after a month in the hospital."

Her shoulders slumped fatalistically. "Anyway, my uncle was long gone by then, ran off with some cocaine whore, and my aunt had pretty much lost her mind, so I lived in a foster home. I dropped out of school and got a job at a Baskin Robbins. After six months, I got fired because they found out I lied about my age. So I left Davenport, took all the money I had and went as far away as a bus would take me. That's how I got to Albuquerque. And right away I got a job at a Starbucks."

Billy was fascinated with her narrative; it was as good as any novel he'd ever read. She continued. "There was this nice guy who came in every morning at nine-fifteen and one day he asked me out. Well, it turned out he was pretty rich and owned this big escort service. He was the first guy I had sex with but, in his defense, I'd convinced him I was over eighteen. We dated for a while but after a couple of months, it sort of fizzled out. By then I knew how much his escort girls made so I asked him if I could work for him.

"His assistant, Tanya, taught me everything I needed to know, how to walk, hold my head up, and how to listen, how to laugh, and how to dress. They even bought me a wardrobe. So I started getting hired out."

Katy looked matter-of-factly at Billy. "Now before you start getting any weird ideas, sex was not part of it. Sometimes, yeah, but as far as the agency was concerned, it wasn't their business. Nelson, the owner, the guy I'd dated, was really strict about that. Now, if you wanted to have sex with a guy, that was up to you; you could say yes or say no."

Her face took on a downhearted, reminiscing look. "Some of them were older men or widowers or businessmen visiting from out of town, and they just wanted some, you know, eye candy on their arm when they went out. The others were rich young guys who wanted to show off to their friends or clients or whatever. I did have sex with some of them, some of their friends, too, and the tips, jewelry most of the time, made it worthwhile."

Katy's voice had become almost monotone. "I was making more money than I ever thought possible. Sometimes thirty thousand a month. I had a nice condo, a red Corvette, bought new clothes every week, and in my off time I could do whatever I wanted. Stayed in every four- and five-star hotel on the planet. And that's what I did for seven years.

"The thing was, when it came to sex, I didn't know how far to go or when to say no, what was acceptable, what wasn't." She had a pleading look on her face and her voice cracked. "Anyway ... " She looked away, holding back tears. "I ended up making some porn films. Five of them. They're pieces of shit, really. More like stupid old fuck flicks taken with a cheap phone."

Katy put her hands over her face and began sobbing. Billy let her get it all out, not moving or taking his eyes off her. After her tears ebbed, Billy put his hand on her arm and they looked at each other for the longest time.

Billy smiled kindly, grabbed a box of Kleenex and waited while she dried the tears. "Was the escort thing how you met Harvey Smith?"

Startled, Katy wondered how Billy knew his name. "Yeah. He was a regular for about a year. He owned a chain of dental offices in the Midwest and wanted to expand into New Mexico and Arizona. What I didn't know was that he had a serious drug problem, designer drugs, and after about five months, sold his business to keep up with his habit. But he kept coming around, paying top dollar, the best restaurants and all that.

"He always wanted sex but I wouldn't because he had this slimy side to him. Gave me the creeps. At first it was easy to say no but as time went on it got harder and harder. Then I found out he had a family and they had just moved to Albuquerque. But I figured as long as we weren't having sex, it was okay.

"Then one night about, I don't know, over a year ago, we were out at this high-end club having drinks. We were ready to leave and he said we should have one for the road and I said okay and he went and got two martinis. Well, he must have put something in mine because I got really woozy right away. The last thing I remember is him saying to the valet that I'd had a bit too much."

Katy covered her eyes, tearless, and shuddered several times. "When I woke up, I was totally naked and gagged and my arms and legs were stretched out and tied to this big, circular thing, like a perverted dream catcher. And he's dancing around, naked, singing some weird shit, all gleeful. Billy, I was so terrified." She looked away, mute and immobile, for some minutes. Billy waited.

"He raped me. Over and over, front and back. He'd drug me and untie me and rape me some more, and when the drugs wore off would tie me up again. He had trouble getting hard so most of the time he used a dildo or a brush handle, sometimes silverware. It just hurt so much. This went on for days or weeks, I don't know, and pretty soon I realized I was in a basement somewhere.

"Sometimes I'd hear him and Mona upstairs and Mona would be crying and telling him it hurt and she wanted him to stop, but he never did. He'd tell her it was okay and that it was just something that fathers and daughters did together."

Both Billy and Katy barely breathed, the only sound the quiet buzz from the electric clock on the side table. "When he was raping me, he'd whisper awful things. Like how he was going to sell me to some sex group in Germany or China or Thailand somewhere. How he had done it four times before and that I'd bring in more money than all the others put together.

"After I don't know how long, he said that if he cut me in hidden places, he'd still be able to get top-dollar, and that's when he started with the X-acto knife. Every time he came in, he'd cut me before raping me. Between my fingers and toes, behind my ears, behind my knees. My armpits. The worst was when he cut the bottoms of my feet. God, that hurt so much. And he always had this giddy laugh and be singing his eerie melodies.

"After a while he told me he'd stop with the X-acto if I'd give him my car. So I did and then he wanted my jewelry so he took my house keys and cleaned me out. Finally, I gave him my bank account numbers and he took all my money.

"I gave him everything, Billy, but after only a couple of days, he told me that he found out that if he cut me length-wise, a plastic surgeon would have an easier time making me pretty again, and he started up with the X-acto again. My legs, arms, breasts, stomach. Sometimes my face and neck. I kept hoping I'd become less sensitive to the pain but never did."

Katy again burst into tears and Billy held her for a long time. When she finally stopped crying, she kept her head on Billy's chest and held him with all her strength.

"I don't know how long it was, but one day he was all frantic, saying he got fucked over and we had to leave, and that's when he drugged me again and stuffed me into that ice chest and locked the lid.

"When I woke up, I was in that trailer and I didn't know where we were going. It was completely dark and I was suffocating. He ran over something and we almost crashed and that's when the chest fell over and the lid broke. I could finally breath, but was still stuck. I tried and tried but I couldn't move."

She sobbed uncontrollably. "He made me eat dog shit, Billy! And he peed on my face and in my mouth!" She continued weeping. "Everything hurt. Everything. And kept hurting more and more. I was in Hell."

With Billy holding her, she cried for the longest time. Finally, she was quiet for some minutes then looked up at Billy. "I don't know how long it was before you came and rescued me. When I first saw you, I knew you were an angel."

FIFTY-THREE

•••

Wᴇʏᴀᴛᴛ ᴀɴᴅ Mᴀᴅᴇʟᴇɪɴᴇ ᴡᴀʟᴋᴇᴅ ᴛᴏ ᴛʜᴇ ʙᴇᴅʀᴏᴏᴍ. Wʏᴀᴛᴛ sᴀᴛ ᴏɴ the edge of the bed looking at the floor. Madeleine apprehensively looked at Wyatt. "There's something else, isn't there?" Wyatt kept looking down. "Tell me. It's okay." She waited.

After several minutes, he looked up at her. What do I have to lose? If she kicks me out, at least I will have had a night of the best sex imaginable. She arranged three pillows against the headboard.

He first told her about bludgeoning the three men in Richmond. About the sounds and the blood and the shooting, about the painful aftermath deaths. He then took a deep breath and told her about the three men in Mexico.

Madeleine assured him that he did the right thing in both instances, and that that's what was important, that he saved two young women from years, possibly lifetimes, of shame and self-condemnation.

Wyatt held her eyes. "The things you say are true and I do take solace in them. But the fact remains that I have killed six men. I remember reading or hearing somewhere that when you kill a man, you not only take away everything he is, you take away everything he will be. Maybe it was Louis L'Amour, I don't know. Anyway, I think about that."

She put a hand on his arm and spoke with earnest. "But Wyatt, any guilt or regret that grows from that is based on the assumption that what will be, will be something better, something good; and that's only a supposition, a vain hope. It's not something that can be known. But what is known, what I know and you know, is that regardless of what they might have become, those were bad men that you killed. Forcing a mother to offer her four-teen-year-old daughter to multiple sex partners? Raping a young woman

221

in a public place? Videotaping it and laughing about it? Then showing it to thousands? Millions?

"I'm not saying you deserve forgiveness or implying a higher order should or will forgive you because there was no wrongness involved, so there's no need for forgiveness. Killing them was necessary, Wyatt. I'm not justifying it, I'm just pointing out the necessity of it. Killing itself is not a necessity of life, but killing them *was* necessary. Do you see the difference?"

He looked at her, hoping for the truth of her assertions. "I do, but didn't I simply stop a vile act with a more vile act? Isn't killing worse than rape?"

Her voice became introspective. "I don't know, Wyatt. When someone is killed, it's over. When you're raped, you get over it, hopefully, but even if you do you always know it could happen again and the thought of that possibility is always with you."

She leaned back and spoke defiantly. "I've been raped, Wyatt. Twice. Gang raped one of the times. You have no idea. We've all been raped, all of us women, raped or we're close to someone who has been. And then afterward, living every day knowing it could happen again. How do you think that affects us?

"What's it like having a daughter and from the very first day thinking it could someday happen to her? Or having a son and wondering if he'll someday be the rapist? Is killing worse than, or not as bad as, rape? I don't know. No one can make that determination so it's futile to compare the two."

Wyatt looked at her a long time. I can't decide if she's more beautiful or wise.

"You're right, Madeleine. You *are* right. But the troublesome thing is this: I don't feel one way or another about killing those guys. Sure, I think about it now and again but how do I feel? I don't know. I don't know that I feel anything. I have no emotions connected with it.

He sighed. "It's not a numbness or an apathy or some sort of denial or renouncing. It's a lacking, maybe a lacking in my character. I think about that, too. Hell, I never even lost any sleep over it, Madeleine. No nightmares or after-the-fact anxieties. Nothing. What does that say about me?"

She stroked the back of his neck. "Oh you dear, beautiful man. Maybe you exist above the riffraff, above the unanswerable questions, above all the mysteries and wonderings. You're not without emotions, my dear, far from it. I mean, we first met in a titty bar and when I mentioned Jane Austen, your eyes welled up."

He looked away and his face softened into a light smile. "Well, I do love my Jane."

He looked back at her. Oh, but this woman! This is the woman I want. I want her, yes, and I do love her. Or am I just being selfish? I don't know. I don't know if it's even possible for me to love. But that's a dodge, isn't it? Or is it? Dammit. Love her, just love her. The want and admiration I feel is love, isn't it? Damn, I wish I knew.

He grasped her hands. "Here's the real crux, Madeleine. When it was going down, I was on the move, taking action. There was no thinking involved, no emotions, no desire to mete out justice or punishment, no curiosity about cause or concern about consequence. I wasn't human, certainly wasn't a god. I wasn't even an animal. I became something else entirely, something not alive, more akin to gravity or the rain falling or tectonic plates settling."

His eyes became laser-like. "It's happened other times, too, the first was in fourth grade, and every time it scared me. But the fear doesn't arrive in the normal way. It starts with a loathing for losing myself, that I'd some-how failed. The fear comes from the possibility that that emotionless *thing* would become permanent. Self-loathing and fear are the reasons I chose a life where it was least possible to happen again."

He let go of her hands and spoke with a cruel self-indictment. "So I got into literature and became a fucking Ivy League professor."

He shook his head trying to get rid of the memories. "It worked or seemed to work for a while, for years, and I never noticed that, probably from the first day, I began to die and every day I died a little more. The art, the literature itself, kept me from insanity and suicide, but the life I was leading was a slowly grinding death."

He again took her hands, gently this time. "The irony is that it's that lack of regret about the violence I've committed, the absence of emotions about them, that lifelessness, that non-human-ness, the possible permanence of it, that somehow makes me want to live." (And makes me want to love you.)

"You say it was necessary to kill them, Madeleine, but was it? What if, over the years, I had developed enough self-control that I didn't lose myself? Knowing the damage I could cause, I should have taken the steps necessary so that I would always be in control of myself, right? Had I done that, I would have gone at those guys as myself and not some un-living thing and maybe they would be alive now. Still bad men, yes, but still with the possibility of becoming good men."

Madeleine spoke with the wisdom of ages. "But now you're back in the realm of what-ifs and that's a place where regret will consume all that you are, a place to die. If we're to live, we have to face up to reality because reality is not only what we're given, it's what we create and give to others, the only place where we *are*."

An extraordinary weight lifted off of Wyatt. The air became lighter, insubstantial, and the colors in the room seemed to glow from within, and he began to realize the immense pleasure of being alive, like he'd just emerged from a coma. I've never told anyone else this before, he thought. She is my confessor and what a glorious thing it is.

Madeleine thought, oh I so love this man. I love him and I want to keep loving him and I want him to love me and, oh god, this is crazy. He is the man I always wanted. This is him. But am I the same person now as I was back when I wanted someone like him. Of course not. In ways I am, though. Either way, can I cross that threshold?

I've given him my body and will do it again and again and again, but can I give him the rest of me? I want to, but am I able to? I don't know if I'm even capable of loving a man. Maybe I never was, never have been. I'm a burden. I'm not good enough but maybe I can be. Oh god! I just want him!

She again put her hands on the back of his neck and felt the coolness of his hair, the symmetric shape of his skull. "Wyatt, I can't pretend to know what it's like to have killed someone."

He stroked her cheek with the back of his fingers. "And I don't know what it's like to have been raped."

Madeleine paused, serene and light. "Together we do."

Wyatt looked at Madeleine more deeply than he'd ever looked at anyone else. "Yes. Together. Together we do know."

FIFTY-FOUR

...

K ATY HAD TO SLEEP OFTEN AND WHEN SHE DID, BILLY WOULD GO BACK to his motel room and search the internet for Harvey Smith, who seemed to have disappeared. He also searched for MasterBlood but other than a gamer geek and a Hip-Hop artist, he found nothing. He even checked out kiddie porn, BDSM and kill sites, but still nothing. Frustrated, he often looked at the computer screen, saying, "I'm gonna find ya, Harvey Smith. And when I do, yer gonna pay and pay big time fer what ya did to my Katy."

Around six weeks later, Billy remembered a friend from school. His nickname was Chewie and he had always been into computers, a diehard geek, and they had formed an odd friendship. Chewie helped him with his math and Billy kept him from being picked on by the school bullies. He still had a number for him in his phone and tried it. Amazingly, Chewie answered on the third ring.

"Chewie?"

"Who is this?"

"Billy."

There was a long silence. "Billy from Lincoln Elementary?"

"The very one."

"The guy who kept getting multiplication and division mixed up?"

"That's me, my friend."

"Well damn!"

For a while, they laughed about the old times and got each other caught up on what had been happening since. After a while, Billy said, "You're still into computers, right?"

"Yeah. Whatcha got in mind?"

"I need your help finding someone. All I know is his name and an old screen name he used to use. Maybe still does. A few other things about him, too. He's into bad stuff. Real bad stuff."

"If it's that bad, the FBI would be the ones."

"Oh, I'm sure they're looking for him, too. But I wanna find him first. It's personal."

Chewie paused and warily said, "I don't know, Billy. That kind of thing could get you into, you know, a bad situation for yourself. Me, too."

"I know, I know. But it's real important, Chewie." Then he said as if the idea just occurred to him, "Say, whereabouts you live? Let me come tell ya about it in person. Maybe I can change your mind."

Chewie sighed. "Well, okay. I'm in Pueblo."

"Colorado?"

"Yeah."

"Great. Give me the address and I'll be there tomorrow afternoon."

After dinner that night, Billy and Katy were in her room and again he looked at her like he had the worst news in the world. "I gotta be gone for a few days."

"Okay." (Please don't let it be anything illegal.) "Some sort of business?"

"You could say that. It's personal."

She waited, expecting the worst. "A wife? Girlfriend?"

"No no, nothing like that." (There ain't nobody but you, Katy.)

"Is it drugs? Tell me if it's a drug deal, Billy." (Please don't let it be drugs.)

"Oh, hell no. I hate that shit." Billy looked around the room then cleared his throat. "I've been looking for him, Katy. Every waking moment when I ain't with you or the girls. Cain't find a trace. Looked everywhere I can think of."

"Who?"

He waited. "Harvey Smith."

Katy stiffened momentarily. A gathering of terrible consequences came to her. She timidly asked, "Why?"

"He's gotta pay. And I don't mean in some cell getting free food and meds. He's gotta pay for what he did, Katy. Two eyes for an eye. And he's going to."

Katy, overcome with anxiety, said, "Oh Billy, I don't know if that's a good idea. He's connected to some powerful people."

"Don't matter. They don't care about me and I don't care about them. But I do care about Harvey Smith getting what he deserves."

This was a significant moment for Katy. The moment when she realized that Billy was more of a man than she had ever hoped for, that he would always protect her, and she decided she would always be there for him and protect him, too, even if he didn't want a permanent (and monogamous!) relationship. She looked around, barely breathing, thoughts confused and short-lived. "Where are you going?"

"Got an old friend living in Pueblo. Knows everything about computers and the internet. If anyone can find the devil, it's him."

FIFTY-FIVE
• • •

WYATT LAID DOWN AND GENTLY KISSED MADELEINE, FEELING THE curves of her temple and cheek. She put her head on the cradle beneath his shoulder and draped her arm across his chest.

Their bodies fit together perfectly, like a stream purling over a bed of moss-covered rocks. In a husky voice, he said, "Those guys who raped you."

"Yes?"

"If we ever come across any one of them, point him out to me."

"Okay."

"Promise?"

"Yes."

"Really. I mean it. Promise me."

She reached up and stroked the scar on his cheek. "I promise thee, my prince."

After lying in silence for some time, Madeleine said, "Wyatt, I . . ." She trailed off, but Wyatt knew.

"And I, thee."

Fifteen minutes later, Madeleine hurried to pack while Wyatt helped with what little he could. In the minutes before the shuttle arrived, he took her in his arms. "I'll be here when you come back."

"It's going to be six weeks."

"I know."

"It's a long time."

"An eternity."

Madeleine leaned back. "I'm not going to ask you to wait. I can't ask you that."

"But . . ."

"No, listen. I know what life is like for a biker. I saw it a lot when my husband was in the Hells Angels."

"Your husband was H.A.?"

"Yeah. He did some sort of initiation for seven months then left for two weeks – missed Brandy's birthday and first ballet recital – and came back with a bunch of tattoos. '81' on his neck, 'ACAB' on his fingers. It took only a month before they kicked him out."

Wyatt squinted his eyes and cocked his head. "They kicked him out?"

"Yeah, they figured out what he was really up to a year before the police did. Anyway, he's not what we're talking about. Look Wyatt, don't change for me, I don't want you to. Just go on being the amazing man you are. That's the man I met and that's, well, that's how I came to feel the way I do." (Will you wait for me?)

"Madeleine, listen ... "

"I love it when you say my full name."

"I love saying it, Madeleine Merry Marks."

"And I yours, Wyatt Hazel Youngblood."

Wyatt kissed her then she kissed him. (Is it too much to hope you'll wait for me?) "I just want you to know that you're free to do all the things you did before we met."

"Thank you, but ... "

"No, really."

"Madeleine, if you're going to wait, then ... "

She gently pushed away from him. "Oh, I'll wait. I'll be staying with my daughter and son-in-law and helping take care of a baby, so I will wait for you." (Please wait for me Wyatt, please.) "But waiting is harder for a man than a woman so I'm not going to ask you to do that. I can't ask you to."

"But ... "

"No. That's it." They held each other. Close, like one. "Kiss me, Wyatt."

FIFTY-SIX

...

CHEWIE OPENED THE FRONT DOOR OF A NONDESCRIPT HOUSE IN A nondescript neighborhood and said, "So you've come running to Chewie to save you from the bullies!"

Billy smiled. "Ain't nobody better with a left hook than you, Chewie."

Chewie was five feet two inches tall, short black hair, wire rimmed glasses, and if you dunked him in the ocean and filled his pockets with sand, he might come up to ninety pounds. The two had been talking small for a while when Chewie asked, "So what ya got going, Billy."

When Billy finished telling him everything, Chewie said, "That's some serious fucked up shit."

"Tell ya what, my friend."

"You looked all over? Google, Yahoo, Dogpile, DuckDuckGo, Yandex?"

"All of 'em, but I ain't never heard of Yandex."

"It's Russian. I'll check it out. But the thing is, this sounds like Dark Web shit. Red Room stuff."

"Ain't never heard of the Red Room."

"It's the internet version of snuff films. Torture and shit. Dangerous to even go to it."

"Well, whatever it is, I gotta find Harvey Smith."

Chewie looked at him for a long time. "Okay, I gotta talk to a guy. Come back tomorrow around noon and I'll have an answer. And bring some lunch this time."

The following day, with a round metal table in the back yard covered with Taco Bell's finest, Chewie introduced Billy to a man in his late thirties named W. He wore sunglasses, was around six feet tall and shaped like a tall version of Chewie. When Billy asked him if W was actually his name, he just nodded once. Billy said, "Well, okay. So Chewie got ya all caught up on everything I know about this guy. Can ya find him?"

W said, "The databases in the Dark Web, especially the Red Room, are heavily encrypted and filled with viruses that'll burn a computer. Sometimes it takes a few tries to get through. We'll need at least three, probably four, virgin PCs."

"Okay. Any specs I need to fulfill?"

"The fastest you can get. Disk space isn't important."

Billy bought the computers straight away and left them with Chewie and W. Chewie said, "I'll call you when we have something."

Two days later Billy got a call. "We found him. Harvey Smith, right? He used to go by MasterBlood but he's using two more legitimate names now."

"What are they?"

"Oh, just a bunch of letters and numbers and symbols. He's gotten smarter."

"Okay, so where is he?"

"Glendale. Nice neighborhood."

"California or Arizona?"

"Arizona. He bought a house a year or so ago with cash, but has never lived there. Until now, anyway. He's going under the name of Frank Fielder." Chewie gave Billy the address. Billy said, "I'll never forget this, Chewie. I owe ya."

"Nah. I think I still owe you, my friend. You saved my ass more times than I could count."

FIFTY-SEVEN

...

WYATT WAS IN THE AIRPORT, PACING NERVOUSLY AT THE BOTTOM OF the escalator. He had rented a car and wondered if he should have bought flowers. Damn! Why didn't I think of flowers! Too late now, but still ....

Madeleine saw him first and her heart leapt. When Wyatt saw her, he looked like he had just found a cache of gold. They hugged for the longest time, saying nothing. Finally, without letting go, Wyatt whispered in her ear, "I waited."

"Oh god Wyatt, I so love you!"

"And I, thee, Madeleine Merry Marks."

For the next three days, they were a combination of puppy love, mature love and lust love, the fervor growing by the hour. They talked about anything and everything and once, while lying naked side by side in bed, Wyatt asked, "How many years have you been working for Al?"

"Wasn't even a year the first time. This time about two years."

"Hmph. What happened in between?"

It was just after sunset, but the warmth of the day still hung undisturbed in the room. Madeleine turned on her side and languorously rested her head on her hand, her breasts lying comfortably on top of one another. "I quit right after Al beat me up. Then I had to quit the drugs, which wasn't easy, believe me. Then I went back to waitressing. Denny's and a couple of steak houses."

"How'd you hook up with Al again?"

"Same way. Working tables at a steak house and one day he walked in. Said he'd changed and wanted me to tend bar for him again and I said okay. It's just me now so I make enough to get by. Wish I didn't have those damned credit cards, though."

"How much?"

"Around thirty thousand."

Wyatt felt the room cool down a notch. "So did Al change?"

"Somewhat. But the one thing that hasn't changed is him taking some of our tip money."

Wyatt was offended. "What!"

"At the end of the night he grabs a handful out of our tip jar. What's left is ours to split."

"What a fucking little prick!"

Madeleine smiled, nodded and raised her eyebrows. "Oh, he is." She went on. "Other than that he did change, but not in a good way. I'm too old for him to have sex with, I wouldn't anyway, but that's not what I'm talking about. The thing is, he's gotten more shrewd and he's onto to bigger things."

"Like what?"

Madeleine turned onto her back again, her breasts taking a few moments to come to rest. "Remember that slick turd asshole I told you about? The one who beat me up and stole my purse when I wouldn't blow him?"

"Yes."

"Well, he's taken over for his daddy and is now the big drug guy in Lansing. He sends the drugs to Al's office, Al sells the stuff and pays him, maybe even helps launder the money, I don't know. The perk for Asshole Son is that he can offer the dancers to his friends and business associates for free."

"Al sells at the bar?"

"No. He may not have a soul but he's not stupid. No one at the Satin Pillow has anything to do with the drugs. He has, I don't know, distributors or whatever do the selling. Like I said, maybe he uses the club for laundering, I don't know."

Wyatt mused. "When does this drug and money exchange happen?"

"Last Wednesday of every month."

A certain potency came over Wyatt, like the intensity before entering a boxing match or the keenness at the beginning of a downhill skiing race. He sat up. "That's the day after tomorrow. And it goes down in Al's office?"

"Yeah."

"How much is involved?"

"A couple of weeks ago I overheard Al brag about clearing fifty grand. He paid Asshole Son around a quarter million."

"So there's a quarter of a million dollars cash in his office right now?"

"At least. Plus maybe Al's fifty."

Wyatt plopped onto his back again. His cell phone buzzed. It was lying on the floor next to his jeans. He reached down and read a text from Billy, and it shocked him into another reality. He thought a few moments. "I'm sorry, Madeleine, I have to answer this." He walked, naked, out to the back porch.

FOUND THAT GUY IN ALBUQUERQUE. INTERESTED?

YES.

WHERE YA AT?

GRAND LEDGE, OUTSIDE OF LANSING.

BEEN TO THE STEEL HORSE IN PHOENIX?

YES.

FRIDAY NIGHT GOOD?

Wyatt thought for a few seconds. SATURDAY OKAY? I'LL HAVE A PASSENGER.

COME TO THINK OF IT, SO WILL I. SATURDAY AT 7.

SEE YOU THEN.

PART III

Vengeance is in my heart, death in my hand,
Blood and revenge are hammering in my head.

—Shakespeare's Titus Andronicus (2:3)

FIFTY-EIGHT

• • •

WYATT STAYED ON THE PORCH LOOKING AT THE DARK SPACES BETWEEN the stars, the cooling night air arousing a restlessness about the coming days, about what needed to be done. Fifteen minutes later he came back inside and said, "I need some data." He then had Madeleine tell him everything she knew about the layout of the Satin Pillow, particularly Al's office.

"Does the outside door open in or out?"

"In."

"Where's Al's desk?"

"In the middle at the back of the room facing the outside door."

Wyatt asked the questions like an auctioneer. "Where's the money?"

"In a safe in the wall behind him. There're oak file cabinets on either side."

"The door's got to be locked." Madeleine nodded. "And bolted." Madeleine nodded again. "Is there another lock on the inside?"

"No, but there's one of those slide thingies with a chain."

"Anything else?"

Her voice had a nervous edge to it. "I don't know. Never noticed anything else but never looked, either."

"How many hinges?"

"I don't know, Wyatt. What's going on in that head of yours?"

"Does he have a bodyguard?"

She sighed in resignation. "Yeah. His name's Trip and he has a gun and some knives. Al makes him stand to his right all day."

"Is he trained?"

"Yeah. I think he's ex-special forces or something. Black Belts and stuff but I've never seen him do anything."

239

The following day, Wyatt had Madeleine take him to the man from whom she rented her house. He was large and balding, hadn't shaved in a week, and wore a dirty white tank top and old black slacks that looked as if they'd been greased down. Madeleine said, "Neal, this is Wyatt. He wants to talk with you."

Neal looked Wyatt down and up. "I'm busy." He started to close the door, but Wyatt pushed it open, stepped past Neal, took a kitchen chair then sat across from his easy chair. He waited.

Neal slowly sat down and said, "Who the fuck're you?"

Wyatt was calm. "Madeleine will be moving out before the weekend's over. You need to refund her security and cleaning deposits."

"She still has over a year left on her lease!"

Wyatt, barely breathing, calmly replied. "She needs her security and cleaning deposits. In cash. Now."

"Fuck you!"

Wyatt stared at him and as he continued to do so, Neal got more and more nervous. He began whimpering. Wyatt kept staring. Finally, Neal said, "I'll have to go to the bank."

"We'll be back in an hour."

When Wyatt and Madeleine got into her car, she asked, "What's going on, Wyatt? What are you planning?"

"Haven't figured it all out yet." He looked at her. "Trust me, okay?"

(God, this man is a pure adrenalin rush.) "Okay. But I'm a little scared."

He nodded. "Me, too." Before they pulled away from the curb, he asked, "Do you know a kid, a good kid, with a driver's license who's looking for some quick cash?"

"Well, there's Helen's son, Mac. She's the one who does my hair."

"Good. Let's give them a visit."

Helen was stout and good-natured, like a sort of mother to Madeleine, though they were about the same age. After Madeleine introduced them, Wyatt asked, "Is Mac around? I'd like to speak with him."

"Oh, he's in his room. I'll get him."

When Mac came out, Wyatt extended his hand and said, "Name's Wyatt."

"I'm Mac." They shook hands.

"So Mac, I need you to do a job. Madeleine's moving out and all of her stuff needs to be put in storage, but she won't be around to do it. I need you to rent a truck and move everything from her house into a storage facility

I'll rent later today. And you need to do it in one day. I'll leave the key on her kitchen table. You'll also need to rent a truck, which I'm figuring may cost around two hundred, probably less. Interested?"

"Sure. But it'll probably take me more than a day."

"Hire a couple of friends to help. And don't forget to feed them."

"Uh, I don't have any money."

"The job pays a thousand plus two hundred for the truck. Cash. In advance. And if you do everything I've asked, you'll get Madeleine's car as a bonus. We'll leave the pink slip next to the key for the storage unit."

"Heck, yeah! I have a couple of friends who'll help."

Wyatt could see that Mac was uncertain about something. "Look, you're the boss, it's your gig. You take four hundred, give each of the others three. But you pay for the food."

"Cool!"

Wyatt reached into his pocket and gave him the twelve hundred dollars.

After they left, Wyatt rented a large storage room for a year, then retrieved Madeleine's security and cleaning deposits.

When they got to her place, Madeleine again said she was a little scared, which was understandable. Here she was, leaving her home and job for good, didn't know where she was going or what was to happen and neither did the man she was going with.

Wyatt looked at her and said, "We're going to have an adventure. It'll be a rush like none other. We'll remember it for years, for the rest of our lives."

FIFTY-NINE
...

KATY STRETCHED LANGUOROUSLY UNDER THE COVERS. SHE HAD SLEPT late and it was a good sleep. Her mind was focused, or rather capable of being focused, but she chose to not put her attention on any one thing. She experienced the kind of comfort that makes one more alive, more attuned to present contentment and future possibilities.

It was mid-morning when Billy got to her room. He had a look she couldn't discern but was untroubled by it. The mere sight of him, his masculinity and his pampering of her, his chivalry, disallowed any anxiety. She reached her arms to him and smiled. He came to her and they held each other in silence and contentedness.

Billy gently withdrew from their embrace and looked at her face as if memorizing every detail before bringing the chair to the bedside.

"We gotta get ya packed up. Time to get moving."

"Oh. Okay." She was crestfallen. "Is it too expensive?"

"No no, nothing like that. But don't ya worry none. It's all good. We're going to Glendale. We'll put your stuff in storage."

Katy looked around her room, her home and sanctuary for the past two months. "California or Arizona?"

"Arizona. We'll take the bike but you'll be okay. We'll take it easy."

"Okay." She took one more look of longing at the room. "Why?"

Billy looked at her for some moments. "I found him."

Katy was still with a mixture of hatred and apprehension. Disconnected images of what had happened to her flashed behind her eyes, like harsh strobe lights. "What are we going to do?"

"Don't know exactly but like I said, he's gonna pay."

She closed her eyes, the bed cold of a sudden. "This is dangerous, isn't it, Billy? And illegal? Even criminal, right?"

He leaned to her and put his hands on her arms. "All three. But it's all on me. Besides, my buddy Wyatt and his girlfriend will be there; he'll back me up all the way. Anyways, you'll be safe, nothing'll happen to you."

(But if something happens to you, Billy, it'll be worse for me.) "Okay, but...." (Do I want to do this? Can I do this? Can I face him again? She looked up at Billy, his eyes unwavering, and she knew. With him I can. With Billy, I can do anything.) "Okay."

"All right. I'll be back after I pack up and get the storage unit. He got up to leave but Katy stopped him. "Wait, Billy. There's something else, something else you haven't told me."

"Something else? Can't imagine what."

Katy had a look of dread. "Those two vials on your keychain. What's in them?"

Billy pulled them out of his pocket. The coolness and weight in his palm. He sat down. "Nobody else has ever touched these." He twirled them around. "Nobody else knows what's in them."

He took them off his keychain then handed them to her. She slowly unscrewed the tops. In the first was an old photo of a young Billy in a gray suit and red bow tie, standing next to his mother just before they went to church. He had a big smile on his face, his mother proud of her son.

In the second vial was a photo of Billy in a little league uniform holding a bat. His green cap was too big and balanced on his ears. His father was standing next to him with his arm around Billy's shoulders. As with his mother, he was proud of his son. Both photos had splotches of dark brown blood on them. She said, "You were a cute kid."

Billy haltingly smiled and his eyes became wet. "My daddy was a lieutenant in the army. He's retired but always kept running things on a tight schedule. Him and my momma bought this new UltraGlide, blue with white pinstripes. They'd had it fer just six months and they looked real fine on it." He was lost in pleasant memories for a time. "They's so happy riding on that thing." His eyes wandered around the room but looked at only the memories. "I'd just got into town and we was gonna meet for lunch. I's running behind so I called 'em and said I'd be ten minutes late."

Billy's eyes began watering. He felt the warmth of Katy's hand on his arm. "Daddy was okay with it. He never minded a change as long as ya let him know. Anyways, they took off ten minutes later than they'd planned and ended up getting hit by a drunk driver. Got run over and died right there. All because I couldn't get my ass in gear."

Billy threw his head on her lap and wept uncontrollably; Katy gently ran her hand through his hair and cried for him. They stayed like that for many minutes, Katy not knowing what to say or what to do, unwilling to upset the precariousness of deep grief.

When Billy's sobbing subsided, he lifted his head but kept his eyes on the tears that wetted Katy's nightgown. He closed his eyes and blessed her for being there, for understanding, though no words had passed between them.

Katy took the photo of Billy and his mother and again uncurled it. A few specks of dried blood fell to the sheet. She froze with apprehension. Billy stared at the drops then took a deep breath and gently scraped off the rest of them. He did the same with the photo of his father then rolled the two photos together and put them in the first vial.

He delicately picked up the dark brown specks of blood and squeezed them into a ball with his tears. He put it into the second vial, screwed on both tops and replaced them on his keychain.

It was later in the afternoon when they visited the girls. After the four hugged, Billy looked at Mary for a few moments then at Mona. He said, "We're gonna be gone for a bit, but we will be back."

Both girls immediately grew downhearted. Mary asked, "Where are you going?"

"Just some place where we got something to do."

"How long will you be gone?"

"Don't know. But we *will* be back, doncha worry."

Mona, her eyes watering, asked, "When are you leaving?"

"Tomorrow morning."

Mona began crying. "You're never coming back. I know it."

Katy held her. "You'll see us again. Promise."

Mona wrestled free. "But why do you have to go? What am I going to do? What's Mary going to do?"

Katy smiled through her sadness. "Be strong. Keep being amazing. Do your homework. Take care of each other. And know you'll see us again. It's a promise."

Mary started crying as well. "It's going to be a long time, isn't it?"

"We have to do something important, Mary, and we don't know how long it will take, but we *will* be back."

Billy held Mary while she quietly sobbed on his shoulder. Mona threw herself back into Katy's arms and stayed there for the longest time, crying.

SIXTY

...

MADELEINE'S HEART RACED WHEN WYATT TOLD HER WHAT THEY WERE going to do. Her imagination kept coming up with all sorts of bad outcomes but she managed to force herself to consider ways it could end well. Wyatt's fearless but Al's ruthless; Wyatt has a heart but Al doesn't. I love Wyatt but do I trust him with my life? I have to. And I do. Love and trust go together, right? Well I guess this is it, can't turn back now. Please let this turn out okay.

She climbed onto the back of his bike and twenty minutes later, they rolled into the Satin Pillow's dirt parking lot. Wyatt pointed the bike toward the street. Madeleine watched how he took off his helmet and gloves, how he checked his .357 and Ruger. Like a machine.

He turned to her and said, "I don't want you in there but I'll need you for a little bit. Only in the beginning, though. When Al looks at you, just look back. Don't look away, don't even flick your eyes away, just look right at him like you're bored. Don't say a word to him, not even "Hi" or even nod. If he says anything, anything at all, don't react and don't answer. Not a word except to me. You're not scared, you're not pissed, you're not anything but bored; not drugged-out bored, just garden variety bored. Got it?" Madeleine nodded.

Madeleine watched as Wyatt walked to the door. It was high quality but old. He looked closely at the door jam. Good solid work but signs of rot. He backed up while continuing to study the door. When he was next to her, he said, "Don't come in until I've disarmed Trip." She nodded. His expression remained hard but he half-smiled. "This is going to be fun."

He breathed deeply three times then rushed full force. Just before reaching the door, he turned halfway around and back-kicked it just below the doorknob. He whipped around and hit the door again with his right shoulder. The door gave way just enough for Wyatt to roll in on the floor and point his .357 at Trip.

Trip shot twice at where Wyatt's heart would have been if he'd been standing. Al slowly moved his hand to the middle drawer of his desk. Wyatt flashed his eyes toward him. "You'll never get there."

Wyatt stood up then motioned his head toward a small coffee table at the back left corner. "Put it there." Trip laid his Glock on the table. "And the knives. All of them." Trip did that, too. Wyatt nodded to a framed photo directly left of Al's desk. "Stand under that picture." Trip went there and put his hands up. Wyatt let out a sigh and said, "Geez man, this isn't a fucking movie. Put down your hands."

Madeleine walked in.

Spittle came out of Al's mouth. "You fucking bitch!"

Neither Trip nor Madeleine nor Al saw any movement. By the time the fact of Al's broken left cheek registered, Wyatt was back standing in front of the desk. Trip relaxed his shoulders. He had thought to wait for Wyatt to let down his guard but after Al's pistol-whipping, he knew that, even if it happened, he didn't have a chance to get his gun before Wyatt shot him. Or pistol-whipped him. Madeleine was stunned. Al was crying.

Wyatt said, "Take the handkerchief out of your jacket."

Al looked at him perplexed. "What?"

"Put it on the desk." Wyatt picked it up and wiped the blood off the handgrip. Then he said, "First, you owe Madeleine for eight days of work. That's seven hundred and twenty dollars. Put it on the desk." Al reached into the inside pocket of his coat and pulled out his wallet without taking his eyes off the .357. He counted out the exact amount and put the rest of the bills back in his wallet and the wallet back in his coat. Wyatt handed the bills to Madeleine then looked back at Al. "How many on your payroll?"

"Seventeen."

"Does that include Madeleine?"

"Yes."

"Are they all here right now?"

"Yes."

"Take a hundred and seventy thousand out of the safe."

Al got a horrified look. "Fuck you! They'll kill me!"

This time Wyatt backhanded him with the pistol, fracturing his right cheek. Al fell to the floor moaning. Madeleine and Trip could do nothing but watch. Wyatt stood above him ready to hit again, but Al held up his hands and brought up his knees. "Okay, okay." He struggled up, worked the combination, counted the money and put it on the desk. The bills, large denominations, were wrapped in stacks of five thousand dollars.

"Empty the trashcan in the corner and put the money in it." Al did it. "Get out another five."

Wyatt turned to Madeleine. "Who locks up at night?"

"Jerry, one of the other bartenders."

"First tell him that the Satin Pillow has closed down. Tell him to turn off the music then get all the customers to leave and leave quickly. No one pays his tab. Then get everyone else, all the employees, into the bar. Tell them that the Satin Pillow has gone out of business and they're each due severance pay. Give them each two stacks and tell them to leave quickly. Don't answer any questions. Two stacks are your severance and the extra five is for the tips Al stole from you.

"Put on your helmet and wait by the bike. When everyone else has left, honk the horn. When Al's business associates show up at the end of the street, honk the horn again. Got all that?" Madeleine nodded again. He pulled the Ruger out of his back pocket, checked that the clip was loaded, chambered a round and held it out for Madeleine.

"Is that necessary?" she asked. Wyatt didn't say anything but kept holding the gun. She finally took it then walked into the bar with the trashcan full of money.

SIXTY-ONE

...

WYATT TURNED HIS ATTENTION BACK TO AL. "GET OUT ANOTHER twenty thousand." Al put four stacks on the desk. "Get out another thirty and put it in a bank bag." Al moved like a tin puppet in a carnival show. "Now get the rest of the money and unwrap all the stacks and sprinkle the bills on the trash." Al whimpered all the while.

When he was done, Wyatt said, "Put your wallet on top." Al did it carefully, as if he were laying the last card on a huge house of cards. Wyatt noticed a large cigarette lighter on the desk. "Get out your lighter fluid and spray it on the stack."

"Are you fucking crazy? That's over eighty thousand dollars!"

Wyatt hit him with a left cross, breaking his nose. Al fell down then reached up, opened a drawer and sprayed the bills and the trash and his wallet. Wyatt fluffed up the pile with his boot. "Keep spraying until it's all gone." Al did so. "Light it." Al began to wail.

The three men watched. The flames snaked and the smoke curled like an ancient sacrifice in an unholy place. Black shards of soot reached up the walls. A death-like stench wafted through the air. As the fire waned, Wyatt heard the horn from his bike. He turned to Trip.

"Have a family?"

"Wife and two boys."

"How long have you been working for Al?"

"Year and a half."

"How much does he pay you?"

"Ten fifty an hour."

Wyatt let out a disgusted grunt and nodded to the twenty thousand dollars on Al's desk. "Ten thousand is your severance pay, five thousand is

251

for the embarrassment of having to protect this pile of snot, and the other five thousand means you quit your job yesterday and you weren't here."

Trip was astonished. "You serious?"

Wyatt smiled. "I'm the one with the gun."

"Damn." Trip grabbed the four stacks and walked toward the door.

"You forgot your Glock. Your knives, too."

"Shit man, you're all right."

After Trip left, Wyatt walked over to the corner and patted down the ashes with his boot until any slightest trace of money was gone, the resulting black smudge like an Old Testament curse.

Wyatt pulled up a chair and sat looking at Al, who was curled up and sobbing. "A few things, Al. When your friends get here, you were alone because Trip quit his job yesterday. You heard what I told him, right?" Al nodded. "You can tell them whatever you want about what happened. They won't believe a word and they certainly won't believe the truth.

"Now, if Trip or any of his family get hurt in any way because of this, I will find you, give you a visit and you will not like it. If Madeleine or her family or any of her friends get hurt in any way because of this, I will find you and keep you alive for a very long time, and it will be painful. All of that assuming, of course, that you're still alive at the end of the night. Do we have an understanding?"

Al nodded and looked at Wyatt through a veil of snot and blood and said, "They're gonna kill you."

"No. They don't give a shit about me. They just want their money and as far as they're concerned, you were the last one to have it." Al continued crying. Wyatt sat and stared. Fifteen minutes later, he heard the second honk from his bike and left.

SIXTY-TWO

...

WITH MADELEINE BEHIND HIM, WYATT RODE LIKE A MEDIEVAL ASsassin in the service of God – or, perhaps, the Devil – his concentration waxing with every mile. He was aware that looming close was the Dark Companion, and at first, having it in proximity to Madeleine worried him.

The more he thought about it, however, the more he felt an unexpected comfort because, to be honest, it had served him well in his confrontation with Al. For a while, he looked into his past and came to realize that the Dark Companion had actually been more of a benefit than a curse. Except for that first time in fourth grade, but even then it had been borne from a desire to make things right, a sense of justice. He remembered his father's words: You did right by defending yourself and Deanna and I'm proud of you for that.

 And for the first time in his life, he began to view the Dark Companion, whatever it was, as an accomplice, an accomplice for the violent good that he must do at times.

After she had walked out of her house for the last time, Madeleine didn't offer up any conversation or ask any questions, even when Wyatt handed her the bank bag with thirty thousand dollars in it and said, "No more credit card debt." The truth of it was that she was happy, thrilled, to be done with her mundane job, drab home and near meaningless existence.

Other than the short ride to the Satin Pillow, she hadn't ridden on a motorcycle for decades, so for the first sixty miles, it was like being on a rollercoaster. Afterward, however, she started getting stiff and sore and by the second gas stop, began to ache all over. But she was with the man she loved, the man who loved her, so she simply held onto him and said nothing.

Throughout the night, the only stops they made were for gas and snacks and to stretch their legs. After dawn, they stripped off a layer of clothes and continued southwest. After lunch, they changed into t-shirts and vests and that evening checked into a motel in Joplin, Missouri.

Wyatt unloaded everything then got some fried chicken and soda. They sat on the bed and while they ate, he told her the whole story. About meeting Billy several times on the road, about the man in the white pickup, about the mother and the two girls, and about finding the woman in the ice chest and how it had changed Billy.

He said, "Here's the thing: Billy is my only friend, so when he asked for my help, I wouldn't say no. Now, I know it's not fair, dragging you into this, but I couldn't stand to be away from you again. It's selfish of me, I know."

She rested her hand on his thigh. "Oh Wyatt, I'll go with you anywhere. And if having me around means you're selfish, I want you to be the most self-centered man on the planet. Just tell me what you need me to do."

"Billy and I will take care of the bastard. I just need to know you'll be there afterward."

"At least that, Wyatt. I'm with you." She kissed him lightly on his lips but remained close. "Always."

Wyatt's face melted into a contented smile, and he thought that it wasn't out of the realm of logic that everything that had happened to him, every-thing he'd done, from playing baseball, to a sham of an existence at Yale, to becoming an itinerant biker, to getting shot, to killing six men, to meeting Billy, all of it, had led to finding this woman. I still don't know what love is, he thought, but I do know I will do anything for her.

Too, Madeleine felt a surge of loyalty to Wyatt, the depth of which she had never conceived possible. I'll do more than just be there for him, she thought. Nothing bad will ever happen to him as long as I'm around. I know he'll always protect me and I'm going to do the same. I'll even kill if I have to.

SIXTY-THREE

...

BILLY AND KATY TOOK OFF A DAY BEFORE WYATT AND MADELEINE, THE reason being that, though the distance wasn't great, Billy was concerned about Katy's stamina and wouldn't ride more than thirty or forty miles at a time. Besides, she was used to taking naps during the day and Billy insisted she keep doing so.

The truth was that Katy had taken to sitting behind Billy as if she had been doing it all her life and other than lying in bed, it was the most comfortable place she could be. But she enjoyed Billy's doting so she had never said anything.

A cheerful and relaxed compatibility grew between them and their conversations had undertones of excitement and optimism about their future together. True, there was still an unpleasant task before them, but there was no need to speak of it so they didn't.

On the night before they reached Phoenix, they stopped at an upscale inn in Payson. Billy got the most expensive room and after dinner, they spent over an hour lounging in the Jacuzzi. The smell of pines and gardenias gently coursed through the open windows, and the night held a profound peace. It was late when, fully content, they climbed into bed.

Katy initiated their first lovemaking and a velvety warmth came over Billy, over and through both of them, and a vast honesty accompanied every touch, every move. At first, he was gentle, but Katy kept urging him to greater and greater strength until they fused into one organism of love-fury.

In the demand for carnal satisfaction they became as wild animals, insistent and hard and relentless, the explosion at the end their only desire. She became intoxicated with his smells of sweat and gasoline and beer and masculine musk, and she gave herself wholly to them.

She kissed the scars on his chest and stomach, stroked his legs and felt the hard but pliant muscles, strong as a bear's, and imagined being taken by a primordial beast more than twice her height, not wanting to stop it but, rather, wanting it and wanting it more and more until she melded with the animal's demands at whatever cost to herself.

Billy pushed back her head and kneaded her throat with his teeth, cupped her breasts and scraped her nipples with his stubble and tasted them. And they rolled and grasped and bit and scratched like ancient savages, feral with want, and they each consumed the salt and blood of the other.

He then seized her hips and brought her onto him, hard and insistent, and they stroked and stroked harder and harder until they were at last raw, their nerves electric, and they hovered, timeless, in the ecstasy between life and oblivion.

Billy and Katy lay in silence and stillness, flushed with lust consumed yet the longing of it beginning anew, the sweat between them clutching skin to skin.

After many minutes, Katy roused herself onto her right elbow and gently massaged the ridge of a scar next to Billy's scrotum, then the chaos of scars across his abdomen and chest. She lightly kissed his cheek and his neck then again rested her head on his shoulder. She asked in a subtle and even voice, "Must we do what we must?"

"Yes." His answer was immediate and certain.

She waited. "Why Wyatt and his girlfriend? Do you think there will be...." She paused. "Problems?"

"No. The dispatching of Harvey Smith will be simple enough. He's a coward, nothing but, but I do hold out a hope that he will fight back, or at least put up some sort of defense." His speech had become classic, his voice distant, but with a new and different strength, an additional certainty, as if he spoke in unison with countless warriors and knights and princes from millennia past. The drone of crickets came through the curtains as murmurs of agreement.

He went on. "Why have Wyatt and his girlfriend there?" He paused. "As witnesses so there will never be any doubt as to the bond between you and me."

She became lightheaded as under a spell. "And me?"

"So you will know by your own eyes and not my telling of it."

She tensed slightly, anxious of anything but the perfect answer. "And you, Billy. Why?"

He looked at her, his shadowed countenance penetrating, his voice like a far away seraph. "I suppose you could reckon it as honor." He deeply sighed. "Y'see, during my year of drunkenness, I told you I blamed myself for what happened to you, Katy, and I did. And as impossible as it sounds, after I finished that bottle of tequila, I knew you were somehow still alive, and I promised myself right then that no harm would ever again come upon you, that no matter what shape you were in, you would be my charge for as long as you or I lived."

She twirled the bristling hairs on his chest. "But he's no longer a danger to me." (Not with you around, certainly.) "He's hiding. On the run. He'll never look for me."

Billy looked at her slender arm. Two scars, one then the other, on the inside of it. "No, he won't. He won't look for you." He looked up and reached for the soft sculpture of her shoulder. "You see, the honor of it is for me. For you there is the justice of it. Whether you need it or not, I don't know, but I do know you deserve it, and it's up to me to deliver it."

SIXTY-FOUR

•••

WYATT AND MADELEINE ARRIVED AT THE STEEL HORSE SALOON A little early. Billy and Katy walked in fifteen minutes later. The two men guy-hugged and when Billy introduced Katy, Wyatt stared at her, then leaned forward and stared some more. He looked at Billy, who had a big smile on his face, then back at Katy and said, "That was you?" She smiled and slightly nodded. Wyatt leaned back like he was looking at the impossible. "Wow."

Katy turned to Madeleine, put out her hand and said, "I'm Katy."

"Oh, I'm sorry," interrupted Wyatt. "This is Madeleine and that's Billy and, well, that's Katy."

Madeleine smiled at both of them and said, "You can call me Maddy."

"Okay, Maddy it is," said Billy.

The women looked into each other's eyes for the longest time, the way that women often do, as if discerning all the past they each held. Finally, they hugged, looked once at the men, then walked to another table. Billy said, "Well, for the time being, I guess we don't exist much."

Wyatt nodded. "That is one hell of a woman, Billy."

"Tell ya what."

"Scars and tattoos, just like you like them."

"Yeah. And she's not even done filling out and I'll be damned if she doesn't already have the finest ass in the country." His eyes went from Katy to Madeleine. "Now, yer Maddy there. Damn. That is one downright, drop-dead gorgeous, voluptuous woman."

"Indeed."

"Little short fer you, ain't she?"

"Took me all of a minute to get over the fact."

Both men stared longingly at their counterparts for a full minute, then sat down. Billy said, "Let's get to business."

"I'm ready, but before that, I need to know what's been happening with you for the past fifteen months."

Billy told him everything. The drinking, the nightmares, the fights. It startled Wyatt when he told him about meeting me. Afterward, Wyatt got Billy caught up on what had happened with him in Mexico and our conversation, which equally startled Billy. Wyatt said, "That tequila was something else, wasn't it?"

"Sure was. I woke up and everything was all good. Bones, muscles, everything."

"Me, too."

"What year was it? I forgot."

"1948."

"Right."

Hiding in the corner, I watched them with a bit of self-satisfaction as they each thought about the physical impossibility of it all.

Finally, Wyatt said, "So. Back to business. What do you know?"

Billy first told him about what Harvey Smith had done to Katy and his plans for selling her. Then about Chewie and W and how they had found him. When Billy had finished, Wyatt slowly shook his head once and said, "So where is he?"

"Glendale. He bought the place with Katy's money. Three-bedroom house with a guesthouse that has a cellar, so that's where he's gotta be doing all his fucked up shit. Rode up there a couple of hours ago and checked it out as best as I could. It's locked up tighter than a seventy-year-old nun, but there's a hill that leads up to his back yard. Figured we'd park a ways away, probably should get a car so he cain't hear us, climb up that hill and break in through a window. I've been visiting with his two girls and ... "

Wyatt threw back his head in surprise. "Wait, you've been seeing those two girls?"

"Yep. The younger one's real cute and real smart. The older one's real nice, too, but she hardly ever spoke a word until she met Katy."

"That's wonderful!"

"Yeah, I'm growing real fond of them. Katy, too. Anyways, the younger one said Harvey liked to do his stuff at night, which works out good for us. I figure most any night he'll be in the basement of that guesthouse doing whatever. We break in through a window without setting off an alarm and kidnap the piece of shit."

"Sounds good to me. Then what?"

"Oh, he's gonna pay and pay big time before he meets his maker."

Wyatt knew Billy had never killed anyone – it wasn't in his nature – but from the sound of his voice, he knew he was capable. "How?"

"Don't know yet. But I can tell ya this: It ain't gonna be fast."

The two men sat in silence while a band played 70s and 80s rock. Some patrons danced. The murmuring of voices, the clacking of balls on a pool table, an occasional outburst of laughter. Two women came over and introduced themselves. Billy said, "Y'all's right fine looking but the two of us are already taken fer the night."

One of them wrote their phone numbers on napkin, handed it to Billy. "If it doesn't work out."

The two men would often look at Madeleine and Katy, who never stopped talking, sometimes seriously, sometimes laughing. Billy said, "Well, I guess we still don't exist much." Men would come over and ask them for a dance, but they always politely refused with a smile. Some would leave them their phone numbers, too.

After three hours and six beers each, Billy looked at the napkins. "Three sets of phone numbers. Not bad."

"Yeah. But the girls probably have twice that."

"I hear ya. Ya think they'll ever stop talking? Remember they deserted their two men, left them to fend off all these other ladies by themselves?"

Finally, the girls looked their way, caught them staring and burst into laughter. They came over. Madeleine said, "Gosh, I'm surprised you're still here!"

"Yeah," said Katy. "We thought you'd be hanging out with at least one of those pairs of hot babes by now."

"Those two blonds were cute."

"And probably fifteen."

"But then, all women are the same age, isn't that right, boys?"

Billy turned red, Wyatt covered his eyes.

SIXTY-FIVE

...

B ILLY RENTED A BROWN, MID-SIZED TOYOTA AND AROUND A HALF PAST eleven, parked it at the bottom of the hill behind Harvey Smith's house. The two men made their way through the weeds and underbrush.

The back of the guesthouse had just one window, about four feet tall and five feet wide. The interior was dark and quiet. Billy took a circular glass cutter, set it at the largest diameter and began cutting. Wyatt took over after a few minutes and after that, they took turns.

They were almost done when the front door opened. A girl walked in and put bags and drinks from Taco Bell on the desk. Following behind her was Harvey Smith, who turned on the light.

Billy broke the window inward and jumped through. Wyatt followed. Harvey Smith ran out the door, slammed it shut and bolted it from the outside. Billy, followed by Wyatt, jumped out the window and ran after him.

Harvey Smith reached his car, got in, and took off as Billy pounded on the driver's side window. "Fuck!" The two men watched, helpless, as he drove away. They went back to the guesthouse.

The girl was in shock. There was a rug in the middle of the floor and Wyatt kicked over half of it, revealing the entry to the basement. Billy went over to the desk. "Computer's still on. Gotta be something on it." He looked at the shelves behind it. "Well, lookie here, a brand new four terabyte hard disk. I'll have everything right quick."

Wyatt pulled up two chairs, sat down and told the girl to sit across from him. "What's your name?"

"Jessica."

"How old are you?"

"Nineteen."

"Right."

She fretted, twisting and intertwining her fingers. "Are you gonna hurt me?"

"No. How'd you end up here?"

"I was just walking home and Frank said he'd give me a ride."

"His real name is Harvey Smith."

She started crying. "I didn't know." Wyatt let her cry and when the tears stopped, she said, "He asked if I was hungry so we went to Taco Bell and he told me about his shell collection."

"Shell collection? In Arizona?"

"Yeah. He said it was one of the best in the world. So we came here." She looked at Wyatt. "You're really not going to hurt me?"

"No, we're not going to hurt you. We'll need a favor, though, but before I tell you what it is, there's something you need to see." He fully pushed aside the rug, lifted up the door to the cellar, walked down a few steps and turned on the light. He turned to Jessica. "Come on down."

Timidly, she followed. Halfway down, she stopped. "What's that?"

"It's a frame. See the hooks at the corners?" She nodded. "What Harvey Smith does is kidnap women, even those under eighteen, and drug them, usually by putting something in their drink. When they wake up, they're completely naked and their arms and legs are stretched out and tied to those hooks. Then for the next couple of weeks, maybe a month or two, he rapes them and cuts them with an X-acto knife. Then he drugs them again and takes them to a plastic surgeon who fixes up the scars. Then he sells them."

Jessica looked in wide-eyed horror. "Sells them? Where?"

"Anywhere. Thailand, China, Germany. Even the United States."

"But you can't sell people."

"These guys do. And when their customers buy women, they can do whatever they want with them. Rape them, hire them out for sex, torture them. Ever hear of snuff films?"

"That was going to happen to me?"

"Yes." Wyatt let the reality of it sink in then said, "Let's go back upstairs."

When they got back to their chairs, Jessica was sobbing. Again, Wyatt let her get it out. He retrieved a box of tissues and she wiped away the tears.

He said, "So this is what we need you to do. After we leave, you can eat some of that Taco Bell but stay away from the drinks. Wait thirty minutes then call 9-1-1. That's important, wait thirty minutes. There is no way Harvey Smith will come back so don't worry about that. When you talk to the 9-1-1 operator, act scared, cry if you can, and tell them you don't know how to get home. They'll be able to find you.

"When the police get here, tell them how you met Frank – and use that name – and how you ended up here. Now this is where you start lying." His voice conveyed a deep compassion. "As soon as he opened the cellar door to show you his shell collection, two burglars broke in through the window. Frank got scared and ran off. The two burglars also ran off. We were wearing ski masks and you were too scared to notice anything about us. Leave the cellar door open. Got all that?" She nodded.

Wyatt looked at Billy. "How's it going?"

"Less than a minute."

Wyatt looked back at the girl with a father's kindness. "Look Jessica, you're going to be fine, but make sure you learn from this. There are evil people in the world; not very many, a minuscule percentage actually, but they do exist. You met one tonight. He gave you a ride, bought you dinner, was probably a little charming, made you laugh. Wanted to show off his shell collection. Sounds all happy and innocent, right?"

She nodded. He went on. "So he gave you nothing to tag him as evil. But as you grow older, you'll learn to spot people like that. Trust your gut, your intuition, and never stop observing and learning. Women are better at it than men, so like I said, you'll be fine."

Billy spoke up. "Got everything. Let's git."

Wyatt got up then looked back at Jessica. "Remember, thirty minutes."

"Yeah. Thirty minutes, I promise. And I'll say everything you said. I'll do it all real good, too, so don't worry."

Wyatt smiled and nodded. The two men left.

SIXTY-SIX

...

THE MOOD WAS SUBDUED WHEN BILLY AND WYATT GOT BACK TO THEIR motel. Billy immediately connected the hard disk to his laptop, then called Chewie and gave him all the data he needed. Chewie said he'd call as soon as he found out anything.

For three days, the four of them stayed inside eating a diet consisting mainly of pizza and soda. Billy paced, Wyatt tapped his foot now and again, and Katy and Madeleine sat on the bed holding hands much of the time. On the third night, just after they had finished another pizza, Chewie called. "We found him."

"Where?"

"Ever hear of a place called Wonder Valley?"

"Rode through there once. Out by Joshua Tree in California."

"Yeah. It's like this modern day ghost town. Lots of abandoned small houses but there's electricity and water. Oh, and Harvey Smith has a new ride. A white Prius." Chewie gave him the license plate number and the address.

"So yer sure he's there?"

"Oh yeah. He logged in a day and a half ago and his computer's been on ever since."

"My friend, I still owe you big time."

"Not a problem, Billy. Good luck."

It took a while, but Katy convinced Billy she was strong enough to ride as long as he could, so the four friends took off around nine o'clock and rode through the night. Of them, Billy's thoughts were the most uncluttered: he wanted vengeance.

In contradistinction, Wyatt's musings were complex. What he had said earlier to Madeleine was true, that Billy was his only friend. But more than that, for six years, Billy had been his only reliable contact with the world and he had seen in his friend a sort of hope, a hope for a future in which he would be free.

Further, during Billy's year of dissipation, Wyatt had always felt that it was temporary. After all, even when things were going well for both of them, they would go months with no communication.

Too, he was finally settled on the Dark Companion's place in his life and had come to the conclusion that it would not fail him, though from having seen how Billy handled himself in a fight, he had no doubt that Billy could, and would, handle the coming violence alone.

However, he now had Madeleine to consider, which changed everything exponentially. How would she hold up? She's tough – God, I love that about her – but how will she react to the violence that was to occur? Sure, she watched me beat the snot out of Al, but Harvey Smith's life will end. How will she handle that? So far, she had been unyieldingly faithful, but will she stay with me afterward?

Madeleine held a mixture of emotions. As short as her time with Katy was, she knew their friendship would endure regardless of what was to happen. She was confident about Katy's resolve and mettle, but nevertheless worried about her. Thinking about and intending retribution is one thing, carrying it out is something entirely different.

Her thoughts turned to Wyatt. The blend of respect and love she had for him was boundless and unblemished – she had never known such a quantity of feelings. He had said that all he wanted was for her to be there when it was over. She smiled when she thought it would be the easiest thing she'd ever done. She again resolved that she would do anything, everything, to back him up and protect him and, in a way, she wished she could.

Katy's mind was the most active. As she rested her head on Billy's shoulder and watched the nighttime desert flow by, she would oftentimes see in a detached way the things that had been done to her. As she fully confronted the horrors, her reactions to them slowly diminished until, eventually, it was as if she were watching a petty parade of paper puppets.

Other times she would see her life since Billy came into it. His nervousness and sometimes uncertainty of what to say or how to act. His honesty. And how they were each connecting with Mary and Mona. She smiled and thought that if she had to have experienced all that she had in order to know those girls and, especially, to be with Billy, it was more than worth it.

Dealing with Harvey Smith would not be troublesome – she harbored no doubts about the reasons for his demise. No, her biggest concern was for Billy, not for his safety but, rather, his emotional wellbeing. It could be, she thought, that her biggest challenge would be to protect him against any after-the-fact regrets. He'd never killed before, of that she was certain, and how would he respond? Would the nightmares come back? Would he start over-drinking again? Would he become numb to any feelings whatsoever?

She decided that she must not allow any of that, that somehow, they would come to the other side of this with no shame or regret. He loved her and she loved him and made him happy, that she knew, and would always do so. It would have to be enough.

She held him closer. Billy gently squeezed her knee.

SIXTY-SEVEN

...

THE FOUR ARRIVED IN TWENTYNINE PALMS AROUND SIX IN THE MORN-
ing. They breakfasted then rode out to Harvey Smith's house in Wonder Valley. His white Prius was parked behind it. They would wait until
midnight.

It wasn't until two in the afternoon when they were able to get two rooms
at a Holiday Inn. They went out for lunch and after they ordered, Billy said,
"I'm thinking we should rent a car again. If he hears our bikes all of a sudden
stop, it might put him on guard."

Wyatt said, "Good idea. But even at that, we should park a ways away.
That way he won't see the headlights."

Wyatt gave Billy a ride to the car rental place, where he got another
medium-sized Toyota. When they got back to the hotel, they were all too
amped up to relax, but finally lay down and went to sleep around six. They
had dinner around nine, but most of it went untouched. The wait for midnight seemed to last forever.

They parked next to an abandoned house a half-mile away. Billy and
Wyatt checked their guns; Billy gave one to Katy, Wyatt one to Madeleine.
They checked their knives and sheathed them. The four then walked in
silence to meet Harvey Smith.

As they stood in front of his house, they heard a thin, shrill melody,
like a deranged witchdoctor singing to demented gods. "What the hell is
that?" Billy asked.

Detached, Katy stared straight ahead. "I've heard it before."

Under the canopy of countless stars and a midnight moon, the desert
took on an eerie persona and they stood as grim wraiths. As the deviant
melody twisted and turned, they became bereft of all humane impulses.

271

Wyatt turned to Billy. "He's alone. I'll break down the door and roll in. He'll be scared shitless. Jump over me and he's yours." Billy nodded.

Wyatt waited some seconds, drew in a deep breath and ran, Billy right behind him. The door crashed into splinters and in the silence, it was like thunder from Hell. Billy jumped over Wyatt only to have a bloodthirsty 160-pound wolf dog knock him onto his back like a swatted mosquito. The wolf dog then lunged straight at Wyatt's throat.

The shot, high and piercing, was similar to the one Wyatt had heard years before in the parking garage in Richmond, the one that had saved his life. The wolf dog whimpered once then landed, dead, on Wyatt's chest. Behind him, Madeleine stood, arms outstretched, the gun in her hands unwavering, her face like that of a remorseless assassin.

The silence in the room was complete, all five people frozen like characters in a grisly tableau.

Soon, Harvey Smith ran to the dish rack and grabbed a meat cleaver, new and razor sharp. Madeleine pointed the gun at him but Wyatt pushed off the wolf-dog, stood up, then gently lowered her arms. Billy stood up. His and Wyatt's eyes met.

Wyatt moved to Harvey Smith's right, Billy to his left. Their eyes met again. Wyatt took one step and bellowed a short and guttural cry. Harvey Smith swung the meat cleaver in a wide arc, slicing Wyatt's t-shirt. Billy exploded toward Harvey Smith and smashed him in the face, breaking his cheek.

Harvey Smith was on his back, barely conscious. Billy stood over him, seething. He got a pitcher, filled it with water then poured it on his face. He choked and coughed. When he saw Billy, it was as if he looked at the devil.

With one hand, Billy picked him up by his shirt and again hit him in the face. "Fight back!" He hit him again. "Fight back, goddammit!" Spittle flew out of his mouth, his face mottled with rage, his eyes full of fire from the Pit itself. "Fight back, you fucking coward! Fight back!"

To Wyatt, Madeleine and Katy, Billy was like an ever-growing beast, a primordial savage, a monster unleashed from Hades. With every punch, Madeleine held onto Wyatt more tightly. He wrapped his arm around her shoulder and she folded herself into the curve of his waist.

Billy hit Harvey Smith two more times in the face then just under his ribs. He dropped him and he crumpled to the floor gasping for breath. He was beyond going unconscious, a fact that gave Billy a grim satisfaction.

Harvey Smith slowly raised himself onto one elbow and knee, and looked at Katy pleading for mercy – he knew there would be none coming from Billy – but she looked at him like a porcelain statue of Santa Muerte, merciless and emotionless and expressionless. A cold darkness infused his soul.

Billy, breathing with loud and grating rasps like a blacksmith's bellows, went over to Katy. They held each other and stayed in their lover's grasp for what seemed an eternity, each giving the other strength.

Eventually, Billy let go of Katy then found the door to the cellar, opened it, turned on the light and walked down. He came back up. "It's a mud floor. I'll shackle him to it. Got a bunch of building stuff in it."

Katy, her eyes still on Harvey Smith, said, "Take his clothes off." Billy nodded then pushed him down the stairs with his foot.

Wyatt picked up the wolf dog by its four legs and he and Madeleine went outside. About fifty yards behind the house, Wyatt dropped it behind a clump of creosote bushes. In but a few days, it would look like nothing more than an old roll of shag carpet.

They looked at each other for a long time, Wyatt's face shadowed, Madeleine's lit by the midnight moon. Finally, Madeleine said, "Nothing will ever hurt you again."

In the basement, Billy removed Harvey Smith's clothes and laid him out spread-eagled, face up. He pounded metal stakes deep into the ground just beyond his hands and feet, which he then tied to the stakes. The stretching roused Harvey Smith and he began to groan. Billy gagged him.

When Wyatt and Madeleine got back to the house, they stood just inside the front door. When Billy got back up the stairs, he stood next to Katy. She held onto his arm and stared straight ahead for a long time, not moving and barely breathing. Billy waited. They all did. And the desert night engulfed them in a menacing silence.

Katy finally took a deep breath and looked around the room. On the counter was a small ice chest. She walked over then opened it. Inside were a loaf of bread, some lunchmeat, jars of mayonnaise and peanut butter, and a large jar of strawberry jam. She picked up the jam, found a spatula in a drawer, took hold of Billy's hand, then together they walked down to the cellar.

They stood over Harvey Smith for minutes. He whimpered and cried and pleaded with muffled syllables. Slowly, the look on his face became more and more terrified. Without taking her eyes off of him, Katy said, "Cut him, Billy."

Billy took out his knife and began on Harvey Smith's face. When he moved down to his chest, Katy placed her hands on Billy's, guiding them, and together they sliced slowly and deeply. When they got to the bottoms of his feet, Harvey Smith looked as if out-of-control electricity raged throughout his body, the long and deep vertical gash in his abdomen like a medieval red death.

When the cutting was done, Katy emptied the jar of jam and with the spatula, spread it all over Harvey Smith. In the corner was a colony of fire ants.

For the next three days, the two couples mostly stayed to themselves except for meals, but even then, little was said, none of it about Harvey Smith. At the end of dinner on the third night, Katy looked at Billy and said, "I need to see. I need to make sure."

Billy nodded. "Okay."

Some hours later, the two couples rode out to Harvey Smith's house. Standing still and silent, Wyatt and Madeleine waited outside, looking over the desolate, midnight desert, Wyatt with his arm around her shoulder, Madeleine with her arms around his waist. The coolness of the air seemed to stop time.

Billy and Katy stepped down to the cellar. Billy stood next to the ladder, Katy sat on the bottom rung, her arms wrapped around Billy's leg. The wan light from the naked bulb glimmered and the smell of rotted blood laced the stale air.

Harvey Smith was still laid out as they had left him. His mouth opened and shut, over and over, like a mechanical doll's. Covering his body was a quivering of flies and ants. His eyes were gone along with much of his skin and internal organs.

They watched and waited. At last, they heard the final expiration of air from his one remaining lung.

SIXTY-EIGHT
...

THE FOLLOWING MORNING, WITHOUT ANY DISCUSSION, THE FOUR HEAD-
ed north and stopped for the night in Visalia. The next day, they rode
west to Cayucos and got two rooms at a bed and breakfast on the beach.
The contemplation of the future is restorative and as the days passed,
all four of our friends slowly adopted forward leaning notions. Thus it was
that the mood lightened. So much so, that one night after dinner, they were
walking along the beach when Katy, out of nowhere, burst out laughing. She
couldn't stop and soon, they were all bent over with tears of joy.

I must say how good it was to see that. You see, it's understandable to
worry about how the aftermath of events like this will affect people. Not
that I had any doubts about the four of them, I didn't, it's just that you never
know what demons lay hidden and by what means they can be aroused.

Billy and Katy will always remember their pasts, of course, but they
were finally free from them. After a life of high dreams that were dashed
time after time, Madeleine was at last free of all of those disappointments.
And Wyatt? Well, Wyatt was always free, it just took meeting Madeleine
for him to realize it.

Our four good friends stayed in Cayucos for three weeks. On the day
they left, they headed out when dawn was but a promise. The roar from
their engines was like the invitation of new destinies and as they rode east,
the indigo sky slowly gave way to splashes of orange and pink. Soon, the
fresh and wholesome blue sky beckoned.

I choose to be happy.

—Voltaire, in a letter to Abbé Trublet

THESE EVENTS ENDED SIX YEARS AGO AND I THOUGHT YOU MIGHT LIKE
to know how everyone is doing these days.

I look in on Wyatt and Madeleine every now and again and sometimes
it takes me days to find them. They still live on the road and average about
thirty thousand riding miles a year. They have now ridden on six continents,
but I don't think they have any plans to visit the seventh, Antarctica. (But
then, with the way they go at it, you never know.)

Fortunately, Wyatt has had to rely on the Dark Companion only a handful of times and it never failed him. True to her promise, Madeleine always
watches his back and there were a number of times he desperately needed
it. Wonder if she ever killed anyone in order to save him? Well, I believe I'll
leave that answer to your imagination.

They are still wildly in love and their lust for each other has never waned.
The most remarkable change is how much they smile and laugh these days.
My, oh my.

After their stay in Cayucos, Billy and Katy rode straight to Albuquerque
and, as you probably predicted, immediately began filing the papers to adopt
Mary and Mona. It took six months and afterward, they went straight to
Georgia where they bought a big house on six wooded acres with a fishing
stream at the back end of it.

Three years later, Katy found out she was three months pregnant, which
was a surprise to everyone. Six months later, the final addition to their family
was a healthy baby boy. At first, they thought about naming him Wyatt,

but eventually settled on Baxter Oliver Oscar Balcomb Junior. Thankfully, everyone calls him Billy J.

Well, there was one more addition to their family. Three weeks after they moved in, a hound dog puppy wandered onto their property and decided to stay. They named him Buck.

Mona is now close to eighteen years old and is thoroughly excited for her first prom date with a nice Georgia boy named Clay. Mary is now eleven and won the Georgia State Spelling Bee last spring and placed third in the nation.

Katy loves being a wife and mother and I cannot think of a more loving or more competent one. Billy still rides often, whenever possible with Katy, and is a founding member of the Baseball, Bacon, and Beer Riding Club.

Wondering about me? Well, I'm just a biker, always will be. And I ride. Oh, do I ride! Anywhere, nowhere and allwheres.

When you awake in the middle of the night amid an infinite silence, you will sometimes begin to hear, a hundred yards or a hundred miles away, the rumble of an engine. You listen as it comes closer and becomes louder and you wonder who it is, who it is riding alone. I pass, and the momentary roar is like the clap of a rifle shot; then, in a long decrescendo, the sound evanesces into nothing.

I am the wind.

I am a wisp of warmth on a cool night, the last chill of dawn before the sun catches hold, the sunlight on your face. I am the comfort of your jeans, the stretch of a leather glove, the scuff of a denim collar. I am the caw of a lone hawk, the low croaking of ravens, the whoosh of bats in the night.

Sometimes, I am laughter and when you turn around, no one is there.

I am the vibration of your handgrips, the warmth of your engine on a cold day, the tick-tick-ticking as it cools down. I am the whisper of dry leaves, the murmur of a stream in a campsite, the crunch of your tires on gravel. I am the shadow of clouds on grass, of an oak tree in the moonlight, of a granite spire on the desert floor.

Sometimes, I am but a reflection on glass. Do you see me?

—END—

Acknowledgments
and Musings

Writing is an activity that is best done while alone. In other words, if you dislike being by yourself only, writing is not for you. That being the case, it is also true that as the actual publishing date slowly approaches (in my case, excruciatingly slowly), others, by necessity, begin to help. And I'm glad they do.

Before publishing, I always ask some friends to spend some hours perusing my scribblings. This serves two purposes, the first being a sort of discipline. It's funny: I can go over a manuscript a dozen, two dozen, three dozen times, fixing errors, rewriting this, revising that until it's all "perfect," but the moment before sending it to someone else, I become beset by doubts. Does that description of clouds need to be there? Is that metaphor too childish? Should it be a moonlight-filled night instead of a moonless one?

The second purpose is simply because I've spent who-knows-how-many-hours alone writing the damn thing and I'm dying to actually communicate it.

Now, when I'm amid creating, I never formally ask for feedback and I certainly don't conduct any surveys. (*After* all the creating it's acceptable, sure, but during it? Never.) The reason I don't ask for feedback or conduct a survey is that when someone *does* say something, I know it's an honest comment, borne of nothing but hey-I-think-I'll-tell-this-to-Foster.

If you're curious if I've ever changed, a story, a plot, because of someone's critique, the answer is "No." Now, that doesn't mean I've never amended anything because of what someone said, but when I have, it was always a minor change.

F'rinstance, some years ago, I had a cat (long black fur, green eyes) named Felicity. Several years after she left us (she loved harassing coyote), I wrote a short story in which the main character was a lady named Felicity. I named her that simply because I liked the name and it came across as ultimately feminine, which she certainly was. So my daughter reads the story and says, "You named her after a cat? Really, Dad?" I changed Felicity's name to Eloise.

Before I sent this manuscript to my editor, five people read it, and their thoughts and observations, though few, were weighty and invaluable. Sometimes funny. (My favorite critiques were along the lines of, "Killer stuff on page xxx, Foster! But uh, what the hell are you talking about?") Anyway, those five genius-friends are Anna Polsinelli, Kirk Steele, Amber Gosling, Linda V. Ferguson, and George Gluchowski. Love you gals and guys!

The first draft had in it much more Spanish than the book does. When I began revising and amending, which was pretty much immediately, the number of Spanish passages gradually became smaller and it got to the point where I considered not having any Spanish at all. Ultimately, however, I felt it was not only justified but necessary because the Poet is, presumably, this ancient Mexican guy and Wyatt spends some time in Mexico. Besides, I liked the idea of it.

The main problem, the only problem, really, was that I know very little Spanish. (And from what I can tell, Google Translate knows even less.) What to do? Easy-peasy. Call on a couple of highly literate and trustworthy friends: Sergio Barer and Eugenio Castillo. ¡Muchísimas gracias, mis amigos!

By the bye, the best way to make a foreign language understandable for the reader and still keep the narrative flow going is to have what comes right after it, explain it. F'rinstance, I'm a mono-linguistic American and were I to have read Wyatt saying, "Disculpe mi torpeza," I would have had no clue what he meant until Darcy replied by saying, "Apology accepted, but you're anything but awkward, big fella." Works, right?

Alas, sometimes it's not possible. With that in mind, here're a few translations off the top of my noggin that you may want or need. "Señorita linda" means "pretty miss" (as in unmarried lady), and when the housekeeper says to Wyatt, "Dios lo bendiga," it means "God bless you." If you find any others that are impossible to figure out, my apologies. Just put those passages into Google Translate and it'll get you close enough.

If first-rate editors are blessings for writers (and they are), then Diane Austin and Rose Albano are divine ones. Comprehensive, uncompromising, and caring, all wrapped up in an I'll-watch-your-back-like-a-bodyguard-assassin-but-I'll-whack-you-upside-the-head-if-I-have-to New York attitude. Love it.

Ronda Taylor (HeartWorkCreative.com) did her usual supreme job of designing the cover and the interior. It all just looks so perfect, doesn't it?

Big time thanks to Melissa Manning for her cover photo of the back of the Poet, and to my life-long pal, Dwight Mikkelsen, for his portrait photo of me (it's atop my bio) and his cover photo of that post-apocalyptic looking road in Montana.

Deeply felt "Thank Yous!!" to Dante Alighieri, Voltaire, and Mr. Shakespeare for allowing me to use their quotes. (I shudder when I think where we would be without them.)

When I think of all the people who have read one of my books or short stories, it warms my heart and I sincerely thank all of them. Really. I look at it this way: When an author sells a book, they're asking someone, a stranger, to spend, what?, ten to twenty hours reading their words. Let's face it, that's asking a big favor. We writers do our best to make it worth their while, of course, but still, ten to twenty hours is a legitimate commitment. So, with my hat off I offer a sweeping bow to all readers everywhere.

Last, my kids (Khalin Egon, Lacee I-hate-my-first-name, and Jasmine Pavane) and grandkids (Travis Riley, Diego Cruz, Ana Lucia, and Vienna Lyn) are constant muses. If I were to claim that I do all that I do because of them, it would not be far from the truth.

Oh, and I shan't ever forget Rosemary.

Love and Respect,
Foster

ABOUT THE AUTHOR

FOSTER KINN is a pen name for Dwight Mikkelsen. He was born in California's San Joaquin Valley and is the son and brother of Danish immigrants. He is a widower, the father of three, and the grandfather of four. He describes himself as "Fundamentally a Freedom guy, Classical music composer, and a not-too-bad raconteur who feels there is never enough time to ride my motorcycle."

He has been a professional musician and composer his entire adult life and has worked with many celebrities including Whitney Houston, Chicago, Quincy Jones, Elmer Bernstein, Patrick Doyle, George Clinton, Barbra Streisand, and Mike Post.

He has written two nonfiction books, *Freedom's Rush* and *Freedom's Rush II*, both of which are about his solo motorcycle rides throughout the United States and Canada. They are published by Hugo House Publishers and are available anywhere you can buy books online.

Many of his photos can be purchased from FosterKinn.zenfolio.com. He can be reached via email through either of his websites.

www.FreedomsRush.com

www.NoteSlinger.com